Guardians Of Earth

Book One: The Argus

P. R. Garcia

This is a work of fiction. Names, characters, places, and incidents are either the product of the author's imagination or are used fictitiously. Any resemblance to any person, living or dead, events or locals is coincidental.

ISBN: 9781948060042

DEDICATION

To my daughter and granddaughter, who always remain in my heart.

To the people who put aside bigotry, greed, hatred, and indifference each day. To the crusaders who are fighting to save our world's wildlife, are developing ways to stop global warming, producing biofriendly fuels, and more humane ways to care for livestock. To the person who says no to a plastic straw and eating utensils, who uses cloth bags instead of plastic bags at the store, who recycles and does a hundred other things to help our planet. Together we are making a difference.

CONTENTS

ACKNOWLEDGMENTS

Mike and William for their support and help while fighting crippling diseases. Both give me the determination to press forward no matter what the obstacles.

Vickie and Denise for helping me find my mistakes. Darlene for her pride in my accomplishments and her help in finding some pretty funny spelling errors.

A SURPRISE VISIT

Sarina had just removed a pan of bubbling lasagna out of the oven when the front doorbell rang.

"Okay, which one of you locked the screen door on your brother again?" she called out to her two younger children watching television in the living room. Neither child answered. "I don't care who locked the door. Just let him in or no lasagna."

Timmy, the youngest, leapt from his chair and made a mad dash to the front door. "It wasn't me."

"I didn't do it," Mary shouted, chasing after her brother. "So, you must have. You're the one always locking the door on Jeremy."

"Uh-uh."

"Yes, Sir!"

Sarina listened to the two arguing until the front door open, then silence. The sound of a stranger's voice wafted in from the living room. Who would call upon them this late at night? "Kids, who is here?"

"I'll get my mom," drifted in Timmy's voice.

Wiping her hands on the kitchen towel, Sarina hurried towards the door. When she turned the corner, she froze, dropping the towel on the floor. Three men dressed in black suits stood in the doorway. Several more waited outside. Men in suits meant only one thing--her husband in Afghanistan was wounded, or worse. Her heart pounding, she walked forward, placing an arm around each child as she paused between them. "Who are you? What do you want?" Holding her breath, Sarina waited for one of the men to say those horrible words every soldier's wife fears.

"Are you the author Mitch Hannigan?" the tall man in the front asked.

Sarina said nothing. She stared at the talking man, then at the one behind him. What did he ask? Weren't they at her home to tell her about her husband? Were they from the publishing company?

"Are you the author Mitch Hannigan?" the man repeated.

Sarina tried to answer, but the dryness of her mouth prevented her from doing so. Swishing her tongue from side to side, she re-moistened her palate. "That's my pen name," she said, returning her gaze to the first man.

"The same Mitch Hannigan who wrote the novel *Guardians of Earth?*"

A sense of danger, uneasiness, and impending doom bubbled up from deep within Sarina as she stood there. It was the same sensitivity she sometimes got while writing her book. Vague, yet undeniable. The hair on her arms stood up as if covered with goosebumps. "Kids, go into the kitchen and start eating. Mary, cut the bread and put it on the table."

"Is Daddy okay?" a frightened Mary asked.

"I think so. Now go eat." Sarina forced the best smile possible onto her face. Once her children were out of sight, she turned her attention to the men before her. "Is my husband okay?"

"Are you the Mitch Hannigan who wrote the novel *Guardians of Earth?* It's a simple question. Yes or no?"

"Yes," Sarina said.

"Let me assure you, Mrs. Spalling, your spouse is fine," a tall man said as he walked from behind the two men, his hand outstretched. "My name is Samuel MacIntosh. I am the Deputy Director of Homeland Security. I apologize for the late visit. And for alarming you. We want to ask you a few questions about your novel."

"My book?" Sarina asked, shaking the man's extended hand, still trying to comprehend they weren't there to deliver bad news about her husband. What interest could Homeland Security have in her book? It was a work of fiction, a sci-fi thriller about a group of aliens who lived inside the moon and protected Earth. Her writing had nothing to do with national security. Did they think she was revealing top secrets? "I'd like to see some identification."

"Of course," Deputy-Director MacIntosh replied. Reaching inside his breast pocket, he removed his credentials and handed them to Sarina.

She examined the identification card, not sure what she should be searching for. The ID stated the man's name was Samuel MacIntosh, and he was the Deputy Director of Homeland Security. An emblem of the government organization embossed the card. Next to the ID was a golden badge like what the Sheriff wore. Sarina couldn't tell if the credentials were real or fake. She returned the identification to their owner. "And their identification?"

"Agents," the Deputy-Director instructed. The two men in front handed their IDs to Sarina. As with the Deputy Director's, she scanned them, then gave them back.

"You see, Mrs. Spalling, we are who we say we are," the Deputy Director said. "If you would come with us, we can straighten things out."

"Straighten what out?" she demanded, her tone more confident and louder. "I'm not going anywhere with you. I want you out of my house this instant." She tried pushing the three men outside the front door, but they did not move.

3

"I am sorry," Deputy Director MacIntosh said. "We must speak with you."

"If you won't leave, I'm calling the police." She reached for her cellphone on the entrance table, but her hand never made contact. An agent grabbed her arm in mid-air and dragged her towards the couch.

"I am afraid I can't permit you to do that," the Deputy Director said. "If you would just let me explain."

"You leave my mom alone," Timmy shouted, charging from within the kitchen. His hands balled into fists, he hit the man restraining his mother.

"Timmy, no," Sarina yelled.

"Come here, you." The second man grabbed Timmy and put him in a secured bear-hold. "We will not hurt your mom. We only want to ask her a few questions."

Timmy raised his arms into the air as his older brother had taught him to do if ever someone tried to snatch him. Within seconds, he slipped through the man's grip, ran over, and began kicking the Deputy Director.

"Will someone do something about this kid?" the Deputy-Director said.

"I got him," said the man holding Sarina. The agent pushed Sarina down onto the couch, then grasped the menacing youngster by his arms. The second man grabbed Timmy's legs. Together, the two agents lifted Timmy off the floor. No matter how he squirmed or kicked, he couldn't break free.

Realizing her brother was in trouble, Mary burst into the room, the bread knife grasped in her hand. She ran forward, preparing to save her sibling. When she saw the expression on the Deputy Director's face, she came to an abrupt halt. He had the same look her mother did when she was about to do something wrong and get into lots of trouble.

"Whatever you're thinking of doing, I wouldn't," he advised.

Sarina reached out and pulled Mary into her arms, grabbing the knife from her hand. Alarmed the children might be harmed, Sarina held her breath as Timmy struggled to free himself. "Please. don't injure my kids."

"I have no desire to hurt your children, Mrs. Spalling," the Deputy Director said. "If everyone would just calm down. Agent Smith, take the children into the kitchen and sit them at the table." A third agent took Mary from her mother's hold and escorted her to a chair in the kitchen. The two men holding Timmy followed suit. But the moment his bottom touched the seat, Timmy was up again. Prepared for such a maneuver, the men grabbed Timmy by the shoulders and forced him back down.

"Tell your children, Mrs. Spalling, to remain seated, or they may get hurt," the man holding Timmy said.

Sarina walked over and knelt in front of her children. "Mary, Timmy, I want you two to behave. Eat your supper before your food gets cold. I'm going outside and talk with these gentlemen."

"No, Momma," Mary cried.

"It'll be all right," Sarina said. "Probably some kind of mistake. I'll be back before you finish your first piece of lasagna."

"I'm scared, Momma," Timmy said.

"Don't be." Sarina hugged her son. "Besides, when do unscrupulous men come to your house in suits?" She gave a little chuckle.

"They always do in movies," Timmy answered. "Please, don't go."

Sarina turned to her daughter. "Mary, call Aunt Cindy. Tell her I need for her to come over right away and stay with you three tonight." Turning towards the Deputy Director, Sarina said, "If you have finished scaring my children and me, I will go outside with you and discuss my book."

Deputy Director MacIntosh glanced at his watch. "One moment, Mrs. Spalling. I have one more matter you need to take care of first." Before she could ask what, the phone rang. "I think you need to answer that call. It should be your husband."

"Tim, answer the phone," Sarina instructed, wondering what her husband had to do with what was transpiring.

"Hello?" Timmy said into the phone's mouthpiece. Upon hearing his father's voice, his eyes lit up. "Dad, there are men in suits here, and they're trying to take mom away. And..." He paused, listening to his father speak. "But... (Pause) Are you sure? (Pause) Yes, I will." He handed the phone to his mother. "Daddy wants to talk to you."

"Steven, what's going on?" Sarina asked.

"Sweetheart, I don't know, but whatever is going on is big. I mean huge. They won't tell me anything. I am being pulled off duty and am being sent home. Sarina, go with these men. They won't harm you."

"Go with them? Why?" She glanced at the Deputy Director. "Why do they want to know about my book?"

"Sweetie, do as they ask. I'll be home in under thirty-six hours. We'll sort out what's happening then."

"Are they discharging you?"

"I don't think so. The only thing I'm being told is this is classified as 'Top Secret', all hush-hush. Even my Commander can't get a straight answer on why I'm being sent home. Is Jeremy there?"

"Not yet. He had practice. I expect him home any moment."

"Then let me talk to Timmy again. I love you."

"I love you too," Sarina said, handing the phone back to her son. "You two stay in the kitchen. I'm going to talk with these men."

Sarina followed the Deputy-Director and another agent outside. She noted two remained in the kitchen to ensure the children did as told. "What do you want to know about my book?"

"Our concern is quite involved," the Deputy Director said. "I need you to come with us downtown for questioning."

Sarina prepared to object, then remembered her husband said to do as asked. "Let me tell the children, grab a few things, and I'll be ready to go with you."

"No need to, Ma'am. We have anything you may need. We must leave. Time is important."

"But I have to inform my children I'm leaving," Sarina interjected. As she turned to go back inside, the Deputy-Director grabbed her arm.

"Mom, what's going on?" Jeremy asked, running towards the house. He recognized the three cars in their driveway as government vehicles. Such sedans were not the bearers of joyful news. "Did something happen to Dad?" The young man stared at the Deputy Director's hand on his mother's arm. Was he trying to force her somewhere? Upon seeing Jeremy, the Deputy Director released Sarina's arm.

"No, your father is fine," Sarina said, trying to diffuse a volatile situation. "These men want to talk to me about my novel. I need to go with them downtown. Aunt Cindy is coming to stay with you until I get back."

"Your book?" a confused Jeremy asked. "What about your book?"

"Jeremy, is it?" the largest man said as he extended his hand. "I am Deputy-Director Samuel MacIntosh of Homeland Security. We have a few questions about your mother's upcoming book. She's agreed to go downtown with us to answer a few questions."

"I don't understand," Jeremy said, ignoring the outstretched hand. "When will you be back?"

"In a few hours. Your Dad's on the phone talking to Timmy. I believe he wants to speak to you."

"Mom, why is Homeland Security taking you?" Jeremy asked, not satisfied with her explanation.

The Deputy Director reached into his breast pocket and removed a business card. He held the card out for Jeremy to take. "Here's my name and private telephone number. If you get worried about your mom, you call this number, and I promise you can talk to her."

"Please, Jeremy, go inside," Sarina said, her lips tight. "I'll be fine. Make sure Mary and Timmy do their homework. And no television until it and the dishes are done." She walked down the sidewalk towards the car where an agent stood with the door opened. She hoped Steven was correct, and there was no danger in going with these men. Summing up her courage, she stepped inside and sat down, too fearful to peek at her son. The Deputy Director entered and sat across from her. When the door slammed shut, the doors lock. What had she agreed to?

Not sure what he should do, Jeremy scrutinized the three black sedans driving away, committing to memory the license plate of the sedan his mom rode in. He then ran into the house, hoping for answers.

THE OFFICE OF
EXTRATERRESTRIAL LIFE

"Mr. MacIntosh, I've done as you asked," Sarina said as they drove away. "I want answers. Why is my husband being sent home six months early?"

"I assure you, Mrs. Spalling, we would not be taking such measures if it were not necessary," the Deputy Director said. "We felt we could further our investigation if your husband was here to help with the children."

"Why is Homeland Security interested in my book?"

The Deputy-Director reached into a side compartment and removed a recording device. He laid it on the seat beside him. "I will record our conversation, so there is no misunderstanding on what was and wasn't said." He pushed the record button. "This is Deputy-Director MacIntosh speaking with Sarina Spalling, aka Mitch Hannigan, author of the book *Guardians of Earth.* Please verify that you are the author and that you use the pen name of Mitch Hannigan."

"Yes."

"Yes, what?"

"Mitch Hannigan is my pen name I write under."

"And did you write the book *Guardians of Earth?*"

"Yes, I wrote the *Guardians of Earth.*"

"In your book, you talk about an undisclosed part of Homeland Security, a division you say is so secret even the President isn't aware of its existence. Is this correct?"

"Yes, that is correct."

"How did you come up with the idea?"

"Sounded like an intriguing notion," Sarina said.

"Did your husband tell you about it?"

"Steven? Why would Steven tell me? I wrote the book, not my husband."

"Then how did you learn about the secret division?"

"I didn't learn about it." She was tired of these ridiculous questions. "You can't find out about something that isn't real."

"Your idea came from somewhere."

"If you must know, I got the idea like I do most of my book plots. I dreamt it."

"You dreamt it?"

"Yes. Do you have a hearing problem?" Sarina sarcastically asked. "Believe it or not, a lot of brilliant authors dream their ideas. Don't you dream when you sleep?"

"Probably, but I don't remember many of them," the Deputy Director said. "You call this organization The Office of Extraterrestrial Life. OEL for short. Am I correct?"

"Yes." The uneasiness in the pit of her stomach returned as Sarina stared at the man before her. A slight ringing filled her ears. How did he know these things? Did someone give him a copy of her book to read before its release?

"In your book, you made the Director of OEL a woman and named her Abbie Santiago." the man continued. "Is this also correct?"

"Who told you these details?" Sarina asked. "Only my publisher knows my characters' names."

"For now, let's say I received a synopsis of your book and the names of its individuals. Is the name of your character Abbie Santiago?"

"Yes."

"Why did you name her Abbie Santiago? Have you overheard that name somewhere?"

"I don't remember how or why I decided on Abbie Santiago." Sarina was becoming more confused. Her mind was reeling, and she couldn't think straight. "More than likely, I made her name up. I invented a few names and picked one I thought sounded adequate. What difference does it make what I called her? I could have named her Denise Monday, Linda Poore, or even Mary Frigging Poppins. In case you don't know, she isn't real. She's a fictional character."

"A fictional character of Native American descent. Why did you make the Director a Native American?"

"I don't know," Sarina shouted, scooting a little forward in the seat. Her patience was wearing thin. "Maybe because I have Native American in me,"

The Deputy Director reached inside his pocket and removed a small piece of paper. He read, "You described her as being slight in stature but muscular, with black hair and eyes. Is this correct?"

Sarina stared out the window, silent. In the distance, she saw the airport lights growing closer. She needed answers now before it was too late. She was done giving them.

"You also wrote she had a slightly noticeable scar running from her jawline to her collarbone, a result of an accident when she was young. Is this also correct?"

"You tell me," Sarina sneered as she sat back in her seat. "You seem to be an expert on my book. I'm not answering any more of your questions until you tell me what's happening. I WANT ANSWERS."

The Deputy Director shifted his position on the seat, bending toward her to give the pretense of authority. "Mrs. Spalling, I wasn't candid with you about where I'm from. I work for Homeland Security, but not one you know. I am the Deputy-Director of OEL--the Office of Extraterrestrial Life. My boss is the Director, and her name is Abigail Santiago. She is Native American with black hair, dark eyes, has a muscular built, stands five-foot-ten inches, and weighs approximately one hundred and forty pounds. She has a scar extending from her left jawline to her collarbone, a souvenir from a drunk driver when she was eight."

Sarina sat there, her mouth agape, staring at the Deputy Director. "You're lying!" The ringing in her ears increased.

The Deputy Director reached in his pocket once more and pulled out a picture. "I assure you, I'm not. I took this photo two days ago of Director Santiago."

In disbelief, Sarina stared at the picture. The photo was an exact representation of the character in her book down. There was even the scar extending down her left side. "This isn't possible. I invented her." She stared at Deputy-Director MacIntosh, her eyes pleading with him to say the picture wasn't real, and this was a military exercise to test her ability to keep confidential anything she may have overheard Steven say. "How could I have invented a character who is real?"

"Something OEL wants to know," he said. "Now, you understand our wish to talk with you. You have revealed top-secret intelligence in your book, knowledge that jeopardizes OEL's existence. How were you able to describe Director Santiago in such detail?" Sarina shook her head, shrugging her shoulders. She hadn't a clue. "Although unlikely, you may have seen Director Santiago on TV in the past before she was the Director. But not OEL. Someone had to of told you about OEL. Who was it?"

Sarina sat there, unable to make sense out of anything the Deputy Director said. She had no explanation. "I made everything up," Sarina whispered.

"I'm sorry, I didn't hear you. What did you say?"

"I made the facts up," she repeated, hoping the Deputy-Director would believe her this time and this would all go away.

"One more matter which has me intrigued," the Deputy Director said. His passenger's shoulders sagged as she sighed, dreading what he would say next. He wondered if she was telling the truth or covering up a plot to expose OEL. "Your hero in the book - I believe his name is Renn?"

"He's real," Sarina blurted out, grateful to have the answer to one question. "I used my father's name. I modeled the hero after him."

"I understand," Deputy-Director MacIntosh said. "You wrote that this Renn person is drawn into protecting Earth because of radio signals he receives? Signals that originate from a precise location on the moon?"

Sarina waited for him to say more, but he didn't. Then she realized if everything else was real, so were the moon transmissions. "Are you saying the signals are real? Aliens are living on the moon?"

"I'm not saying anything, Mrs. Spalling. I'm trying to get down to the truth. Your husband works in Special Ops, doesn't he? In the top security division?"

Sarina slid forward again, meeting the man on equal ground. This stranger would not accuse her husband of any wrongdoing. "You think Steven told me military secrets."

"You tell me."

Not sure how to answer, Sarina peered outside the window. Had Steven talked one night in his sleep, giving her the idea? Her head reeled with questions and doubts. No, she had made up the story. All of it: the alien base on the moon, the mysterious radio signals, the OEL, Director Santiago, the threat from another alien race. Every word she wrote was fiction. But if not true, why was this man accusing her husband of telling her classified military secrets? Why was there a real agency called OEL with a Director named Santiago?

As the outside world whizzed by, something caught her attention - a gas station and restaurant. She recognized both. She and the children had stopped and eaten at the restaurant two days earlier when they were out by the airport. But both were east of downtown. Were there two such locations? As she watched, an airport sign passed outside the window confirming her fear that they weren't going downtown but heading to the airport.

"Where are you taking me?" she shouted, pressing her hands up against the window. "You said you were taking me downtown to your office."

"A little white lie," the Deputy Director explained. "We need to go somewhere where we can get down to the truth of your book. I am taking you somewhere private, somewhere secure. We have a secret hangar out west where we can talk freely."

"No, I'm not going," Sarina screamed. She unhooked her seat belt and pulled on the door handle, but the bar wouldn't open. Desperately, she searched for a lock. But there wasn't one. "Let me out. I have rights and want a lawyer. I..." A slight sting pricked her neck. Within seconds, her eyelids grew heavy, and she slumped over, sound asleep.

The front seat agent removed the hypodermic needle from Sarina's neck. He had slipped through an open window behind the driver's seat without her noticing. "She'll stay asleep until we reach our location."

"Hopefully, Director Santiago will have better luck than I did figuring out what in the hell is going on," the Deputy Director said.

CALL HOME

Sarina tossed in her bed. She was standing alongside a small spaceship with a group of tall, muscular, metal men. Robots. They were fighting with aliens for the dominance of Earth. She fired her weapon as the aliens advanced, killing two.

"Run, Mrs. Spalling," the robot beside her shouted. "Run to the ship."

She didn't move.

"Mrs. Spalling."

"Mrs. Spalling?" came a voice from somewhere outside her dream.

Opening her eyes, she tried to get her bearings, but her mind was a little fuzzy. Her head hurt. What day was today? Was it a school day or the weekend? Had she forgotten to set her alarm, or hadn't the ringer gone off yet? So many questions she didn't have answers to. As she laid there, she focused on the dark, drab walls surrounding her on three sides. The fourth side was a long mirror. Where was she? Then she remembered. Her book. The car. The Deputy-Director.

Sarina bolted into a sitting position. The walls danced around her in erratic motions. The pounding in her head grew louder, as did the ringing in her ears. Why were her ears ringing all the time? She belched. Raising her hand to her mouth, she feared she would vomit.

"Dangle your feet over the edge of the bed, but don't stand," came a soft, feminine voice. Sarina opened her eyes to view a lady standing a few inches away. "I've got something which will help with the room spinning and the upset stomach." The stranger held up a syringe filled with some medication.

"You're not sticking that thing in me," Sarina said, although she was too weak to put up much of a fight.

"You decide," the female said. "You can either feel better in about fifteen minutes or puke your guts out for the next twenty-four hours. Me, I'd rather feel better in fifteen. So, which do you want?" Sarina tried to think, but the headache was too intense. "The meds will also take your horrible headache away."

Not wanting to vomit for twenty-four hours or keep the headache, Sarina held out her arm for the injection. She hoped they didn't bring her all this way to keep her sedated, wherever here was. At least that was what she told herself.

"My name is Sally Rushmore." She injected the needle into Sarina's arm.

"Like the monument?"

"Yeah, but no relation." Sally laughed. She removed the needle and rubbed the area with her finger before applying a band-aid. "You need to sit there for at least ten minutes before you try to get up." She walked over to a nearby nightstand and retrieved a glass of water. "Drink this; it will help." Sarina eyes the liquid. "It's only water. I promise."

"Where am I?"

"Somewhere safe," Sally said. "I'm not allowed to say anything more. The Director will talk to you about what happened and your book."

"So, you know about my book too?"

Sally leaned in closer and whispered, "We all do. Now, drink the water. I will get you something to eat. Be back in about five minutes."

After the stranger left, Sarina drank, allowing her eyes to scour the room. It sure was an ugly, unfriendly place. The only bright spot was the white blanket and flowered sheets on the bed. Her thoughts drifted to her family, wondering if the kids were okay. Had Steven arrived home? What time was it? What day was it? They must be freaking out.

The door opened again, and this time, a soldier stepped inside, holding the door open for Sally. The soldier's presence confirmed her suspicion she was on a military base. And under guard.

Sally pushed a small cart inside and over to the bed. "How are your nausea and room spinning?"

"Much better."

"The serum does wonders for counteracting the effects of the drug they gave you," Sally said. "I wasn't sure what you liked, so I brought an array of stuff. I have coffee, orange juice, and water. A variety of sandwiches. Some pudding, a banana, and grapes. Don't want to put anything too heavy into your stomach." Sarina's stomach growled at the sight of the sandwiches. She didn't realize how hungry she was. With the nausea lessening, she scarfed down a sandwich. "When you're done eating, you can get changed. A bathroom is located behind the door against the right wall. I'll take you down to Director Santiago when you're ready."

"Is her name really Santiago?"

"Your book got her name right."

"But how?"

"Beats me," Sally said. "I believe Director Santiago is hoping to help you find the answer to that and a few more questions. For now, finish eating and get dressed. When you're ready, push the red button by the door. Take your time. We are in no huge hurry."

"But...", was all Sarina said before Sally left. "Did my kids call?" she called out, but Sally did not answer. The Deputy Director gave Jeremy his card and told him to call if he became worried. Had she missed her son's call?

Sarina skidded to a stop when she entered the Director's office, unable to comprehend what she saw. Sitting at a desk was a perfect representation of the OEL Director in her book. She even had the small streak of gray hair on her left side. Deputy-Director MacIntosh hadn't lied.

"I am glad to meet you, Mrs. Spalling." The Director stood, extending her hand. "I am sorry we are meeting under such circumstances."

Sarina held her breath and reached out and grabbed the Director's hand. Her hand was warm and soft. It felt real. If the hand was real, did that mean the woman was real too? "I want to go home."

"I assure you; we will return you to your family as soon as we can."

"When?"

"As soon as we can."

"Unsatisfactory. I want a time. I want a date. I want you to tell me what is going on. Why are you people so damn interested in my book? Why was I kidnapped against my will? I WANT SOME FRICKING ANSWERS!"

"I apologize for Deputy-Director MacIntosh's actions," the Director said, motioning for Sarina to have a seat. "His handling of the situation is appalling. You were to receive your husband's call before the Deputy Director's arrival, not after. He arrived a few minutes too early."

"Why is Steven involved in this? He has nothing to do with my book."

"Why you are here is complicated."

"Then uncomplicate it," Sarina demanded.

"Let's start by going over the statement you gave to Deputy-Director MacIntosh in the car," Director Santiago said, ignoring Sarina's request.

"No," Sarina said, her voice strong and confident. "I said uncomplicate it."

The time had arrived for the truth. Mrs. Spalling would be pushed no further. "As you wish. On page one hundred and sixteen in your book, you describe the Command Center at the heart of OEL in detail. You describe the carpet colors, the number of desks, and their arrangement, the technical equipment, and the vast viewing screen on the front wall. You described what any Command Center in our government looks like. Except for one major addition. A red Coke machine at the right end of row four. Am I correct?"

"Yes." Sarina laughed inside. She knew the Coke machine wasn't real.

Director Santiago picked up a control panel on her desk and pressed a button. The blinds covering a window to the left lifted. As they raised, Sarina saw a massive room on the other side. The area was dark, too dark to make out much. But she did witness the shapes of people inside.

Director Santiago pushed another button. "Sergeant Willis, raise the lights in the Command Center. Mrs. Spalling, if you would direct your attention to the wall to your left, please."

Sarina surveyed the room as the light illuminated the area. Precisely as she described, the room was filled with desks and computers. A massive screen was suspended from the ceiling at the front of the room containing a feed of the moon. She glanced at the floor and saw the carpeting as described in her book. Holding her breath in fear of what awaited her, her eyes darted to the enormous screen, then counted back four rows and down to the end of the row. Sarina gasped, refusing to believe what she saw. In all its glory, there stood the full-sized red Coke vending machine she described in her book.

"It can't be," Sarina whispered, unable to stop looking at the red box.

"I have a horrible addiction to Coke," the Director said. "For my birthday, the staff surprised me with a Coke machine. You don't even have to use any money. They tell me I'm not as irritable if I have a Coke in hand."

The room spun as Sarina grew flushed. Nauseated again, she wished she hadn't eaten those last two sandwiches. Every nerve in her body tingled. To keep from fainting, she placed her head on the table. "This can't be happening."

Director Santiago reached over and grabbed the pitcher of ice water. She poured a glass and pushed the liquid towards Sarina. "Have a drink. It should help."

Sarina waited a few minutes, not sure she could return to a sitting position. When the dizziness stopped, she sat up and took several sips of water.

"I have uncomplicated the situation for you," the Director said. "As you see for yourself, the things you wrote in your book are real. I need to understand how you know these things. Do you know how?"

"No."

"Well, that makes two of us. Deputy Director MacIntosh recorded your statement on your way to the airport. I had it transcribed. My secretary, Sally, will read what you told him. You can then tell me if your testimony is correct."

Sarina listened as the secretary read what she had said in the car. As far as she knew, what Sally read was correct. "Yes, that is what I said."

"And you still claim you dreamed your book?"

"I did. I dreamt most of my story and imagined other parts."

"Are you psychic?"

"Excuse me?"

"Are you clairvoyant? Are you able to gain information about objects, people, locations, or events by extrasensory perception?"

"I don't believe so. Sometimes I get a funny sensation in my stomach when something's about to happen. And lately, I've been getting a lot of ringing in my ears." She glanced back at the Coke machine to make sure the apparatus was still there. It was.

"Are you experiencing that sensation now?"

"No, but I did earlier."

"Did you have this sensation when you wrote your book?"

"Yes, all the time. Sometimes the feeling was so intense I feared I wouldn't be able to finish the book."

"Did your mother have these feelings?"

"I don't think so. Mom sensed when I was in trouble or bothered about something. Drove me crazy when I was a teen. I always assumed it was because she was a single mom."

"One, perhaps two, secrets in your book we can overlook." The Director stood up and walked around her desk. She sat on the edge of the desk facing Sarina. "But not two hundred and thirty-six pages of them. The most logical explanation is we have a mole, and he or she has told you about OEL."

"No, no one told me anything about OEL," Sarina said in defense. "I must have heard about the agency on the news."

"I can assure you, you haven't. OEL is an organization of the government which doesn't exist — not on paper, not in funding. And even if the agency did, there is no way you could find anything describing the Command Center. You got its appearance right, even down to the Coke machine and the geometrical design in the carpeting. Any idea how?"

"I wondered the same thing the moment the lights came on in the other room," Sarina said. "How did I write such details about a place I've never seen?"

"How indeed. Let's try something else. What can you tell me about the rock formation on the moon?"

"The arch is real too?" Sarina asked.

21

"Afraid so. Since the formation is a natural structure, you might have seen a picture of the rocks somehow. But we can't find a single picture or diagram of it. Not even at NASA. But a lack of proof doesn't mean the evidence doesn't exist. Do you recall ever seeing the structure?"

"Not only do I remember, but I can even tell you the date," Sarina said with joy. "The date was July 26th of last year. I remember because that day is my birthday. Steven was home on leave, and the two of us went out for my birthday. I had a few drinks and was a little tipsy, so we retired to bed shortly after returning home. During the night, I had this vivid dream of the moon and the rock formation. At first, the structure appeared to be just a plain wall of rock. But as I drew closer, I distinguished a band of blue rock forming an arch. And from within the formation came an eerie yellow glow from lights. I remember walking through the arch down a long tunnel to a hidden underground hangar. Then I realized the room was more than a hangar; it was an underground space station. Someone touched my shoulder and called out my name. His touch startled me so much I bolted up in bed. Nearly scared Steven half to death. I tried going back to sleep, but I couldn't. All I thought about was the arch and the space station. Fearing I wouldn't remember the dream in the morning, I got up and wrote the description down. I was still writing when Steven woke up four hours later. That's the day I started writing my book."

"Did you visualize the fighter planes then also?" the Director asked.

"Yes, they filled the hanger. Most were small fighters, but I saw larger spacecraft mixed amongst them."

The Director nodded to the secretary. Sally reached inside her briefcase on the floor, removed a paper, and placed it on the table before Sarina. Sarina stared at a perfect representation of the space aircraft in her book.

"Is this what the small fighters looked like?"

"Yes," Sarina said, her excitement disappearing. "You had someone draw a picture of the fighters in my book?"

"What you are looking at is not a drawing," the Director said. "But an actual picture of a spacecraft seen flying into your arch on the moon."

"No way," Sarina shouted, jumping to her feet. "There is no way I dreamt about a real spaceship on the moon." She searched her mind for an explanation, any explanation. "All starships appear the same. I probably saw this one in the new *Star Wars* movie. I've seen it four times. Or from a *Star Trek* episode. There must be tons of movie and TV starships that have this design."

"True," a calm Director said. "But they don't have your designation."

Sarina lifted the picture for a closer view. There, in bright red letters below the cockpit, was the designation UPB45. That was the identical lettering on her heroes' aircraft. Her eyes diverted to the right of the insignia, praying the double star image was not there. It was.

"What the hell," Sarina dropped the picture onto the floor. "What are you people trying to do? Convince me my book is real? I don't buy it. I want to go home! This is bullshit." Grabbing her coffee cup, she carried it to the back table where a soldier had left a carafe of coffee. Her hands trembled, spilling the coffee she poured. She had to get it together.

"One more thing," the Director said while Sarina kept her back towards her. "As Deputy-Director Macintosh told you, we have been picking up radio signals coming from the moon. Until last night, we had no luck in deciphering them. The moment you arrived, we received a coherent message. It said, 'Flimflam Girl, call home'."

The sound of breaking china broke the stillness of the air as Sarina dropped her coffee cup. She sat down on the nearest chair; her legs too weak to return to her seat. The blood drained from her face. She blinked at the Director. "You are wrong. Such a message is not possible."

"As you have stated many times," the Director said. "Yet it is a fact. Can you tell us who or what the Flimflam Girl is?"

Sarina tried to speak, but her words would not come out. She was afraid. No, afraid was too mild a word. She was terrorized, traumatized beyond belief. If she answered, then this was reality. But she had to answer, had to learn the truth. She tried again, and this time, her words emerged, although faint. "It's me."

"I'm sorry, I didn't hear you," the Director said.

"It's me," Sarina said, louder this time. "I'm the Flimflam Girl. At least I was. Flimglam Girl was a special word my mother called me, a name only she and I knew."

"Might one of your siblings know the secret word?" Director Santiago asked.

"As I am sure you are aware of, Director, I have no siblings. But the words were more than a pet name. It was a code."

"A code?"

"Yes. My mother gave me the word to protect me. Do you know how parents give their kids a secret word in case of an emergency and someone else needs to pick them up from school? The name is like that. The difference is this word meant I was in terrible danger, and I needed to hide."

"What kind of danger?" Deputy Santiago asked.

"She would never tell me. She would only say it meant something bad was going to happen. Really bad. Are you sure that's what the message said?"

The Director reached over to the remote control and pushed a button. "Harry, play the message we received from the moon at 0-one hundred."

"Yes, Ma'am."

A few seconds later, over the loudspeaker in the room, came a female's voice. "Flimflam Girl, call home." The message repeated five times, with a fifteen-second pause between the announcements.

"Do you recognize the voice?" the Director asked.

"It almost sounds like my mother."

"Isn't she dead?"

"Yes, she died fifteen years ago."

"Does your childhood home still exist?"

"No. Contractors demolished the house about five years ago to make room for some condos. Might we take a break? I have a horrible headache."

Realizing how stressful this examination was, the Director agreed. "Of course. I've given you a lot to ponder. Perhaps some coffee or something else to drink? And a call to your children?"

Sarina took a sip of water. As the liquid washed down her throat, so did her fear. Somehow, the words "Flimflam Girl" were quieting her insides, replacing her worry with intrigue and wonder. She realized the things she wrote in her book couldn't harm her. They were only words.

"I've changed my mind. If you have no objections, I'd like to do what the message said. I want to call home."

"Are you sure?" The Director asked.

"Oh, yes," Sarina giggled. "I can't quit now."

"Sally, get us a telephone and an outgoing line," the Director ordered. She wanted Sarina to make the call before she changed her mind.

"Yes, Ma'am," Sally said. She hurried from the room, returning with an old fashion push-button phone. After plugging the phone into the phone jack, she sat the communication device on the table beside Sarina. "All set."

Sarina rose and walked over to the waiting phone. Her legs shaking, she thought it best to sit down. "I hope I remember the number," she whispered as she dialed the digits. 1--847 -. She stood, too nervous to sit still. 632. The Director and Sally scrutinized Sarina's actions. 8525.

"The phone is ringing," she said, sitting once more. How was this possible? The phone didn't exist anymore. She counted the rings. One, two, three. Then she hung up. "We had a calling code. Three rings, then one, then two." She redialed the number. 1-847632-8525. As soon as she detected the first ring, she hung up. Last dial. Too eager to sit, she stood and pushed the buttons and counted. One, two.

The phone click and a voice say, "Hello? Flimflam Girl?" There was no doubt in Sarina's mind who the voice belonged to. It WAS her mother. Her legs gave way, and she collapsed into the chair, unconscious from realizing the truth.

―――――――

"Mrs. Spalling? Mrs. Spalling, are you all right?" Director Santiago asked as Sally put cool washcloths on Sarina's face.

"You should call me Sarina," she said, sitting forward in the chair. She hung her head between her knees for a moment, clearing her head. When she felt better, she raised her eyes and beheld a room of questioning faces before her.

"Did someone answer?" the Director asked, praying the answer was yes.

"As I've said several times, it's impossible." Sarina took a sip of water from the glass on the table. "The voice was my mother. She answered the phone."

"But you stated your mother died fifteen years ago."

"She did because I was there. I held her hand and kissed her goodbye. I observed them bury her. But that voice was her. I'd recognize her voice anywhere."

"You're positive?"

"Without a doubt."

"Only one way to find out for sure," Sally said. "We need to exhume Mrs. Tensley's coffin and discover if her body is inside."

Sarina didn't hesitate. "Do it."

"Sargent Tillerson, I need to have a body exhumed," the Director said into the intercom. "A Jenny Tensley at... Where is your mom buried?"

"St. Joseph Cemetery in Erie, Michigan," Sarina said.

"The body is in St. Joseph Cemetery in Erie, Michigan," the Director repeated. "I need this to be fast and quiet. Bring the body to the bunker."

"Yes, Ma'am."

"We should have an answer on your mother's body within six hours," Director Santiago said. "Your profile states your father died before you were born. Did your mother tell you anything about him?" A perplexed expression overshadowed Sarina's face again. "I wouldn't be an efficient investigator, Sarina, if I didn't investigate your background: your mother, her parents, your husband, and his parents. But we found no information about your father except the marriage license to your mother. There is no birth certificate, no Social Security number, no bank accounts, no school records, no nothing. It's like he was from another world."

"Mom never spoke much about him," Sarina said. "The mention of him pained her, so I didn't ask many questions. I remember her saying they had a whirlwind romance. And he died in a farm accident. When my mom died, I found several love letters he wrote to her."

"Would you mind if we analyzed the letters?"

"I don't mind, except they're back at the house. Perhaps you can answer some questions I have about him."

The Director glanced at her secretary. "I'll have someone retrieve them," Sally said.

"His name was John? John Andrew Tensley?" the Director asked.

"Yes."

"Can you confirm his birth date?"

"July 26, 1949. I was born on his birthday."

"Do you remember, by any chance, the date of his death?"

"No," Sarina said. "But he died before I was born, so I'm estimating the end of 1975 or before July 1976."

"Sally, check the local newspaper for that period," the Director said. "Search for anything about a farm accident. There might be an obituary."

"Yes, Ma'am. I'll get right on both items." She left the room.

"If you don't mind, Director, I'd like to call my children now," Sarina said.

"Of course. Feel free to use the phone."

Sarina studied the black object on the table. "If you wouldn't mind, I'd rather use a different phone. That one spooks me out."

"I understand." The Director pressed the intercom button again. "Sam, I need another phone in here."

"On my way."

"Have you changed your mind about going home?" the Director asked.

"I still want to go home. But now, I'd rather go later than sooner. I have to figure out what in the hell is going on," Sarina said.

"Then welcome to the OEL's rollercoaster."

––––––––––

For a few minutes, Sarina reveled in the sound of the kids' voices. She talked to each one, assuring them she was fine, and they'd be seeing each other soon. Jeremy told her he had spoken with their father, and he had arrived at Fort Bragg. He should be home by 0-nine hundred the following morning. Sarina talked to her sister-in-law last. Aunt Cindy was a little freaked out by what was happening at the house, especially by the two soldiers standing guard outside the home. And they forbid the children from going to school or from leaving the house. Jeremy even had to miss practice, and it was doubtful they would allow him to attend his game on Friday. Sarina assured her Steven would sort the problems out when he arrived home. She asked for her husband to call her as soon as possible.

Sarina surveyed the faces in the Command Center for the Director. She needed answers. Why were her children being kept home? Jeremy couldn't miss the game on Friday night. But neither the Director nor Sally was anywhere in sight.

"Mrs. Spalling, the Director asked me to show you to your quarters," said a tall dark-haired man in uniform. "She thought you'd want to lie down for a while, then freshen up before dinner."

"Might I see the Director?" Sarina asked. "I want to speak to her about my family."

"She will see you at dinner," the soldier said, speaking in a way that told Sarina the subject was closed.

"What about Deputy-Director MacIntosh?" Sarina figured he was the next best thing.

"He will see you at dinner as well."

Thinking Sally would not be available either, Sarina dropped her line of inquiry. In silence, she followed the soldier. After several corridors and two airlifts, the soldier stopped at a door. Taking out a key from his pocket, he inserted the key into the lock and opened the door. "This is your room. If you need anything, push number 6 on the desk phone. Someone will assist you. Dinner is at seventeen hundred. Someone will return to escort you to the dining hall."

Sarina stepped into the room and placed her jacket and purse on the table. When the door closed, the unmistakable sound of a lock turning sounded. Was she a prisoner? Was the soldier standing guard outside? What did they think she would do, try to escape? Escape to where? She didn't even know where she was.

Sarina awoke to the sound of a soft knock on her door. Her eyes darted to the clock on the wall. Sixteen-thirty. She had been asleep for several hours.

"One moment," she said as she scrambled to the bathroom to check her appearance. Seeing she was still presentable, she proceeded to the door. To her surprise, the structure opened when she turned the doorknob.

"I'm to escort you to the dining hall," the soldier said. As they walked down the stone corridor, Sarina tried to memorize the way. But the dull floors and walls blurred together, making it impossible to distinguish their route. Was this the same way they went before? Realizing it was useless to learn the path, she followed behind the soldier in silence. Upon entering the hall, the soldier spoke to a civilian. "Mrs. Spalling is joining the Director for dinner."

"If you would follow me," the man said. Doing as requested, Sarina stepped into the dining hall. The room was more of a military mess hall than a regular dining room. It was small, not much bigger than Mary's school cafeteria, filled with rows of tables with benches. At the end of the rows was an area devoid of furniture except for one round table and six chairs. Seated were Director Santiago, Deputy-Director MacIntosh, and Sally.

"Is your room to your liking?" Director Santiago asked.

"Yes," Sarina answered, taking the seat the greeter pulled out for her. "I was surprised at how well furnished my room was. I expected something more military."

"The crew's quarters are less elegant," the Deputy Director said. "We try to keep our guests' quarters somewhat nicer."

"Do you have lots of guests?" Sarina asked.

Deputy-Director MacIntosh laughed. "Now that you mention it, no. You're the first." He paused for a moment. "I owe you an apology for the way I handled our meeting, Mrs. Spalling. I am sorry if I scared you and your family." Sarina searched his face for sincerity, wondering if he apologized on his own or if the Director ordered him to. "I'm more accustomed to interrogating criminals and terrorists than civilians. Please forgive me."

"If you had told me what you wanted to know about my book and why, I would have come more willingly," Sarina said. "Apology accepted."

"Were you able to speak to your children?" Director Santiago asked.

"Yes. Jeremy said they are being made to stay at home: no school and no basketball practice. My son is up for a college sports scholarship. It is imperative he goes to practice and attends his game on Friday night."

"I'm afraid that is impossible," the Director said. "Until we can understand what is going on, your children are safer if I keep them under our protection."

"Under protection?" a surprised Sarina asked. "From what? An alien spaceship? Do you think a ship from the moon will come down and steal my children?"

"No, not from the moon," Deputy Director Macintosh replied.

"Then, from where? Earth?"

This time the Director answered. "Sarina, your book is out there for the world to read. Others are going to realize that what you wrote in your book is real, describes places and events you should have no knowledge of. These people will want to know how you know what you know, and they will want your knowledge. You have opened a Pandora's box." The Director paused, the muscles on her face tensing. "Sarina, the people I speak of are ruthless and will stop at nothing to get to the truth, including using your children as bargaining chips."

"For the hundredth time, my book is FICTION," Sarina screamed, wondering why no one believed her. A hush came over the room as those present paused because of Sarina's outburst. Realizing everyone in the room was looking at her and sensing their surprise, she lowered her voice. "Why won't you believe me?"

"It's not a question of believing you. It's about what is real and what isn't. Can you sit there and still say your book is only fiction? After everything you wrote? Me, the OEL, the moon arch, the radio message, your mom answering the phone? And the Coke machine?"

Sarina wanted to scream at the top of her lungs that her story was a creation of her imagination, but she couldn't. Not anymore. "I can't. Do you think my family is in danger?"

"Without a doubt," the Director said. "And not only from opposing governments. Underground organizations such as the Illuminati, the Seven, the Serpico, and other groups will hunt you, and them, down. They are relentless, Sarina. They do not stop until they get what or who they want."

"Those organizations are real?" Sarina asked, unable to hide her vocal elevation. She heard stories about those organizations, their unscrupulous ways of doing things, how they tortured people, worked outside the law. Were Steven and the children in danger?

"I assure you, Sarina, they exist," the Director said. "Already, we're getting reports of your name being uttered in the underground. Agencies are receiving requests for pictures of the moon. Even the Soviet astronauts aboard the International Space Station are showing renewed interest in Earth's lunar sphere."

"Then why aren't my children and husband under your protection?" a concerned mother asked.

"I am working on it," the Director said. "In the meantime, I'd like you to try calling your mother's home again after dinner. We tried calling the number back and doing the code, but no one would speak. Whoever or whatever is on the other end will only respond to you."

"And if my mom answers again?"

"You need to speak with her, find out what she wants, what we do next," Director Santiago said. "We're at a dead end with nowhere to go. Can you call her?"

"I can try. When will you receive word if my mother is in her grave or not?"

"Her casket is being exhumed as we speak. I expect a report within the hour."

After dinner, the four returned to the Conference Room beside the Control Room. Sarina sat next to the phone, trying to summon strength enough to make the call. Taking a deep breath, she dialed the number. After three rings, she hung up. She dialed again, letting the phone ring just once. Dialing a third time, the first ring sounded. Her heart pounded, and a slight ringing returned to her ears. Ring two. She held her breath. Ring three. Ring four? Had she done something wrong?

"Try again," Director Santiago said.

Sarina repeated the process, but the outcome was the same. No one answered the phone. She tried two more times with the same result.

"Maybe they've stepped out for the evening," Sarina nervously giggled.

"Perhaps," Director Santiago said. "There are a million reasons why no one is answering. We'll try again tomorrow."

MOTHER AND DAUGHTER MEET

Robots in shiny silver armor surrounded Sarina, keeping her safe inside their circle. Those on the outside of the ring clashed with an unknown enemy to save Earth. She fired her weapon, killing the blurred aliens determined to annihilate her. Somewhere in the distance, a constant ringing sounded. The robot beside her told her to run to the ship as before. She didn't see a means of transport and asked him where her ride was. But instead of words, the ringing of an alarm clock emerged from his mouth.

The fogginess in Sarina's mind cleared as she awakened. Time to get up and get the kids ready for school. She wanted to remain cozy and warm beneath the covers for a few more minutes, but not with that annoying sound. Lordy, how she hated the ring. The sound dug into her nerves, vibrated her eardrum. She reached over to hit the snooze button but could not find the knob. Where in the heck was the stupid button? Begrudgingly, she opened her eyes. There was no alarm, just the starkness of the walls that imprisoned her. She was at the Compound. Her mother! She had called home, and her mother answered. Now awake, she sat up and viewed the clock. O-nine thirty hours. She never slept this late. Even on the weekends, she was up by 0-seven hundred hours.

Since the hour was late, she passed on the shower. She brushed her teeth, put a little makeup on, got dressed, and grabbed the small packet of medication on the table. Popping the pills in her mouth, she drank several sips of water. Turning, she walked to the door. Upon opening it, she saw Fred waiting.

"Morning, Fred," Sarina greeted.

"Good morning, Mrs. Spalling. Ready for another exciting day in the bunker?"

"Is that what you call them? Exciting?" Sarina laughed. She wouldn't characterize her stay so far in the secret installation as exciting, more like a page out of an alien mystery.

"I consider everything that has happened fascinating," Fred said. "The thought of aliens living on the moon electrifies me so much I can barely stand. I've always accepted intelligent life out there in space. It's so logical. Why would God create such a vast expanse as the universe and put life on only one planet? Astronomers estimate for each star we see, there's a ten percent chance the glowing dot is a sun with three to eight planets orbiting it. If even one percent of those planets contain life, that would mean there are millions of life forms for us to meet."

"Sounds like you've given this a lot of consideration, Fred."

"I've dreamed of nothing else since I was a little kid. That's why I joined the military and requested this assignment the moment I was old enough. I knew it was just a matter of time before we'd make contact."

"Any ideas on why the story I fantasized is real?"

Fred stopped. He turned around and snickered at the woman behind him. "Because you didn't."

"I didn't what?" Sarina asked.

"You didn't make your story up." A strange smile spread across the soldier's face as if an idea had formed in his mind. "You don't know, do you? You're too close to the problem to see the truth."

"See what?" Sarina asked, intrigued by Fred's line of logic.

"They told you what to write," Fred said, leaning down and whispering the words so no one else heard. "They contacted you through your dreams."

"Do you think so?"

"If they are advanced enough to be living on the moon without our detection, they can send us messages. Do you ever get ringing in your ears, ringing you can't explain?"

"Yes," Sarina said. "Lately, often. And now that I think of it, the ringing started about the time I began dreaming about the story."

"That's them trying to contact you," Fred peered around the corridor as if aliens would emerge from the walls. "Something is about to happen, and they needed to get in touch with us without freaking everyone out. At least it's what I assume."

"But what's the message? And why me?"

"I don't have the answers to either of those questions," Fred said, continuing his way to the dining hall. "My advice is to be patient. Let them call the shots."

"Not much else I can do."

"Here you are, Ma'am," Fred said when they reached the dining hall. "I leave you in the capable hands of Ms. Rushmore."

"Good morning, Sarina," Sally greeted. "Did you sleep well?"

"Too well," Sarina laughed. "It's the reason I'm late for breakfast." She searched the room for the Director and Deputy Director, but neither were visible. "I suppose both Directors have already eaten?"

"Yes, Director Santiago ate at 0-seven hundred after her usual hour exercise regimen in the gym," Sally said. "Deputy-Director MacIntosh left last night after you retired. He should be back in several days."

Sarina wondered who he would drag out of their homes now. "You have a gym?"

"Yes. You are more than welcome to use the equipment. Director Santiago asked me to bring you to the Command Center after breakfast," Sally added. "I have your coffee ready." The secretary waved her hand to the right. A nearby table contained a cup of coffee, a glass of orange juice, and water.

"Any word on my mother's grave?" Sarina asked as she sat on a bench.

"The report came in this morning at 0-three hundred. I believe what it says is one item Director Santiago wishes to discuss with you."

"What did it say?"

"I don't have the information." Sarina wondered if the woman was telling the truth.

"What's worth ordering on the menu?"

"Chef can cook anything you'd want: pancakes, waffles, oatmeal, omelets, eggs, and meat. You name what you want. We also have a variety of cold cereals."

"By any chance, can he make a Farmer's omelet?" Sarina sheepishly asked. She seldom indulged in such things unless she was on vacation or for her birthday. Her current situation was like a vacation-a forced, against-your-will vacation. She decided to splurge this one time.

"It's one of his specialties," Sally said, a smile on her face. "No one orders them, except the Director on Sundays. The chef would be ecstatic to make one." The secretary called an aide over and gave him Sarina's order. While they waited, they chatted about little things: how long Sally had been the Director's secretary, did she have a family, how did she not go crazy cooped up down there, etc. In return, Sarina told her about her three children, her military husband, and her life as an author.

After eating the best omelet ever, the two women proceeded to the Command Center. The Director was talking to an elderly gray-haired man on the overhead screen. By the decorations on his uniform, Sarina figured he must be a Brigadier General or

Admiral. She always had trouble determining an officer's rank by his pins.

"I'll call you this evening, Sir," Director Santiago said as Sarina entered the room. "Twenty-one hundred."

"Looking forward to hearing what you have," the man said. He shot Sarina a glance before the screen went dark. After thirty seconds, the screen reverted to an image of the moon.

"Good morning, Sarina," the Director greeted. "I see you are a late sleeper."

"Not usually," Sarina said, a flash of embarrassment crossing her face. "Normally, I'm up by 0-six-thirty during the week, 0-seven-thirty on the weekends."

Ignoring Sarina's response, the Director said, "We have a lot of work to do today, but let's try calling home again first. Then Sally will go through your book with you page by page. See if you remember anything specific on how you imagined the storyline." Before Sarina asked, she added, "Oh, I received the report on your mother's grave. The coffin was empty. No body. My men will question the funeral home to discover why."

Empty? Why was the coffin empty? She was present when they lowered the lid with her mother inside. "Are they sure?" Sarina saw the disapproving glance in the Director's eyes. Of course, she was sure. Agents had conducted the exhumation. They didn't make mistakes.

The subject of her mother's missing body closed, the Director turned and walked into the Conference Room. When Sarina didn't follow, the Director stopped and glared at her. "Well, aren't you coming?"

"Yes, yes." Was the Director acting differently than she had the previous day? More reserved, colder, more like Sarina was a problem she didn't want to deal with? Had the man on the screen said something to upset her? Or was she always cranky in the morning? The Director had stated that was the reason her staff bought her the Coke machine.

Sarina called her childhood home. The results were the same as the day before and continued to be each time afterward. No one answered.

Sally and Sarina spent the rest of the day going through her book. The work was tedious. Why did she have the secret team meet on Yale Street in the heart of Chinatown? How did she come up with the idea of the space aircraft? Time and time again, she had no explanation, but Sally pressed on. Also included in the discussions were recordings of her conversations with Stephen while stationed in Afghanistan. There were copies of the phone calls coming into and out of her residence for the past year. Realizing the depth to which OEL had penetrated her personal life, Sarina questioned the legality of the government organization's actions. Sally said they were Homeland Security and could do whatever they wanted in the name of terrorism. And having aliens on the moon fell into that realm. Besides, since the organization didn't exist, no one could complain about their operating tactics. Sally regretted ever writing the damn book.

Before returning to her room, Sarina called home and spoke with Steven and the kids. Timmy and Mary were thrilled to stay at home from school, except for the homework their teachers sent. But Jeremy was furious. His confinement to the house would cost him his college scholarship. Determined not to lose his dreams, he tried several times to sneak out of a bedroom or basement window. No matter how quiet and careful he was, a guard always caught him and brought him inside. Steven realized how important Jeremy's basketball career was to his son. He explained there would be other opportunities but going outside was too dangerous. Jeremy didn't listen.

At nineteen hundred two days later, a guard escorted Sarina to the Command Center. She was surprised to see Director Santiago waiting for her in the Conference Room. Ever since the Director spoke to the officer on the viewing screen, Sarina had seen nothing of her. From her expression, Sarina surmised she was not happy.

"Please sit down, Sarina," Director Santiago said. On the table beside the Director sat an advance copy of her book.

"Did something else happened?" Sarina asked, hoping the answer was no. Her nerves frayed, and her stamina dwindling, she wasn't sure how much more she could take.

Ignoring the question, Director Santiago slid Sarina's book towards her. "Please open to page two hundred and forty-two." Sarina did as asked. "Describe the scene taking place."

This page opened with a description of an alien starship drilling a sample hole in California. They were extracting massive amounts of gold buried deep within the earth. She and Sally had already discussed this in some detail. The Director had to know.

"Sally and I went over this. I..."

"Yes, but I would like you to tell me," Director Santiago interrupted. Sarina tried to read the Director's face. What was she thinking? But her expression was emotionless, almost statue-like. The Director was searching for something.

"As I told Sally, I had the book almost done," Sarina said. "I was proofing the book and got this idea of the aliens wanting to test the purity of our minerals before strip-mining the Earth. I chose gold because that element is such a fantastic heat conductor. Gold is a desirable mineral."

"How did they dig the hole?"

"With their advanced technology." Sarina gave a slight giggle, but the Director wasn't amused. Becoming sober, Sarina continued. "Lasers and sound drills dig mile-wide holes in a matter of seconds. They drill into the earth at the rate of a foot per minute. An enormous tube siphons up ground-up dirt and rock and dumps into a holding area where it's examined and separated. When complete, the only thing remaining is a hole with polished sides and no debris."

"Like this?" Abigail pushed a paper across the table. Sarina gawked at a picture of a drilled hole precisely as she described in her book. The opening extended downward for miles, the sides smooth and shiny as if polished to a high gloss. The area around the entrance was undisturbed. Not even a rock appeared out of place.

Sarina shook her head, refusing to admit another part of her book was reality. "I don't know what to say. I made the drilling up."

"LIAR," the Director shouted, slamming her fist on the table. Startled by the Director's sudden action, Sarina pushed herself and her chair several inches away from the table. "Tell me how you know these things. How did you write about events which haven't even happened yet?"

Something inside Sarina snapped. She was tired of being scared, afraid of what other truths her book might reveal. She decided at that moment that if the book was real, real it was. If aliens had communicated with her in her sleep to write it, so be it. The Director or anyone else would no longer intimidate her. Sarina looked her in the eyes, an expression of determination and strength on her face. "I'm not a liar. That picture could be of anything. An alternative way to mine using lasers. Even a photo constructed in Photoshop. Where on Earth was the picture taken?"

"It's not a picture from Earth," the Director said. "It's on Enceladus. NASA's Cassini spacecraft took the shot a few weeks ago when the craft flew by Saturn. NASA received several images of the drilled hole at 0-nine hundred this morning. I received a copy an hour ago."

"Enceladus? One of Saturn's moons? I don't understand. My book has nothing to do with Saturn. How was I able to describe a hole billions of miles away? NASA knew nothing about this before last night?" The ringing in her ears returned.

"No. And the hole wasn't there six months ago when Cassini took pictures of the same area. Who, or should I say, what are you?"

"What am I?" Sarina screamed, jumping to her feet, and staring down at the Director. "I'm a human like you." Doubt crossed the Director's face. "You think I'm an alien, don't you? Or I'm connected to them. I'm not!"

"Then, perhaps you can explain this." Director Santiago threw a report on the table, letting the pages slide to Sarina. She studied the writer's face to see if she already knew what the report disclosed. As she read, Sarina's facial expression turned from surprise to disbelief, then drained to an ashy white. "That report says you are NOT completely human. You have a gene never seen before. So, I ask again, who are you?"

Sarina slowly sat back down in her chair, unable to accept the information. How could she be different? She WAS human; she was sure of it. Her mother was human. Her father was human. At least she believed he was. That's ridiculous; of course he was. But what if they didn't believe her? Thoughts of government experiments and alien abductions crept into her mind. Anticipating they would not allow her to leave, Sarina defiantly said, "I want to go home now."

"I'm afraid we're way past you going home," the Director said. "Not until...". A soldier rushed in after a brief knock. "Get out."

"Director, we're getting another message from the moon," the soldier said.

"Bring her," the Director commanded. With a guard on each side, Sarina followed the Director to the Command Center. Upon entering the room, Director Santiago voiced her orders before anyone even sat down. "Play the message."

The sound of a female's voice came over the speaker. "Flimflam Girl, call home now. I am waiting." Then silence.

"Is this the voice you heard before?" the Director asked, her heart racing. Were they finally going to make contact?

"Yes. It's my mom."

"Get the phone," Director Santiago said. "And make sure the recording equipment is rolling. I want this all on audio and video."

The ringing in Sarina's ears grew louder. She remembered what Fred said about what the ringing meant. Were they trying to reach her? She didn't have time to speculate about the cause now. Glaring at the phone on the desk, Sarina debated her options. The phone gave her leverage, a bargaining chip, an opportunity to go home.

"Call home," the Director ordered. Sarina didn't move. "I said, call home."

"No."

"What do you mean, no?"

"I want a written statement saying I can go home today, or no phone call," Sarina said. "I also want to call my husband, and you will tell him I am coming home TODAY. Not tomorrow, not next week, but today."

"You do not dictate to me when you are going home," the Director angrily said. "Plus, as I already told you, it is too dangerous for you to leave our protection."

"I'll take my chances."

"No."

"Then dial the number yourself."

"Lieutenant, call the number and use the code," the Director ordered.

"Ma'am, we've tried numerous times," the soldier said. "No one answers when we call."

"Dial it."

Doing as instructed, the Lieutenant dialed the phone number. He did as Sarina had, letting the phone ring three times, then once and then twice. Nothing happened. Understanding the expression on the Director's face, he tried again. Same results. When he placed the receiver back on the phone cradle, the receiver burst into flames. Sarina pushed her chair away from the inferno on the desk. The ringing in Sarina's ears intensified, almost to the point of causing pain.

Everyone jumped when the intercom crackled. Within seconds, the room filled with the same high-pitched hum as in

Sarina's ears. Unable to bear the sound, everyone covered their ears in pain.

"Only she may call," came the female voice. "Only she."

The ringing in Sarina's ears disappeared. "Do you want to write the note first or talk with my husband?" Sarina asked the Director.

"She'll write the note," said a stranger who walked into the room. He wore a green uniform with many medals and stripes. He had gray hair and a beard, although shorter than when he had appeared on the screen several days earlier. Perhaps the Director had been in such a foul mood because someone else was calling the shots.

"And you are?" Sarina asked.

The man smiled. He liked her spunk. "I am Major General Thomas Hancock. I am now in charge of this operation." Sarina didn't like the change in authority. The Major General tilted his head towards Abigail. "Director."

She nodded, "Major General. I wasn't expecting you until tomorrow."

"I got away early," he said. "Sally, is it? Would you get Director Santiago a pen and paper? And someone get Mrs. Spalling a phone which is not burning." When the new phone arrived, the Major General handed Sarina the receiver. "If you would call your husband so I may speak to him.".

"Not until I have the written statement by Director Santiago," Sarina said, audacity in her voice.

"Abigail, are you done yet?" the Major General asked.

"Signing my name now," she said. Her signature complete, she handed the letter to Sarina, who skimmed over the document.

"I need a cell phone to send a copy of this to my oldest son and husband," Sarina said. A signed paper saying she could go home was useless unless someone on the outside had a copy.

"I'm afraid, Mrs. Spalling, we cannot use a cell phone here," the Major General said. "We only have landlines."

"You're lying again, Major General." Sarina took a step towards him, standing as tall as possible. "There's a way of getting information in and out of this facility. I received a report about my DNA a short while ago. That report came from Virginia."

The Major General turned and gave Abigail a disapproving glance. "It may be true the report is from Virginia, but if so, it arrived by the good old U. S. mail service. We still get mail here."

"You're still lying," Sarina said. "No fax, no call."

"No call, no fax," the Major General sneered. "No fax, no going home."

"Oh, stop, Thomas." Abigail grabbed the signed paper. "She has us, and she knows it. We don't know how long we have to make the call, how long they'll wait." She walked over and sat down at the desk next to Sarina. After typing in a password, she walked over to the scanner and took a copy which immediately appeared on the computer screen. "There you are, Sarina. A copy of my signed letter. The line is open. You can email both your husband and son." She stepped back, eyeing the Major General, daring him to stop either of them.

Before the Major General changed his mind, Sarina entered the email addresses. Within seconds, a copy of the letter was racing to her son's and husband's emails.

"I'll take that phone now." Sarina dialed her phone number, wondering who would answer. It was Mary. "Hi, Mary. It's Mom. I need to speak to Daddy. Yes, I'm fine. I'll talk to you after I speak with Daddy. (pause) Yes, I promise."

"Dad, Mom's on the phone."

"Sarina?" Steven asked.

"Hi. I have someone who wants to speak with you," Sarina said. She stared at the officer before her. "But first, I have to tell you I sent you and Jeremy a signed letter by Director Santiago stating I get to come home today. There's been some debate about me having to stay here. (pause) No, I don't want to stay. (pause) Yes, I'm okay."

The Major General held out his hand. "Allow me." Begrudgingly, she placed the phone in his palm. "Captain Spalling, this is Major General Thomas Hancock. Because of some recent developments, we need to keep your wife a little longer. I am sure you understand." Steven's outraged voice erupted from the phone. "I assure you; she is being taken care of. (pause) Unfortunately, I am now in command, so the letter Director Santiago gave your wife is null and void. Good Night." He hung up the phone.

Sarina's face flushed a deep red. "I told my daughter I would speak to her. And I wasn't finished speaking to my husband."

"The time for idle chitchat is over," the Major General said. "We have more important matters to attend to. We kept our end of the bargain; it's time for you to keep yours. Or must I remind you your husband is still an active officer in the U. S. military, and I can have him reassigned anywhere in the world? Perhaps as an adviser with the Iranian troops on the front line? Or fighting insurgents in Africa? If you don't want your children left with no parent, I suggest you cooperate."

Rage swelled inside Sarina. How dare this man threaten her husband and family? The Major General had won this round, but she was determined to win the next one. Thinking she had no options if she wanted to keep Steven home, Sarina dialed the number. After the third ring, her mother, or whom she suspected was her mother, answered.

"Flimflam Girl?"

"It's me," Sarina said. "I've been trying to call you."

"Sorry. There were things we needed to complete before we accepted your call," Sarina's mother replied. "Plus, your location must be within sight of the moon for you to receive our transmissions." Without warning, the display on the wall went blank. After fifteen seconds, the screen flashed bright orange, filling the room with a blinding light. As fast as the luminosity appeared, the brightness vanished, leaving an image of her mother on the screen. At least the being resembled her mother, but a younger version. Her mom was sixty-two when she died. The mother on the screen appeared in her forties. Sarina's eyes filled with tears.

"Momma, is that you?" Sarina asked.

"Not exactly." A man walked into the picture. "She's a duplicate of who your mother was. Same face, same voice, but a synthetic life form. We hoped contacting you would be easier if you saw someone you were familiar with."

"So, there are more of you?" the Major General butted in.

"I am not speaking to you," the man said, authority audible in his voice. "I will converse with you later. Until then, shut up, or I will end this conversation, and you can go screw yourself and your government."

Sarina laughed, as did Abigail, at seeing the anger on the Major General's face.

"Sarina, have you taken shelter?" her mother asked. "Are my grandbabies and son-in-law safe with you?"

"No," Sarina said. "I'm being held at some military facility. Steven and the kids are still at home in Michigan."

"We cannot allow this," her mother said. "Steven and my grand-babies must join you immediately."

"Are you being held there against your will?" the man on the screen asked.

Before Sarina answered, the Major General spoke up again. "Mrs. Spalling is our guest for a few days. I assure you..." The screen went blank. "What in the hell happened?"

"You opened your mouth again, Thomas," the Director said, doing her best to hide her glee. "He told you to keep quiet."

"Get them back," the Major General ordered.

"I have no way of reconnecting with the moon, Sir," the communications officer replied.

"Then someone dial the damn phone number," he bellowed.

"They won't answer, Sir," the officer said. "Only Mrs. Spalling can dial the number. They won't answer if anyone else tries."

The Major General glared at Sarina. "Let me guess. You will not call them back until your family arrives."

"That is correct!"

AN ALIEN CONVERSATION

As the officer had predicted, no one answered the phone if someone other than Sarina made the call. How did they determine it wasn't Sarina calling? After two days, the Major General had to concede. He ordered the Spalling family be brought to the facility.

As soon as her family was safe in their quarters, Sarina told the Major General she would make the call. But with one stipulation--her husband would be at her side. The Major General refused, stating Commander Spalling did not have clearance. Abigail reminded him he had no choice and should be grateful she wanted nothing else. He didn't like his commands ignored, but he gave in. Sarina and the people on the screen had the upper hand for the moment.

With Steven beside her, Sarina dialed home. This time, the screen came alive after the first ring. Standing there, bigger than life, was Sarina's mother and the man they had seen before. Unsettled by seeing his dead mother-in-law, Steven gasped and sat down. The woman on the screen was a younger version of Jenny.

"Steven, I am so glad to see you," Sarina's mom said upon seeing him. "I assume my grand-babies are with you and safe?"

"Ah, yes." Steven stared. "They send their love." Could you send love to an artificial life form?

The man now spoke. "Major General, I see it only took you three days to realize we will only deal with your base through our daughter. Our disconnection was the only warning you will receive. Repeat your performance, and we will end all correspondence--permanently."

"Your daughter?" Sarina fell into the chair beside Steven. She stared at the man on the screen. Was he her father? A chill ran through Sarina's body at the thought. One ran through the Major General's too, but for a different reason. He thought Sarina was a threat to national security before the stranger spoke. Upon hearing she was this man's daughter, he knew she was a danger to the world.

"It's not possible," Sarina said softly, again fearing to speak the words out loud made them a reality. "My father's dead. He died before I was born."

"Your mother fabricated my death."

"You didn't die?"

"No."

His answer brought a whole new set of emotions into Sarina's body--anger, resentment, betrayal. "Then, you abandoned us?" Sarina stood, staring at the man, her words filled with rage. "You abandoned her when she needed you the most? She was pregnant with your child. What? The mighty spaceman couldn't stand the pressure of fatherhood?"

"Sarina, let him explain." Steven touched his wife's arm.

"No. Do you have any idea how hard Mom worked to support us, what she went without? She missed you every day she was alive. Even on her deathbed, she called for you. And now, after almost forty years, you've returned with open arms?"

"It wasn't like that," the man said. "I met and fell in love with your mother. The result is you. I did not know your mother was pregnant until her funeral."

"The hell with you," Sarina sat down, turning her back to the screen.

"Is, ah, is Sarina part, ah, alien?" Steven stuttered as he had trouble forming his words.

The man on the screen laughed. Not a little laugh, but a full belly laugh; a loud, hearty laugh of amusement. "Why would you say that? Do I look like an alien?"

"No, but you're up there," Steven wasn't sure why this was funny.

"I assure you, Sarina and I are as human as you," the father said. "Well, she is. Space changes people a little. After you live up here for a while, one of your genes usually mutates into something else. We believe the change allows you to thrive in space."

"Is that why my tests came back wrong?" Realizing the truth, Sarina forgot her anger for the moment.

Her father gave both the Major General and former Director Santiago a disapproving expression. "So, they've already done tests on you. Trying to figure out who and what you are? Typical Earth humans. So threatened, so scared. But I am surprised the mutation showed up in your DNA analysis. To my knowledge, you have never lived in space. There is no reason your DNA sequence should have changed. The fact it did is an exciting development, something we need to investigate."

"Sir, I'm Steven Spalling, Sarina's husband," Steven said. "Before we go any further, I believe introductions and a small explanation of what in the hell is going on is necessary."

"Yes, we seem to have gotten off the reason for our contact," the man said. "As for you, Steven, you are not a stranger to us. You're a Commander in the military, a loving husband, and a wonderful father. Serving your second tour in Afghanistan. You suffered an injury during your first deployment when a roadside bomb went off."

Sarina glanced at her husband. "You told me it was a car accident."

"It appears you kept the truth from your wife," the man said. "I did not mean to reveal your secret."

Steven stared at the screen. "How did you get this information? It's military and confidential."

"For now, all I can say is we do. Yes, Major General, you have a question?" The General raised his hand. So, Earth humans could be taught to respond appropriately.

"You've mentioned 'we' several times," the Major General said. "How many of you live up there?"

"A sound military question, Major General. One we will get to momentarily. For now, let's finish with Steven's request. Might I suggest those still standing take a seat? We may be here for a while. And some of what I will tell you might be a little shocking. No matter what you hear, please remember this: Neither you nor your planet are in any danger from us."

The few standing individuals sat down, except for the Major General. He remained standing, his eyes fixated upon the supposedly "human" on the screen.

"My name is Renn," he said. "By Earth years, I am one hundred and thirty-six years old. Our life expectancy is three hundred. As I mentioned before, I am as human as you. My parents were born on Earth and brought here during your Civil War. As with most humans, they met, fell in love, and produced my two siblings and me. We sometimes traveled to Earth, and on one of my missions, I met Jenny. For me, I fell in love with her the moment I met her. I married her two weeks later. We couldn't have been happier, but our joy soon turned to sorrow when a month after we married, I became deathly ill. My body had become poisoned by the pollutants I breathed, drank in the water, and ate in the food. I was dying. My only recourse was to return to the station for medical treatment. I begged your mother to return with me, but she wouldn't. She insisted her place was on Earth. I didn't know the real reason; she never told me she was carrying my child." He wiped a tear from his eye.

"It was several months before I was well enough for a brief trip back to Earth. I planned to bring your mother back with me no matter what her argument was. But when I arrived, I couldn't find My Jenny anywhere. I searched, but she had vanished without a trace. Over the years, I continued to search for her, but to no avail. She understood I would never stop trying to find her, so she hid well. I never knew where she was until her death notice appeared in the paper. Sarina, I never stopped loving her. I do so today."

"As I stated several days ago, the woman beside me is a biological artificial intelligent life form. I couldn't bear the thought of Jenny not being in this world. So, I took her body the night of her burial. I brought her here, where our scientists used her DNA to make a robotic replica of her. In her, they also placed her memories. She would be a blessing in disguise."

"But enough of sentimental by-gone days. I am sure the Major General is wondering who brought my parents and the other humans up and why," Renn said. "I believe the Commander of this station and my best friend can address those fears. His name is Glogg. For those of you in the military, don't go all Rambo on me. For the rest, don't be frightened. He's sizeable, but he's a pushover. Glogg, you're up."

Walking onto the screen was a ten-foot alien who was a cross between a grasshopper and an ant. He had colossal, black oval eyes which glistened with life. His face narrowed to a set of small pinchers. Above his head rose two long antennae covered in tiny black hairs. His skin was a shiny blue-black. He had two sets of arms and one pair of long legs. He wore a magenta-colored uniform. Sarina beheld a beautiful creature while the Major General gazed upon an enemy he needed to eradicate.

"I am delighted to meet you," Glogg said. "As Renn told you, I may appear fearful, but my race is not an aggressive species. I wish there were another way to make this introduction, but time is of the essence, as you will see."

"We call my species %IE**#+, but the humans refer to us as Caelifera. We are from a planet a hundred and thirty light-years away. As you can see, my species developed into something resembling what you call an insect, a grasshopper. At least, it's what I've been told. We are an old species, by your standards, going back some fifteen million years. We are a peace-loving nation devoted to the arts and sciences. About six million years ago, we used our intellect to further our world, and we developed the ability for space flight. We encountered other species, other civilizations, both ethical and corrupted. Determined to live in a free, safe world, some of us banded together to form the Interstellar Space Coalition. Collectively, we protect planets from marauding beings who strip planets of their water and minerals for resale. Humans are not the only ones driven by greed and desire for wealth. The worst of these marauders is a species called the Kett."

"Luckily for you, Earth is so far out in the galaxy that almost no one comes out this far. Your remoteness has kept you safe all these millennia. But about five thousand years ago, a Kett surveyor discovered Earth and her bounty. He reported back to his commander what he had found--a world full of water. And beneath her soil, untold amounts of gold, uranium, silver, precious stones, salt, and so much more. The moment they received the news, a harvesting fleet set sail for your planet."

"The International Space Coalition got wind of their excursion and became aware of your extraordinary planet," Glogg said. "A fleet intercepted and defeated them. But we realized they would return one day to complete their harvest. To keep this solar system safe, a group stayed behind and built a base inside your moon. From there, we have monitored your world and protected you."

"After two hundred years, our ancestors realized our bodies did not do well living under the conditions in your solar system. They started to die. A force of eight thousand soon became a crew of two thousand. They had to do something or abandon this post."

"Understanding Earth was too precious to leave unprotected, they opted to find reinforcements. We tried androids first, but they didn't have the empathy component to make responsible decisions. The only other option was humans. Our ancestors visited Earth, searching for beings who might be worthy of joining our crusade. They searched among the abandoned children your society had forgotten, people who lived simple lives and even some on death's door. Those deemed worthy we brought to the station. But we kept none against their will. Those who wanted to return, we brought back. We incorporated those who wished to stay in our way of life. Today on this station, there are six hundred and sixteen descendants of the original crew, two hundred and eighty-four of which are Caelifera. There are also three thousand, two hundred, and two humans. And yes, Major General, we do occasionally still recruit humans from Earth."

"That's what you call your kidnapping of citizens?" the Major General asked.

"Thomas, this isn't the time," Director Santiago whispered.

"It's okay, Director Santiago," Glogg said. "Renn warned me about your military personnel. They believe all aliens are bad and must be destroyed. He also advised me they would only see the negativity in our story, which I believe is correct at the moment."

The Major General grunted in disapproval.

"I've told you the who and the when," Glogg said. "Now for the why. As I explained, we constructed the base because we believed the Kett would return one day. That day has arrived. We have detected a vast fleet of their ships at the edge of your galaxy." A screen behind Glogg, Renn, and Jenny activated, showing a fleet of fifteen enormous alien ships, with several smaller vessels spaced intermittently throughout. Even at their reduced size, everyone could see they were predators; machines made to tear a planet apart. This time even the Major General was intimidated. "Meet the Kett and their planet destroyers. They build these ships for demolition and can eradicate a planet the size of Earth in four days. The six more-rounded ships with all the equipment extending out the sides and on top are the mining ships. They will siphon off the water and dig out huge chunks of earth to process. Minerals and gems are extracted from the dirt and, together with the water, pumped into the larger, somewhat dull cargo ships, of which there are nine. These ships have one purpose - to hold as much as possible. The ships push the left-over dirt into space to either drift away or rain back down onto the destroyed planet. No planet can survive their mining."

"They have already processed Neptune and the last three planets before her, planets you didn't even know existed. Next is Uranus. In the past, they were more interested in natural minerals and elements, so we assume they will bypass Saturn and Jupiter, but they will process most of their moons and Saturn's rings. We estimate they will reach Earth within eight months. If we hope to save Earth, we need to engage the Kett the moment they clear the Kuiper belt. To do so, we must release our fleet of destroyers and fighters. This means opening up the moon."

"Open up the moon?" a shocked Sarina asked. "You mean, pop the top off?"

Glogg laughed. "Not exactly, but we will lift a significant portion. And now, Major General, you know why we have contacted you. Our fleet's emergence will be something the people of Earth will see. We cannot hide their departure. You humans don't do well with what you don't understand, so we thought if we contacted you, explained to you what would happen, that knowledge might eliminate a lot of the panic."

"You think so?" the Major General snickered. "Do you believe our people won't panic when the moon opens, and a fleet of alien warships emerge?"

Glogg continued. "I must advise you we no longer have enough firepower to annihilate the Kett fleet. We have sent word out for reinforcements, but we do not know if they will arrive in time. Our best hope is to do enough damage to make them turn around and leave."

"And if they don't?" Steven asked.

"Then Earth and the rest of your planets will be no more."

"You don't paint a bright future," the Major General said.

"It's worse. If we cannot stop the Kett, and if reinforcements do not arrive, we will have no alternative but to abandon this post and leave."

"Go. Who's stopping you?"

"If we leave, Major General, so does our base."

"Your base? You mean the moon?" former Director Santiago asked.

"No, what's inside the moon. Our space station. Releasing the station will involve destroying a chunk of the moon."

"Then it's true?" Sarina asked. "The space station is real?"

"Yes, she's real," Glogg said.

"But the moon influences so much on Earth," Stephen said. "Not only the tides but cycles, life itself. Can the Earth survive without the moon?"

"That, we do not know," Glogg said. "We will do our best to minimize our emergence's impact. Even if she survives our departure, eliminating the other planets will drastically affect this system's gravity. We estimate such destruction will knock the Earth out of her orbit long before the Kett arrive. Plus, with all the space debris expelled, the chances are high that a massive meteor will hit and destroy her."

"Now the truth comes out," the Major General roared. "This is all a hoax. There's no mining fleet, no Kett. They want to steal our moon."

Glogg's huge oval eyes tightened and glowed around the edges. His cheeks flare in and out as his breathing increased. "You arrogant human. Do you have any conception of how many worlds we sacrificed so we could keep this planet protected? And for what? Your kind is as bad as the Kett, taking what you want, when you want, with no consideration of what life you are destroying. Your oceans are so polluted life is barely existing. Trust me; Earth will soon end. You cut down the rainforests, pollute your ground and air. Even if the Kett weren't coming, your planet is doomed."

"Then why did you stay?"

"Because we had hope, hope you would realize your mistakes and do better," Glogg said.

"Some are trying," Sarina stood up.

"But many are not," Glogg said.

"I think we are getting off the subject," Renn interrupted. "We will discuss the subject of man's destruction of Earth later. Right now, we need to discuss the Kett and their attack."

"Right," Glogg said. "To reach the Kett fleet in time, we must launch our fleet within the next week."

"One week to get the world ready for what you're proposing? You're kidding," the Major General said.

"I don't kid about such important matters," Glogg said. "We have one week. Possibly less."

"Impossible!"

"Everything's impossible until you try," Abigail said. "Seventy years ago, they said we could not go to the moon, but we did."

"Hey, you guys were already there when Armstrong and Aldrin stepped on the moon in 1969," Steven said, imagining the astronauts encountering the aliens. For all he knew, they did.

"Yes, we were there," Glogg said. "Their arrival was quite a day for us as well. They landed not too far from one of our major entrances. We feared they would discover it."

"So, what, Mr. Glogg, do you need from us?" Abigail asked, bypassing the Major General.

"It's only Glogg. No Mister. We don't have such designations. I'll let Renn tell you our proposal. It is his creation."

"I believe we can agree the people of Earth will panic if they see all these alien ships coming out of the moon, let alone a section of the moon opening up? We need to give them a head's up. We can do this in two ways: Meet with the heads of state from countries worldwide and have them notify their people. Or we can take over your airways and broadcast our existence through every telephone, computer, tablet, and television."

"I don't think your last one would go over too well," Steven said. "A lot of possible hysteria there."

"I agree. Option one is the better choice. Any suggestions on how to accomplish it?"

"The United Nations can call an emergency session," former Director Santiago said. "The organization represents all but six or seven of the world's nations, and we can give them an individual invite. The representatives will take your message to their leaders who would notify the people."

"I suggest we don't mention an alien fleet is heading towards Earth to mine its terra into nonexistence," Steven said. "It's one thing to accept there are aliens on the moon, another they're coming to destroy your world."

"I agree," former Director Santiago added. "Today, most people believe in alien life. I believe a significant number will see you as a friend if introduced correctly. But the idea of an advancing dangerous alien race would reflect on you. You too will be seen as an enemy."

"If Earth will end, her citizens have a right to know," Glogg said. "They have the right to be told about the Kett and us. They need time to make peace with their family, children, themselves, and their Creator."

"How soon would you want to meet with the representatives?" Steven asked.

"As soon as possible. Say, in three days?"

"To arrange such a meeting will take days to schedule," the former Director said.

"We'd be lucky to put something together in three months, let alone three days," the Major General said. "But I will take your proposal to Washington and discuss it with the President. He'll decide."

"With all due respect to your leader, Major General, he has no say in this matter," Glogg said. His tone was one of command, with the implication his words were not up for discussion. They were fact. "This concerns the people of Earth, not only the United States. The sole reason for contacting your country is because Renn's daughter lives there. Had Sarina lived in France, we would have contacted their government. And while on the subject of authority, while I respect yours, Major General, I have no desire to deal with you. Your thinking is too restricted, too military, to accomplish anything agreeable. We will deal with Director Santiago on needed matters. If this is not agreeable with you, we will end any further discussion and do things as we see fit."

The Major General's face turned bright red. Those in the room feared a blood vessel in his face would burst. How dare that insect alien tell him he wouldn't speak with him? He oversaw this operation, not the female.

"Before you speak, Major General, remember if we cut off our communication, it's gone forever," Renn warned.

"So, speak wisely, Thomas," Abigale cautioned.

His fingers digging into his palms as he clenched his fists, his teeth grinding, the Major General said only two words. "Your call." He then turned and left the room.

A PLAN OF ESCAPE

The Major General left immediately to advise the President on what had occurred. The President was flabbergasted and outraged to learn of the secret division of Homeland Security. He called its Director, the Director of the FBI, the Secretary of Defense, the Attorney General, plus the four-star general in charge of the station's private financings and fired them all on the spot. He would not tolerate secrecy in his cabinet and demanded to meet with this alien.

Former Director Santiago spent the next day planning for Glogg to speak with the United Nations. She wrote an announcement for a "must attend" meeting at twenty-two hundred in three days. After they sent the invitations, the staff would call the countries to verify they received the invite. They were ready to go. The only thing preventing them from executing their plan was the President's approval.

That evening when the moon came within range, Sarina called the station. The front screen filled with Renn's and Glogg's faces. Sarina's mother was not present. Former Director Santiago informed the alien and moon human of the plan, the meeting's date and time, and their wait on the President's approval.

"How soon before he gives his consent?" Renn asked.

"I expect to receive confirmation any moment," former Director Santiago said. "Is there anything else you need?"

"Only the coordinates of where the meeting will take place," Glogg answered. "Once we have them, we will have no problem projecting into the room, as we do with you."

"Will we be able to see the broadcast?" Sarina asked. She wanted to attend the talk but knew it was far too dangerous.

Renn smiled. "You possess your mother's sense of adventure. We will broadcast the session live. It will be as if you are there."

"Thank you."

As Glogg and the former Director went over the details once more, the humming returned to Sarina's ears. This time the sound was a lower frequency and more intense. She shook her head as it grew louder, then a voice filled her mind. "Sarina, it's your father. Nod yes or no if you still have the stone your mother gave you." Afraid to eye the screen, Sarina gave a slight nod, reaching up and touching the stone on the chain around her neck. She wondered how Renn knew she had the necklace. "Is there any way you can get access to the outside?" Again, she nodded a tiny yes. Under military escort, the Director allowed her to take the children outside the day before for some fresh air. She was sure she would permit them to go outside again. "Great. Next time you're outside, squeeze the stone three times. I will know you are free to speak. Until then." Renn vanished, as did the humming.

Partaking in a late dinner after the phone call, the Spalling family gathered in the cafeteria. Chef served his normal second Tuesday lasagna. As was his custom, he came out of the kitchen and mingled with those eating in the dining hall, getting their feedback on the food, suggesting what they would like him to serve, or general conversation. This evening he stopped at the table where the Spalling family sat. He noticed the three children had not finished their lasagna.

"Is the meal not to your satisfaction?" Chef asked.

"I'd rather eat a hamburger," Timmy said.

"Timmy, mind your manners," Sarina's cheeks flushed pink with embarrassment. "This lasagna is fantastic."

"Not as delicious as yours, Momma." Timmy glanced up at the Chef. "My mom makes the best lasagna in the entire world."

Mary added. "Yours isn't bad, but hers is better."

"Chef, I'm sorry," Sarina said.

"No need to apology." Chef smiled, placing his hand over his heart to pretend Mary wounded him. "Although your words hurt, I can take criticism." Everyone laughed. "But I must have your recipe, so I, too, can cook the best lasagna in the world."

"Gladly, Chef." Sarina rattled off her recipe. Her ingredients were like Chef's except for the red peppers and tomatoes.

"I am sorry to say I am all out of red peppers," Chef said. "But I'm sure there might be a few in my garden which are ripe."

"You have a garden?" Timmy asked. He loved gardening. "Is it down here?"

"Down here? No," Chef said. "Vegetables need sunlight to grow and taste wonderful. Real sunlight, not the artificial light illuminating our rooms. But above? Yes. She's small but sufficient. Would you like to go with me tomorrow when I pick them?"

"Yes, yes," shouted Timmy and Mary. "Can we go, Momma? PLEASE!!"

Sarina was glad to see her youngest two thrilled about doing something. Activities for children their ages were limited, especially since most of the offspring were in school during the day. Timmy and Mary would not start their lessons until the following week. For Jeremy, there was the gym and the opportunity to flirt with females.

"I'll ask Director Santiago and see if we can go with Chef," Sarina promised.

"I need to do some weeding and fertilizing too," Chef said. "Perhaps you would like to help?"

"I'd love to," Sarina said. What could be better? An innocent trip to the garden with Chef at the cook's invitation. Such an invitation was the opportunity she needed to speak with her father.

"Then, tomorrow night, I will cook the best lasagna in the world," the Chef boasted. "But only for the Spalling family. Personnel gets upset if I serve the same thing two days in a row."

As she had hoped, the former Director had no problem with Sarina and the two children going with Chef. She warned the children to be careful. Sometimes unwanted critters got into the open area above the compound. That possibility excited the children, especially Timmy. The thought of unwelcomed creatures made Sarina want to cancel the entire expedition. If there were another way to talk with her father, she would have.

The next day, as soon as Timmy and Mary finished breakfast, they and their mother accompanied Chef outside. But instead of exiting on the ground level as they had earlier, they rose to the top of a small plateau. When the elevator opened, they did not believe their eyes. There, planted on the plateau a thousand feet above the desert floor, was an extensive vegetable garden with tomatoes, lettuce, cucumbers, snow peas, beans, eggplant, and so much more. It reminded Sarina of the rooftop gardens she had seen in the city.

"Chef, this is amazing," Sarina said.

"Director Abigail gave me permission to plant a garden as long as I assured her someone would not find it," Chef said. "So, we planted the garden way up here. Who comes this high except for the birds? And there is an electrical force field to keep them from eating the vegetables. It's some prototype the government wanted to test. If it's successful, they will use the concept in Africa to keep the elephants out of the farmers' gardens."

"Is it working?" Timmy asked.

"Haven't lost even a pea yet," Chef chuckled. "However, scorpions and spiders do get inside, so you must wear your gloves. Be careful. Check under the leaves before you pick something."

"We will," the kids yelled as they hurried off with their baskets.

"Are you sure it's safe?" Sarina asked.

"Yes. But the scorpions and spiders aren't usually poisonous to humans. I was bitten once and stung twice. No consequences." The Chef's words didn't make Sarina feel any better about their outing. But she was on a mission. Taking her basket, she moved to the end of the garden where carrots were growing - the perfect place for pretending to be working.

Sarina walked down the path, keeping her back to the guards. Careful they did not see her, she reached up and grabbed the stone around her neck, squeezing it three times. Within seconds, she heard her father's voice.

"Wow, you're fast. I didn't expect you this soon."

"I got lucky. The kids got invited to come outside with Chef and pick vegetables."

"They may be watching you, so I'll make this quick. In case this thing doesn't go as we hope, I need to get you, Steven, and the kids out and up here."

"Up there?" Sarina dropped her basket. She knelt, checking for any creepy crawlies first, and righted her basket. She pulled a carrot.

"You didn't think I'd leave my family on Earth if we have to leave, did you?"

"I never thought of it."

"Well, I'm not. Do all five of you ever go outside together?"

"No. I don't believe Abigail would allow all of us outside together at the same time. "

"She's a smart Director. Finding a way inside to retrieve you five will take some doing."

"Take the kids."

"No, I won't leave you or Steven behind. You're the only family I have."

"You cannot get inside and back out safely."

"Don't underestimate your old man. Remember, I have thousands of years of Caelifera's knowledge to work with. What you've seen us do so far is kids' play. For a human, your facility is a fortress. For a Caelifera, it's a cardboard box with both ends opened. All I need to know is when all five of you are together."

"We eat our meals together in the dining hall," Sarina glanced at the closest guard. He was walking towards her.

"Too many eyes watching. What about your living quarters?"

"Sometimes, when watching television or playing a board game. But lately, Jeremy just sulks in his room and doesn't join the family." The guard was getting closer. She pulled another carrot.

"Make him join you. Next time all five of you are in the same room, squeeze your stone twice. I will know your location."

"There's an easier way to pull those carrots," the armed guard said as he drew near. He knelt and used the spade he had brought. "Push the spade into the soil around the carrot to loosen the root. And tada, the carrot pulls right out." He held up a fresh carrot.

"Thanks. I've never gardened before."

"Your kids seem to be naturals," the guard said. Sarina smiled at him as he stood up and walked back towards his post.

"Dad, are you still there?" she said in her mind. There was no answer. They lost the connection. She sighed, wondering what magic her father had in store.

After dinner, Sarina took her husband into the shower stall. Even if the bathroom wasn't safe, the sound of the shower should hide their words from any listening devices. Holding him close, she whispered what had transpired in the garden. Together they made plans for a family movie night with the kids the following evening. Steven cautioned her to be careful. If any military personnel found out what they were up to, they might separate them or, worse, send the children away.

Using the excuse that Sarina was ill, the family stayed in their room for breakfast the following day. Steven knew there were too many ears able to listen in on their conversation in the mess hall who could hinder their plans. Both he and Sarina understood the dangers laying ahead for their family, the sophisticated network of security they had to navigate, and the outcome if they failed.

"Hey, kids. I thought that we'd have a family movie night tonight. What do you think?"

"Let's watch *Mary Poppins*," Mary shouted.

"That's a baby's movie," Timmy said.

"Is not." Mary gave her younger brother the evil eye.

"Is too," Timmy argued. "Let's view something fun, like *Jumanji*."

"We watched that last time," a more mature Jeremy said. "I want something more grownup. The movie about the inner-city basketball team came out three days ago. Let's see if we have internet access so we can rent it."

"No, I hate sport's movies," Mary cried.

"I want *Jumanji*," Timmy said.

"I don't think they have *Jumanji*," Steven said, hoping to stop an argument before one erupted.

"It's okay. I brought *Jumanji* with me, Dad.".

Mary gave him another stern glance. "Well, I brought *Mary Poppins*. And since you got to choose the movie last time and Jeremy the time before, it's my turn." She stuck her tongue out.

"Mom, Mary stuck her tongue out at me," Timmy hollered.

"Did not," Mary said.

"Mary?" Sarina gave her daughter a disciplinary stare.

"How about this?" Steven suggested. "We let Mom choose the movie this time? Mom's working hard all day with the military and could use a relaxing evening at home."

"I agree." Jeremy knew he couldn't sit through *Mary Poppins* or *Jumanji* one more time. "Besides, you two can watch your movies during the day when Mom's gone."

Steven rose from the table to refill his and Sarina's coffee cups. As he poured the hot liquid a knock on the door sounded. Not waiting for an invitation to come in, Sally entered with her coffee cup and notebook in hand. "Sorry to barge in so early. I understand you're not feeling well, Mrs. Spalling?"

"Just a little upset stomach," Sarina lied. "I feel better now that I ate."

"Great. Director Santiago asked to speak with you in the Command Center. Are you up to meeting with her, Mrs. Spalling?"

"Yes."

Steven poured Sarina's coffee into a portable coffee mug. He handed it to his wife, kissing her goodbye. "The kids and I will get things ready for tonight's movie night."

"You two behave yourselves," Sarina said, giving the two youngest scolding looks. "Perhaps, if you behave yourselves, you can go work with Chef in the kitchen and help prepare things for tonight's dinner." She gave each child a kiss on the cheek and an extra-long hug. She then kissed her husband one more time.

"Stay strong," he whispered.

With coffee in hand, Sarina followed Sally into the hallway. "What's up this morning?"

"The President fired Major General Hancock," Sally said. "Director Santiago is the director again."

"Did the President agree to honor my father's wishes about the meeting at the United Nations?"

"Not yet. He was mad as hell at not knowing about OEL, this facility, or what's been happening on the moon.," Sally bit her top lip, trying her best not to laugh.

Sarina wondered what her father might do if the President refused to cooperate. Her steps became quicker as she hurried down the hallway to the elevator. After a brief ride, she emerged onto the floor of the Command Center.

"Sorry for the early hour, Sarina." The Director was standing at the elevator entrance waiting for Sarina to exit the elevator. "I need you to contact your father. And we only have a short time before we lose our ability to communicate with them until tonight. We have a situation."

"What situation?" Sarina asked.

"I'd rather tell your father myself."

Sarina sighed. "Remember, Director, we're in this together, and we need to trust each other. I need all the facts to present them to my father correctly. If I'm startled by what you tell him, he might sense my surprise. Plus, I've never tried contacting him on my own. I'm not sure he'll hear me."

"Now, who's not being truthful?" Director Santiago asked. "I can't prove it, but I believe your father is in contact with you in some form all the time." Sarina prepared to protest. "I'm not saying you're always aware of him, but somewhere deep inside you realize I'm telling the truth. That stone around your neck has something to do with contacting him."

Instinctively, Sarina grasped the stone hidden beneath her shirt. Was the Director planning on taking her necklace away? Did she suspect the stone was a form of communication? If so, why did she let her keep it?

The Director walked nearby and stopped for a second beside Sarina. Leaning in, she whispered, "Unlike our President and the Major General, I comprehend you are Earth's only hope. Keep your stone safe and hidden." She then proceeded on, turning when she reached the end of the aisle.

"The news is not positive. The President refuses to allow us to contact the various nations and inform them of the mandatory meeting. We are not to say a word to anyone about aliens, the Kett, or the moon. He wants more time to plan a strategy, HIS strategy."

"A strategy?" Sarina asked in horror. "What does he think he or anyone can do? This situation is out of his hands."

"You do not tell this President he can't do anything, especially if the action will make him the most important person in the entire world. Or the stupidest," Director Santiago said. "He wants proof this is real."

"What kind of proof?" Sarina asked, an uneasiness swelling in her stomach.

"He wants to talk with your father and Glogg," the Director said. "He wants to hear about the danger and their colony on the moon firsthand."

"And then he'll contact the other nations?"

"He didn't say."

"What do you want me to do?"

"Contact your father," Director Santiago said. "Inform him the President wants to meet him before deciding anything. Explain the President's way is the only way."

"When do you want me to contact him?"

Abigail checked the digital clock on the wall. It read 0-seven hundred forty. "I would say now. The President will arrive in fifteen minutes."

"Fifteen minutes?" a shocked Sarina asked. "What if I can't reach him?"

"Try, Sarina," the Director said. This was Abigail's chance to discover if Sarina and Renn were in communication with each other. If she was, things just got a lot more complicated. But she hoped she was right; she needed to be right. Their future depended on Sarina.

Taking a deep breath, Sarina walked to the front, keeping her back to those in the room. She stared at the screen filled with thousands of stars, hoping the Director was right-someone was listening. Trying her best to lift her hand to her amulet unseen, she silently said, "Dad, are you there?" Using what strength she could summon, she propelled her voice out into the universe displayed on the screen. "Dad, I need to speak with you. It's important."

Startled, she jumped back when the screen crackled. Millions of tiny beads of light appeared, circling, creating an out-of-focus picture. The dots solidified into shapes of color, revealing a face. As the seconds ticked by, the image became more distinct until she glanced into her mother's face.

"Mom," she sputtered. The robot representation of her mother still unsettled her. She didn't think she would ever be comfortable with the A-I. "I need to speak to my father."

"He will arrive momentarily," the robot said. "He was not expecting your call and was unprepared. Are you in need of help?"

"No, I'm fine."

"And Steven and the children?"

"They're fine too," Sarina said. She did not wish to speak with the android about her family.

"Here is your father." The nonhuman female stepped aside as Renn stepped into the viewing area.

"Your mother says you and the family are okay?"

"She is not my mother," Sarina said, tears in her eyes. "Please don't refer to her as such."

"She may not be your biological mother, but she has all of your mother's memories and feelings," Renn said. "She possesses the elements of what made your mother, Jenny Tensley. But I can see the subject still upsets you. I am here. Tell me what you need."

"I asked her to contact you," Director Santiago said. "Might I speak?"

Renn glanced at his daughter, who nodded. Silently she said, "You can trust her."

"I am not sure how familiar you are about how our country and other Earth countries operate, Renn," the Director said. "In our country, we elect a person to lead our nation. We call him the President."

"We are familiar with how the various countries of your world operate," Renn stated. "Some, like the United States and Canada, are democratic and elect a leader. Some, like England, use monarchs, such as kings and queens, who rule by bloodline. Others have dictators who either seized control or were born into the ruling family. We've monitored humanity's progress for thousands of years and have a deep knowledge of how things work down there."

"Then, perhaps, you can understand the President's opinion," the Director said. "This facility is on U.S. land. As such, he has jurisdiction over its territory."

"To a degree."

"And our President decides what will and will not transpire diplomatically."

"Again, to a degree."

"What Director Santiago is trying to say is the President has your proposal," Sarina clarified. "Before he decides, he wants to talk with you and Glogg himself."

"We can arrange a conference. When would the President like to meet?"

"He will arrive in about eight minutes," the Director said.

Renn turned right and gave orders in a language Sarina nor Abigail understood. "Jenny will tell Glogg we need his presence. He should be here shortly."

"The sooner, the better," came a bellowing voice as the President stepped into the Command Center. "I want to see who this alien fellow is."

A PRESIDENTIAL REFUSAL

"Mr. President, meet Renn, a member of the moon team," Director Santiago said.

"I understand you are human like us," the President said, foregoing any greeting.

"Yes."

"And those insect aliens kidnapped you and raised you on the moon."

"Wrong, Mr. President," Renn said. "My parents arrived at the station during the Civil War. I was born up here."

"So, the aliens captured your parents and forced them to remain up there."

"I assure you, we never forced them," Glogg said as he stepped into view. The President gasped and took a step back, bumping into the desk behind him. He studied the alien, analyzing his capabilities and weaknesses. "We've kept no human against their will. Like Renn, each had the choice to return to Earth to live out his or her life."

"And how many humans have supposedly chosen to stay with you?" the President asked.

"Why do you ask what you already know, Mr. President," Glogg said, staring at the terrified human. "I gave this information to your Director and Major General at our first meeting. I know they forwarded the report to you."

"Just checking my facts. Plus, I find it baffling humans would willingly live with your kind up there."

"Why, Mr. President?" Renn asked. "Is Earth such a wonderful place to live? Global warming plagues your planet, as does water and air pollution, human trafficking, devastation from wars, overpopulation, and starvation. I'd say most humans would prefer to live somewhere else."

"Mr. President, I don't imagine you came to argue the point of why humans are living on the moon," Sarina interrupted, trying to get the conversation back on point. "Perhaps Glogg and Renn can explain the Kett's impending destruction of Earth and the need to launch the moon's fleet. And the necessity of addressing the various nations of Earth to prepare them for these events."

Realizing the futility of arguing with the male human, Glogg explained once more who and what the Kett were, the International Space Coalition's mission to protect the solar system, and their wish not to terrify the citizens of Earth when they launched their fleet.

The President listened, occasionally scribbling on a pad on the desk where he sat. When Renn and Glogg finished speaking, he only had one question. "And why should I believe you?"

"Excuse me?" Renn asked in disbelief.

"I can make up a story as ludicrous as yours," the President said. "I've seen no proof to back up your statements."

Glogg held up the picture of the advancing Kett fleet. "Here's your proof. Pictures of the advanced ships which will tear your planet apart piece by piece."

"So you say," the President said. "With a few hours, I can fabricate some pictures too. Probably design even scarier ships."

"Mr. President, why would I lie to you?" Glogg asked.

"To make us think you're our friends so you can come down and take control of Earth. You've admitted you've been kidnapping our people for centuries."

"He's impossible." Glogg turned towards Renn. "This is a waste of time."

"Wait one moment," Sarina said. "We have satellites out in space. If I'm not mistaken, Jupiter III isn't far from where we estimate the fleet to be. Can't we reprogram her to intercept the ships? She could send back proof Glogg and Renn are telling the truth."

"While an excellent suggestion, it would take several weeks before they could reprogram the satellite to send back pictures," Director Santiago said. "And another few days to receive and process the data once they're taken."

"By that time, it would be too late to launch our fleet," Glogg said. "Our latest findings mandate we must launch in one week if we want to intercept them in time. Our meeting must take place no later than Tuesday evening."

"Tell you what, Mr. Glogg," the President said. "I'll arrange your meeting--but under one condition. If you are telling the truth and the Kett might destroy this planet, I want passage aboard your space station for me, my family, and other important associates. I'm sure other world leaders will wish sanctuary. After all, the humans at the base will need a leader."

Renn stared at the human, his mouth agape, acid churning in his stomach. "You've got to be kidding me. After what Glogg said, all you can think about is your own hide?"

"You can't become the richest man and the best president in our history by not thinking ahead," the President said. "What do you say? Do we agree?"

"What do I say?" Glogg asked, trying not to grind his mandibles. "I say we were fools even to consider working with humans. You are a pathetic race who doesn't deserve saving." The screen went blank.

"Mr. President, how could you?" Sarina asked.

"Someone has to lead those humans they've taken," the President said, unaware he had said anything wrong. "We'll start a new colony somewhere, and we'll need leadership. My friends and I can provide such guidance."

———————————

"The nerve of that human." Glogg picked up a bowl that sat on the desk beside him and flung it against the wall, smashing the pottery into pieces. "He didn't hear a word we said. He has no concern for others. Only himself."

"And how he can get rich from what's about to happen," Renn said. "The nerve of him to say we need someone to lead us. Who does he think has been leading us all these years?"

"I'm tempted to move the station and let the Kett take the planet," Glogg said.

"I agree, but the innocent shouldn't pay for his greed and ignorance." Renn paused and took a deep, cleansing breath, allowing his anger and frustration to flow from his body. "There are millions of wonderful humans on Earth. People have devoted their lives to restoring their planet to her greatness. We can't abandon them. Not yet."

"Besides, remember our directive," Jenny picked up the broken pieces of the dish. "Our mission is to protect this solar system, especially the Blue Planet. Do not forget its diversity of life; life found nowhere else in all the known galaxies."

"True, but we have samples of Earth's life preserved inside the station," Glogg said. "They will not disappear."

"We collected the seeds, eggs, and embryos as a precautionary measure in case the planet is ever lost," Jenny said. "Although not a perfect creature, humankind is learning. More people are seeing their leaders' folly and are trying to change things for the better. We owe those individuals a chance to succeed."

"So, how do you suggest we proceed?" Glogg asked.

"We contact the various countries on our own," Renn said.

"And again, how?"

An idea came to Renn. "Their Internet. The web connects the entire globe twenty-four hours a day. We can bombard the waves with a message stating a representative from each nation must meet at the United Nations Building in New York Tuesday at twenty-two hundred hours. The message will state the meeting is a matter of global survival."

"That doesn't give some representatives much time to reach New York," Renn said. "Some must travel long distances. I fear if held on Tuesday, only half of the countries would be represented."

"What do you suggest?" Glogg asked. "Postpone the meeting for another twenty-four hours? Such a delay would mean launching the fleet late."

"I don't see what choice we have," Renn said. "It's either that or meet with half the delegates. "

"Agreed. Move the meeting to Wednesday so all can attend. Now, for the message. What should the words be? It should be something that won't scare them too much yet makes them understand the seriousness of the situation." Renn's scrunched his forehead creating ripples of skin. The gesture did not go unnoticed by Glogg. "Do you not agree with me, Renn?"

"I do, but I see one flaw in our plan. People understand they can't believe everything they see on the Internet. The waves are full of lies, hoaxes, and scam artists. How do we convince them our words are true and not a terrorist's plot or sleaze bag trying to scare them?"

"We need something which will convince them," Glogg said. "Something no human can do."

"What about something here on the moon?" Renn suggested. "A bright light or something."

"No. Only part of the Earth would see such a display," Jenny said. "Those countries in daylight would miss it and might not trust those countries in the dark. Every person on Earth must see or experience the display simultaneously."

"Too bad we can't do what Klatoo did in *The Day the Earth Stood Still*," Renn said. He saw the blank expression on Glogg's face. "It's a movie. Klatoo was an alien. He neutralized electricity for a half-hour to convince the people of Earth he was serious."

"Can you neutralize electricity?" Glogg asked. "How would you even start?"

"I don't think it's possible. But I have an idea which might work," Jenny said.

"Don't worry, they'll be back," the President said in confidence.

"No, they won't," Director Santiago said. "These are superior beings who do not take orders from us. We need to work with them, not against them."

"You forget we have an ace up our sleeve." Sarina felt the President's icy stare and cringed at the thought of what he might be thinking. "Mrs. Spalling is a unique interest to this Renn fellow. I understand her entire family is. I'm sure he'll cooperate if he thinks they're in danger."

"You can't," Sarina stepped forward. She kept her eyes on the president as two MPs grabbed her by the arms, stopping her advancement. "I'll never help you."

"I think I can persuade you," the President said. "Major, I want her family separated. Put the husband and the two boys together in a secured room with a twenty-four-hour guard. Place Mrs. Spalling and her daughter in another room far from the others. I don't want them silently communicating with each other."

"We're humans, not aliens," Sarina said. "We can't speak to each other telepathically."

"I'm not stupid, Mrs. Spalling," the President sneered. "Your father was the man on the right. And your gene sequencing is abnormal." He smiled at the surprised expression on the female's face. "I know a lot more than you may think I do." He paused for a moment, turning to gaze at the Director. "And, Major, put Director Santiago under house arrest too."

"For what?" Abigail demanded.

"For espionage," the President said. "For conspiring with the enemy."

Steven rechecked the wall clock, then compared its time against his timepiece. Both stated the time was eighteen hundred hours, the time they were to dine with Chef. Where was Sarina? If something came up, she would have contacted him. Something was wrong. He felt it.

"Dad, when's mom coming home?" Timmy asked as he zoomed into the room with his space fighter. "I'm starving."

"Me too," Mary said, her toy aircraft flying in alongside her brother's.

"Some work must have delayed her," Steven said. "Go washed up, and we'll head to the dining hall and eat. Your mom can join us there."

As soon as the younger two were out of sight, Jeremy whispered, "Dad, Mom would have sent us word if she could not join us or if she got delayed. She wouldn't leave us in the dark."

"I agree. But I don't want to frighten your brother and sister. Stay alert."

"All ready," Timmy shouted as he and Mary burst back into the room.

"The last one to the dining hall is a pooper-scooper," Mary yelled as she ran to the door. The glee on her face vanished the moment she opened the door and encountered three MPs standing outside.

"We're going to get a bite to eat." Steven placed himself between the guards and his children.

"We have a change of plans, Captain Spalling," one guard said. "I must move you to another chamber with your sons. You will take all your meals in your room."

"And what of my daughter?" Steven asked.

"She will stay with her mother down the hall," the MP said.

"The hell she will." Jeremy charged the three soldiers. "We're through being pushed around by you guys. "

Without hesitation, the two guards in the back raised their guns. Steven's heart sank when he heard them release their weapons' locks.

"Stop, Jeremy," Steven shouted, placing his arms out in front to stop his son's advancement. He addressed the front soldier, whom he thought might be in charge. "There's no need for violence, Sergeant. He's stressed out, confused, even scared of what the future will be. Give him a break."

"Tell your son that."

"Calm down." Holding a food tray, Sally pushed her way past the three guards. "Chef sends his apologies. Something came up, and he cannot join you for dinner tonight. But he didn't want you to miss tasting his creation." She waved to two women in the hallway, each with a cart of food and drinks. "Sargent, if you would allow the kitchen helpers to do their job." Inspecting the carts and noting nothing out of the ordinary, the Sargent waved them through. The two soldiers in the back kept their weapons aimed.

"Come and eat," Sally said, waving her hand to show the family should have a seat.

"Where's my Mom?" Timmy asked, unwilling to budge.

The expression on Sally's face told Steven and Jeremy they needed to follow her instructions. "Kids, sit down and eat."

"Not the girl," the Sargent said. "She's joining her mother."

"Daddy, I don't want to go with them." Mary grasped her father's arm. "Don't let them take me."

Before Steven stepped in, Sally walked over to the two armed guards. She placed her hands on both gun barrels and lowered their weapons. "You guys are frightening her. Malcolm, you have a little girl. And Sam, you have two little sisters.

Imagine how they'd feel if some strangers came and tried to take them away."

"We have our orders."

"Yes, you do," Sally said. "But your orders didn't specify she has to go this moment. Let Mary eat dinner with her father and brothers while you three wait out in the hallway where you won't scare her. If you behave, I'll even bring you out a piece of lasagna. Then, when she's finished, I will escort her with you down to her mother. Deal?" She did not give the Sargent time to answer before pushing him past the door and closed it.

"Ladies, put the food on the table. Then return to the kitchen." She turned to Mary and Timmy. "Do you know where your mom keeps the plates and silverware?" They nodded yes. "Please get them for me." She turned to Jeremy. "And perhaps you can get the glasses and napkins."

Steven nodded at Jeremy to do as asked. He realized Sally was trying to restore peace, so he allowed her to continue.

"Your mom asked me to inform you something unexpected has come up, and she isn't able to join you for dinner," Sally said. "She said she was sorry, but she won't be home in time for family movie night either. She suggested the kids finish the board game you started last night while your father finishes reading *Extinction 2038*." Sally monitored the man's face. Would he believe her?

Steven's mind raced. Sarina sent him the book the first week he was in Afghanistan. He had forgotten to pack it when sent home, so there was no way their capturers knew about the gift. And if Sally knew, it was because Sarina told her. Mentioning the book was his wife's way of telling Steven he needed to trust Sally. It also meant something happened which was preventing her from returning.

"The President was here today," Sally said as the children set the table. Once more, she turned her attention to Steven, trying to tell him what was happening without alarming the children. "Your mother's work impressed him. He wants her to do a job for him, but it involves being away from you. Since the President

81

doesn't want your mom to be all alone, he thought Mary might stay with her tonight."

"Did the President say how long we will be separated?" Steven asked as he sat down and served the children.

"Just for a little while," Sally said, trying to keep a smile on her face.

The children's worries calmed down some as they consumed the lasagna. Timmy and Mary both had to admit the Chef's creation was as delicious as their mom's. The fresh red peppers and tomatoes they had picked had done the trick. Sally also brought the ingredients for banana splits, hoping to distract the children. As they finished the dessert, a knock on the door reminded them the guards were still waiting outside. It was time for Mary to leave.

"I don't want to go," Mary cried. "I want to stay with you, Daddy."

"You don't want to disappoint Mom, do you?" Steven asked his young daughter, fearful of what was about to happen. Why were they being split up? Without answers, the only thing he could do was trust Sally. "Let's go pack your bag."

Father and daughter walked into the children's bedroom and gathered Mary's nightshirt and a change of clothing for the next day. Steven also packed her favorite blanket. Even though she was ten, she still carried her coverlet with her.

"Daddy, I'm scared," Mary said. "I don't like being here anymore. Can't we go home?"

"Soon, Sweetheart." Steven took his daughter into his arms. "But you and Mommy will have a wonderful time tonight. Imagine an entire evening with only you two. No Timmy to bug you."

"Or no Dad snoring," Mary said. Steven chuckled. He held up *The Hobbit* and *Mary Poppins*. "Take these with you so you and mom can have your movie night. Now, go kiss your brothers."

"Do I have to?" Mary asked, her face scrunched up.

"Yes, you have to," Steven said, lightly smacking her on the behind. She raced into the other room and kissed each brother. Then she kissed and hugged her father.

"Ready, Mary? Sally asked, holding out her hand.

"Give your mom a kiss for me." Steven forced the biggest smile he could manage onto his face as Sally took Mary's hand. "Take care of my daughter."

"Always."

PINK WATER AND BACK
FLOWING WATERFALLS

At 0-six hundred and thirty-six hours the following day, a message went out across the Internet. The communique appeared in every email box, every Twitter feed, every Facebook posting, and every Instagram. Each person heard or read the message in their native tongue. As Glogg had requested, the bulletin was a simple but direct message. One meant not to terrify people but to assure them this was real and important.

It read:

Dear Friends of Earth,

We are a body of humans and extraterrestrials who banded together five thousand years ago to protect your planet and solar system from hostile forces. From your moon, we have kept watch over you without interfering in your daily activity, keeping our presence a secret. Circumstances dictate we now change our tactics.

A hostile species called the Kett has entered your solar system to harvest minerals. All the planets are in danger. We are ready to defend this system and repel the invaders. Our fleet is ready to launch, but we must exit our hiding place on the moon.

To understand what is happening, we ask every nation to send a representative to meet with us at the United Nations in New York City at twenty-one hundred hours Eastern Standard Time on May 7th. There, we will explain our plan to protect Earth and how we will launch our fleet. Those present will take our message to their people.

Because of our advanced technology, you will not need interpreters. Each of you will hear us in your language.

So you will know we speak the truth, in two hours, the oceans, seas, lakes, and rivers of Earth will turn a neon pink for one hour. As the moon rises on the magnificent waterfalls of Earth, each will flow backward for twenty minutes. Be assured; we do this not to frighten you but to show you we speak the truth.

Remember, we will meet with you in three days at twenty-one hundred hours EST at the United Nations. We apologize for the late hour; the meeting must occur when the moon is over the United States.

Signed, Your Friends on the Moon

The planet almost came to a halt as people reacted to the message. The Internet crashed within minutes of the message's receipt as readers forwarded the message, debating its authenticity. Scared people jammed nations' communications trying to get answers. Worshipers crowded into churches, synagogues, and mosques, fearing the end of the world. Neighbors frustrated at not being able to get any information gathered in town meetings. Friends and family discussed what were possible truths, what were exaggerations, what were lies. As for the world's militaries, they prepared to defend the planet, positive the Internet invaders were enemies determined to end humanity.

At the secret military base in New Mexico, those locked away knew nothing of what happened globally. Sarina was confined in her living quarters with Mary while Steven was on the other side of the complex with Timmy and Jeremy. Each wondered how the others were doing. Mary cried. Not even watching *Mary Poppins* cheered her up.

Director Santiago paced her room, fuming over the President placing her under arrest. Why did he think she was trying to sabotage the mission? Was he crazy? For the hundredth time, she tried her computer. The tiny dots went round and around, refusing to connect. Why wasn't the internet working? Had the President ordered her connection terminated too? She was in the dark, ignorant of what was happening, and it infuriated her. Why hadn't Sally come by to advise her of what was happening? Was she sequestered also?

While those at the bunker wondered in ignorance, the President raged with knowledge. His morning snack was interrupted with the notification the aliens had sent a worldwide message across the Internet, informing the world of their existence. Hoping to hide his refusal to arrange a meeting with the aliens, the President ordered his aides to call the world leaders now. But with all the people trying to get information, his attempts were futile. Their calls were not going through. His aggravation increased when he tried to say something on Twitter. He couldn't even sign in.

"Brian, tell Andrew to write a press release," the President said. "Have carriers deliver it to the Washington Post, the New York Times, and the Free Press. I don't want to take a chance on a fax not working. Inform the populous we are working with other countries to rectify the situation."

"Do you want me to call a Special Assembly of Congress?"

"Why would I want a Special Meeting?".

"Won't we need a plan of action for the United Nations' meeting?"

"I do not care what those idiots have to say," the President said. "It's Dorothy's job to speak at the UN, not mine. I want my plane ready in twenty minutes."

"Where are you going, Sir?"

"Back to New Mexico," the President said, his face flushed and sweaty. " I must speak with that woman immediately."

As the President's plane lifted off, he received a hand-written bulletin. It stated the Atlantic and Pacific Oceans were glowing a neon pink. So were the Great Lakes, the Mississippi

River, and the Potomac River. For twenty minutes, the Victoria Falls in Africa, the South Region in Ireland, and other significant waterfalls experiencing night had flowed backward. Actually flowed backward. How was such a thing possible? Did this really happen?

"Fly us over the Potomac," the President ordered.

"Our flight plan does not allow such a detour," the pilot said.

"I said, fly over the damn Potomac. And stay low enough so I can get a decent view." As his plane rounded the Washington monument, he briefly scanned the communique. Peering out the window, he saw the river glowing a neon pink. Damn those aliens. Who did they think they were dealing with? He was the President of the Free World, the most important man on Earth. He promised himself he'd make them pay for this.

Renn and Glogg glimpsed out the window at the blue planet below them, except the Earth wasn't blue anymore. The planet was neon pink. Even the ice at the polar caps was the same beautiful color. Both wondered how the President was reacting to their little stunt. More importantly, how were Earth's inhabitants doing? Did the pink waters frighten the people of Earth or help them realize they had spoken the truth in the message?

"Jenny, I have to give you credit," Glogg said. "The idea of adding *quinset* to Earth's atmosphere was pure genius."

"It was a straightforward solution," Jenny said. "Much simpler than neutralizing the electrical field, as Renn suggested. And since *quinset* is a mineral unfamiliar to Earth, it gave us the wonder aspect we needed. The hardest part was hiding the fliers as they seeded the skies around Earth."

"A job well done," Glogg said.

"Have you received any signal from Sarina?" Jenny asked.

"No, and I'm worried," Renn said. "She never signaled me last night as we planned. I tried locating her signal. The feedback showed she was in an area on the other side of the complex. I fear something may be wrong."

"I agree.," Glogg said. "Something has happened."

"Or that crazy President is taking out his revenge on our family," Jenny said, unaware of the implications her statement conjured up in Renn's mind. Getting Sarina and the others just became priority number one.

The bunker received only a twenty-minute warning of the President's arrival. Like the rest of the world, their communications were slow, intermittent, and jammed.

"Where is she?" the President screamed upon entering the bunker. "I want to speak to her immediately."

"Are you referring to Mrs. Spalling or Director Santiago?" temporary Director Harrington asked.

"That Spalling woman."

"She's locked in her living quarters as you ordered. Would you like me to get her?"

The President stopped in his tracks and stared at the human before him. "Surely, you're not that stupid."

"Ah, no, Mr. President," Director Harrington stuttered. He turned and ordered the closest MP to retrieve Mrs. Spalling.

While they waited for Sarina's arrival, the Director led the President to the Conference Room. But the President was too impatient to sit. He paced back and forth, watching the clock on the wall. What was taking them so long? Finally, the MP returned, but alone.

"Well, where is she?"

"She refuses to meet with you," the soldier said, bracing for the outburst to come.

"She what?" the President screamed in rage. "How dare she refuse my request? I'm the damn President. Take me to her. I'll tell her when she is to meet with me." The guard turned and walked back towards her room.

"You must remember, Mr. President, Mrs. Spalling is a civilian, not military personnel," the Director said as he ran after the President. "You can't make her do anything she doesn't want to do. She has rights under our constitution."

"To hell with her rights. I need answers."

After what he considered a long walk and breathing heavily, they arrived at the living quarters. The President pounded on the door. "Mrs. Spalling, this is the President of the United States. I order you to open this door." There was silence. He turned to the colonel. "Break the door down."

Director Harrington walked over to the door and inserted a key, unlocking the door. He turned the knob, allowing the door to swing open. "No need, Mr. President. The door only locks from the outside."

Ignoring the Director's words, the President walked into the living area. Sarina was sitting on the couch with her daughter held tightly in her arms. "Mr. President. Let me assure you; I am not pleased to be in your company once again."

"What happened?" the President yelled. "How did they make the Earth waters glow pink? And how in the hell were they able to invade the Internet and cut off all forms of communication?"

"I do not know what you are speaking of." Sarina wondered what had transpired during her incarceration. "They locked me inside this room since you ordered it yesterday. I have no information about anything outside these four walls."

"You expect me to believe you?" the President asked.

"Frankly, Mr. President, I don't give a damn what you believe."

Before the President exploded again, Sally slipped past the guards. "I assure you, Mr. President, Mrs. Spalling is speaking the truth. She has had no contact with either the outside world or her husband since fifteen hundred yesterday."

"What about the person who brought them breakfast and lunch?" the President asked. "They could have told her something."

"I was the person, and I can assure you I mentioned nothing of the happenings in the world," Sally stated.

"From your demeanor, something significant has happened," Sarina said. "What, may I ask?"

"That so-called alien father of yours hacked into the world's Internet. He told everyone about their base on the moon, our impending doom, and their desire to meet with the world's nations," the President said.

Sarina lowered her head and chuckled. Renn had done precisely what he had asked the President to do. When he refused, Renn did it himself. "And now you're afraid of what will happen if the world leaders learn you tried to cut a deal for yourself instead of informing them of what was about to happen."

"I never tried to cut a deal," the President shouted. "I asked for more time to arrange the meeting."

"Don't lie, Mr. President," Sarina kept her voice soft so as not to frighten her daughter any more than she was. "You forget, I was there. I remember what you said." She paused for a moment, gathering her thoughts. "And now you want my help in getting you out of this mess, don't you?"

"I don't need your help."

"Oh, I think you do," Sarina said. "Let's see, what might you need? I know. You want me to contact my father and ask him not to mention the meeting between him, Glogg, and you. Am I right? You want to cover up what you did like you cover up the other crap you've pulled."

The President's face became taut and stern. "I do not know what you're talking about."

"Mr. President, if you want to live in your delusional world, so be it," Sarina said. "But I have a daughter and sons I must protect. I must live in the actual world."

"What do you want?"

"Excuse me?"

The President took a breath. "What do you want?"

"I want to join my husband and sons," Sarina said. "And I want your guarantee they will not separate us again. Secondly, I want Director Santiago reinstated as Director."

"No. I will try her for treason."

"Then I have no more to say." Sarina reached down and took her daughter's hand. "Come, Mary, let's go play in the bedroom." Holding her mother's hand for support, Mary turned around and stuck her tongue out at the President. The mother and child walked into the adjoining bedroom and closed the door. Sarina closed the lock.

"Is she serious?" the President asked.

"Mr. President, if you want her cooperation, you must agree to her terms." Sally felt the icy stare of the President. "They are simple terms. We can't contact the aliens without her help."

"We're the United States frigging military," the President yelled. "We have the top scientists and electronic equipment in the entire world. There must be someone who has a way to contact them."

"Yes, someone does," Sally said. "And she's sitting in the next room. Believe me, Sir, we've tried many times to contact the base on the moon. We can't do it. Only she can."

"She's right, Mr. President," the new Director added. "Should I go inform Ms. Santiago she is the Director again?"

"Not yet," the President said. "Separate the mother from the child and see if she still refuses."

"You can't use a child like a pawn in a game of chess," Sally immediately said. "She's only ten years old."

"I would not hurt her," the President said. "Scare the mother is all."

"And frighten an already terrified little girl. No, Mr. President. I won't allow such actions."

"Nor will I," came a deep, loud voice. The voice seemed to originate from nowhere yet audible throughout the room.

"And who are you?" the President demanded.

"Rear Admiral Paine," came the voice. "I have been listening and recording your conversation. I figured you pulled something like this. If you do anything to harm or frighten the child or her brothers, I will make sure every newspaper worldwide receives a copy of your conversation. Your presidency will be over within the week."

Upon hearing the Rear Admiral's name, the President froze. He and Paine were archenemies, and the Rear Admiral didn't bluff. "I should have surmised the Democrats were behind this."

"Don't even go there, Gerald," the Rear Admiral said. "If we should blame anyone for what happened today, I'd say we blame you. I know about your meeting with Glogg. Unite the family and reinstate Director Santiago."

"You don't give me orders." The President pressed his tiny lips tightly together. "I am the President of the United States."

"So you told Mrs. Spalling. I'm not giving you an order, Gerald. I'm giving you a choice. Either make the situation right, or I go to the papers."

"It's not much of a choice."

"They're the only two I have."

———————

"Mrs. Spalling, it's Sally." The secretary softly knocked on the bedroom door. "The President has agreed to your terms. I'm to take Mary to her father while you meet with him. He will leave shortly to return to the White House."

Sally cracked the door. "They reinstated director Santiago?"

"As we speak."

"How can I be sure you'll take Mary to her father? I don't know who to trust anymore."

"Nor would I," Sally said, offering the woman behind the door a reassuring smile. "We've given you no reason to trust us. If you'd like, you can accompany her to your family. After which, perhaps you would meet with the President."

"Why would I want to see him?"

"Because he understands you are our only hope."

"You said he's returning to Washington?"

"Yes," Sally said. "His plane will depart within the hour."

"Mary, gather up your things," Sarina said to her daughter. "Sally will take us back to Daddy and your brothers."

"Hurray!" Mary yelled, quickly gathering the few toys she had brought. "Are we going to go home too?"

"Not yet." Sally noted the disappointment on the child's face. "But I don't think it will be long before you're home." She retrieved the small overnight case from the closet. "I'll help you pack your nightgown and change of clothes."

Still not sure this wasn't another of the President's tricks, Sarina breathed a sigh of relief when they stepped out of the living quarters, and the guards were gone. She trusted Sally before. Could she trust her now? Sarina saved her decision until they were back with their family and in her husband's arms.

"Mary, would you like to sit up front with me?" Sally asked as she lifted their suitcases into the back of a cart.

"Can I, Mommy?" Mary asked in excitement. "I promise to behave."

Skeptical, Sarina decided against the child's request. "Maybe next time. Mommy doesn't enjoy riding in these carts. I was hoping you would sit beside me and hold my hand."

"Okay," Mary said, jumping into the seat.

"Mrs. Spalling, I apologize for the happenings over the last few days. We've given you no reason to trust me. I'd like to remedy that. Perhaps spending some time with your husband and sons before the meeting with the President would show you my sincerity. Even have a meal together?"

"But I thought the President was leaving within the hour?"

"Is he?" Sally said, keeping her face emotionless. "Guess he'll have to speak with you next time he shows up unannounced."

RENN MEETS HIS GRANDCHILDREN

The Director told Stephen and Sarina the details of the message and explained the world's reaction. "The people of Earth accepted the fact aliens live inside the moon better than I expected."

"Do you think they believed Glogg's message?" Stephen asked. "Perhaps people thought the message was a hoax or a joke."

"From what we surmised, they believed the message."

"Incredible. And no panicking?"

"Some, but nothing the authorities couldn't contain." Director Santiago twisted in her seat. "I thought that since the rest of the world knows the truth, perhaps we should give your children the message as well. I believe they would like to meet their grandfather."

"Stephen and I discussed that very fact last night," Sarina said.

"And I'm sure Renn would like to meet his grandchildren," Director Santiago said. "How do you think they'll react?"

"Timmy will be ecstatic," Stephen said. "He's a huge fan of *Star Wars*, *Star Trek*, and other space adventures. He'd think having a grandfather living on the moon was awesome. And the fact he is a hundred and thirty-six years old will make the news even better."

"What about Glogg?"

"He'll probably ask how soon he can meet him in person." Sarina laughed. "Jeremy will be cautious and skeptical. But he'll probably accept the facts. Mary's the one that worries me."

"The separation from her brothers traumatized her," Stephen said. "I'm not sure she can handle something so dramatic this soon."

"I believe it would be scarier for her to be excluded," Sally volunteered. "I can remain with her and the boys behind the glass petition. She can feel safe there, with no threat of danger."

"Sounds like a plan," Stephen said. "What about your Mom?"

"She's not my Mom."

"Sorry."

"My mother died when Jeremy was two. Mary and Timmy have only seen her pictures on the mantle. I don't believe they will realize who or what she is."

"I agree," Stephen said. "They'll probably be thrilled to learn she is an android."

"Then we agree," the Director said. "I will plan on the three being present tonight when we talk to the moon."

After dinner, Steven and Sarina sat the three children down in the living room. "Today, something happened we think you should know. Our news might sound scary at first but listen to everything we say."

"Have aliens landed?" Timmy shouted, making a joke.

"In a way, yes," Sarina said.

"Cool," Timmy said. "How many are coming?"

Mary snuggled a little closer to her mom, wrapping her arms around hers.

"Actually, they won't be landing," Stephen said. "These aliens are living in our moon, inside a space station. They live with humans and have been there for centuries, protecting and guarding us. Something has happened that has made it necessary for them to advise us of their existence."

"What was that?" Jeremy asked.

"Let me read the message everyone received today. It will answer a lot of your questions." Stephen read the message.

The three children sat there motionless with no expressions on their faces. Finally, Jeremy asked, "Did the water really turn pink?"

"Yes. And some of Earth's largest waterfalls flowed backward. But no one got hurt. These people mean us no harm."

"How can you be sure?" Jeremy asked.

"Because your father and I have been speaking to them. In fact, one of them turns out to be my father," Sarina said.

"Your father? I thought he was dead."

"So did I." A small giggle escaping Sarina's throat. "Turns out he's not. He couldn't remain on Earth because of the polluted air. He never knew my Mom was pregnant."

"Does this father have a name?"

"You know his name. It's Renn, just like I've always told you."

"You mean I have a grandfather, and he's a spaceman?" Timmy asked.

"Yes."

"And he lives on the moon?"

"Yes. And guess how old he is?"

"Eight hundred years," Timmy guessed.

"Not that old."

"Two hundred," Mary said.

"A little lower."

"One hundred?"

"Almost. He's one hundred and thirty-six years old."

"Boy, Grandma liked them old, didn't she," Jeremy snickered.

"He doesn't appear much older than me," Steven said.

"That's logical," a mature Timmy said. "People age differently in space. The further you go into space, the slower you age. A year in space might equal twenty on Earth."

"And when did you become an expert on space aging?" Steven asked his son.

"It's common knowledge among us Sci-Fi geeks," Timmy said.

Sarina nodded her approval for Stephen to continue. "We have one more thing you need to know."

"Besides aliens living in the moon and different aliens coming to harvest Earth?" Jeremy asked. "What else is there to know? Are you two aliens?"

"No, we're human, as your grandfather is," Sarina said. "You three all know that my mother died when Jeremy was a baby. Well, my father stole my mother's body and had her memories incorporated into an android. The A-I appears identical to my mom."

"You're telling us our dead grandmother is now a robot?" Jeremy asked.

"No. Well, sort of. I'll let your Grandfather explain it," Sarina said.

"When can we meet them?" Timmy asked.

Steven peeked at his watch. "Renn and Glogg are calling the bunker in thirty minutes. Director Santiago gave permission for you three to attend the meeting in the Command Center. You may meet Renn if you wish."

"Yes, yes," Timmy jumped up and down. "And Glogg too?"

"Yes. What about you, Mary? Do you want to meet them?"

Mary remained silent, not sure what to say. Fearing her unwillingness might jeopardize his chances of seeing an alien, Timmy shouted out, "Think, Mary. After you meet them, you can brag to that mean ol' Rita Collingsworth you met a real-life alien. She'll be pea-green with envy. You'll be the most popular kid in your class."

Reluctantly, Mary agreed.

"What about you, Jeremy?" Steven asked.

"Sure. Why not? I might as well meet the person who has destroyed my life. Plus, it's not every day one meets a real live spaceman."

"He's not the one responsible for this," Sarina said.

"Whatever, Mom."

Timmy poked at Mary as they walked towards the Command Center in hopes she wouldn't change her mind. She giggled, forgetting what awaited them. To avoid their excess energy, Jeremy walked a few feet behind the group, doing his best to be dispassionate. The closer they came to the Command Center, the more their excitement grew. When they rounded the last corner, there stood Director Santiago. Timmy and Mary ran to her.

"Hello," she greeted. "Are you three ready?"

"I would say that's an understatement," Sarina said. "They can barely hold still."

"So, I see." A sober expression crossed the Director's face. She addressed all three children but kept her eyes on the youngest two. "Sometimes, when we are excited to do something, we discover the reality of it differs from what we imagined. It might be scary, unsettling, even boring. And sometimes, we change our minds and no longer want to do it. Sometimes it's better if we wait a bit."

"Mom, you promised we could meet them," Timmy whined, fearing his moment was being taken from him.

"Listen to what the Director has to say," Sarina said.

"I remember when I first met Glogg; he terrified me," the Director continued. "I realized I was frightened because I didn't know him or what he was. It's easy to become frightened by the unknown. But once I met him, I wasn't afraid anymore. So, to help you three, you will wait inside my room with Sally." She noted the disappointment on their faces. "But don't worry, you won't miss anything. You will be behind a one-way glass wall. You can see and hear what happens, but those on the screen can't see you. It's completely safe. After Renn and Glogg appear on the screen, you can decide if you meet them or not."

"And I don't have to come out if I don't want to?" Mary asked.

"No, you don't," the Director said.

"I won't be afraid," Timmy said.

"I'm sure you won't. Sally, if you'd take these three brave children into the Conference Room. Sarina and Steven, please follow me."

Sally led the children to the adjacent room. The youngsters rushed to the glass wall and stared in wonder at the busy place on the other side. A group of military personnel and civilians bustled around their desks, doing whatever their jobs were. It was so exciting. They drew their eyes to the viewing screen hanging against the front wall as they scoured the room. Jeremy was sure the screen was broader than the one at their IMAX theater. He and his siblings stared in wonder at the moon's image.

The children watched as the Director and their parents walked up the aisle and stood before the screen. Sarina and Steven both turned and saw their children pressed up against the glass.

"I thought they were behind a one-way mirror," Steven said.

"I told them a little lie," the Director said. "I thought they would feel safer if they thought no one could see them."

"Nice call." Sarina waved. "Can you guys see and hear us?" Their mother's voice filled the Conference Room.

"Push the red button on the console there." Sally pointed to a panel of knobs and buttons. "Your parents can hear you when it's down. To hear them, let the button go."

Timmy hurried and beat Mary to the panel. "Mom, Dad, can you hear me?"

Their mouths move, but no sound entered the room.

"Tim, let go of the button," Jeremy said.

"Oh, yeah. I forgot." Timmy held the button. "I didn't let go. Can you repeat?" This time he released the control.

"We said we hear you." Sarina smiled.

"Are you ready?" Director Santiago asked.

"Yes, Yes."

"Remember, you have nothing to fear. You are completely safe behind the wall." She turned to Sarina. "It is time."

Sarina closed her eyes and grasped the stone around her neck. Within seconds, two figures appeared on the screen--Jenny and Renn.

"Sarina, are you okay?" Renn asked. "We've been so worried."

"Yes, I am fine."

"And you, Steven? And my grandchildren?"

"Yes, we are fine," Steven said.

"What happened?" Renn scanned the room. "Where is your horrible President person?"

"He is gone," Director Santiago said.

"It is a pleasure to see you again, Director," Renn said. "And an even greater joy to learn he is not here. We find him to be an unyielding, spoiled, arrogant bureaucrat."

"And me?" the Director asked.

"We find you to be a trustworthy human, although a little unyielding at times."

"It is nice to be seen," the Director said. "And you are not the first to describe me as such."

"Where have you been, Sarina?" Jenny asked. "Why didn't you contact your father? We thought you would contact us once the communique went out."

"A little misunderstanding with the President""

"What kind of misunderstanding?" Renn asked.

"He was calling the shots when it came to you," Steven said. "He thought he had the upper hand and could use us to get what he wanted."

"I hope he now realizes he was in error," Jenny said.

"I think he's beginning to," Steven chuckled. "He understands this is a global matter, not only an American issue. And he has to deal with Sarina if he wants to speak with you."

"Are we ready for the meeting?" Renn asked.

"Yes," Director Santiago said. "Most of the nations are sending a representative. Speculation and fear are growing about what you will say. Although an effective means of showing them your sincerity, turning the Earth's oceans and lakes pink may not have been the best idea. Nor having waterfalls flow backward. The people now see you as a threat, not as a friend."

"The show of force was necessary." Glogg stepped onto the screen.

"HOLY SHIT!" Timmy yelled. "It's an ant. No, a grasshopper. He's HUGE!"

Mary took a step towards Sally and slipped her child's hand inside the woman's. Even Jeremy gasped and took a step backward.

Upon hearing the child's words, Glogg directed his vision towards the glass partition. "I see we have visitors today."

"Who?" Renn asked, scouring the room for unfamiliar faces.

"Behind the glass wall," Jenny said. "Two females: one an adult and one a child. Two males: one a sub-adult and one child. The children resemble Sarina and Steven."

"My grandchildren?" Renn asked.

"May I meet them?"

"Since most of Earth's children know about you, we thought our children should be told of your existence also," Sarina said. "Each can decide if they wish to come forward or not."

"I hope my appearance does not frighten them." Glogg gazed at the glass wall. "Children, I assure you, I mean you no harm. I may appear huge and a little frightening, but I assure you I am not. In fact, Renn tells me I'm a... what do you call me?"

"A kitty cat," Renn said.

"Yes, a kitty cat," Glogg said. "Whatever that is. Perhaps one day I can meet one. But today, I, Renn, and even Jenny would like to meet you."

The moment Sally gave the children the okay to depart, Timmy darted from the room and ran to his father. "Are you an ant?"

"My species is called %IE**#+. Humans call us Caelifera. I understand we resemble an Earth species you call insects. As you said, an ant. Although Renn says I have grasshopper in me too."

"How tall are you?" Timmy asked in awe.

"Believe it or not, I am actually on the short side," Glogg said, delighted at Timmy's astonished mien. "By your Earth standards, I am ten feet, but I hope to grow a little more."

"How tall are the other guys?" Timmy asked, searching the screen in excitement for the others.

"The males of my species average around twelve feet," Glogg said. "Females grow a little larger. They average close to fifteen feet."

"Fifteen feet?" Timmy said. "I want to meet one of them."

"Perhaps one day," Renn smiled. "My name is Renn. I am a human like you. I am your grandfather."

"Mom told us. Dad said you were born on the moon." Timmy said.

"Yes, I was," Renn said. "It is a pleasure to meet you, Timmy." Jeremy emerged from the observation room and walked toward the screen. "You must be Jeremy. Your mother tells me you are an exceptionally talented basketball player."

"Hope to make State Champion this year," Jeremy kept his eye on Glogg. "Are there many aliens up there like Glogg?"

"A few," Renn said. "And representatives from five other worlds."

"And you will not harm us?" Jeremy asked.

"No," Glogg said. "We are all committed to protecting this system, especially your world."

"May I ask why? Or why I should believe you?"

Although both Steven and Sarina thought Jeremy was a little aggressive, they did not stop his line of questioning. He did not see the tall alien as some fascinating extraterrestrial as his younger sibling did. Jeremy considered Glogg as a threat, someone who could destroy his future.

"I realize you have many questions," Renn said. "And I Glogg and I will answer them. But our time is short. We have much to discuss before our session tomorrow night. Jeremy, Timmy, and Mary, would you wait on your questions? If neither your parents nor Director Santiago has any objections, Glogg and I will meet with you after the UN meeting. We will answer as many questions as we can. Is that agreeable with you?"

"I suppose," Jeremy said.

"Can't we stay for the rest of your meeting?" Timmy whined.

"Not this time," Renn said. "We have grown up stuff to discuss. Hopefully, the next time we meet, Mary will be less afraid and will allow me to greet her." Mary pressed harder into Sally in the Conference Room.

"Fred, take the Spalling children back to their room," Director Santiago said. "Sally, I'd like you to stay with them until their parents return."

"Yes, Ma'am." Fred rose from his seat. "Jeremy and Timmy, follow me." Mary followed Sally, then let go of her hand. She ran up the aisle to the front. "Thank you for protecting Earth," Mary blurted out. She turned and ran after her siblings.

"They're beautiful children, Sarina," Renn said. Tears filled his eyes.

"If we could return to business," the Director suggested. "We have little time before the meeting."

"Is the room prepared as we requested?" Glogg asked.

"Yes, everything is arranged as you asked," Director Santiago said. "I won't lie to you. My government is not happy. The fact you can penetrate our airways and communications is unsettling. And not only to our government."

"Earth does not have the technology for the needed communications," Glogg said. "Plus, if we depend on your government to do the broadcasting, we can't ascertain if all the various nations received our message. With us controlling the meeting, we know they are hearing us. Although unsettling to you, this is the way it has to be."

"My government wants a breakdown of what you plan to say," the Director said.

"I'm sorry, I cannot comply," Glogg said. "All nations must receive the message at the same time. No one will be told ahead of the others."

"What about those representatives who do not speak English?" Steven asked.

"English?" A confused Glogg asked.

"What we are speaking now," Steven clarified.

"I am not speaking English," Glogg said. "I am speaking the Universal language, Hi-Kee."

"But I hear English," the Director said.

"Hi-Kee is an advanced form of communication," Renn explained. "It allows each recipient to hear in his or her language. As I speak, Glogg hears the Caelifera's language of clicks and snaps. So it will be when we sent the meeting message; each human will experience our message in their native tongue. This way, we left no one out."

"Does Glogg intend on being present?" the Director asked.

"Yes."

"Don't you think he will scare those attending? Might it not be better to have Renn deliver your message?"

"Possibly, but again, we don't have time for games," Renn said. "The Kett grow closer with each minute ticking by."

"The people of Earth have the right to the truth," Glogg explained. "And I am part of the truth. I cannot expect them to trust us if I am not willing to trust them."

"You have more faith in humanity than we deserve," an individual in the second row said. The Director shot him a disapproving semblance.

Glogg turned to the human. "Do I scare you?"

The non-uniformed man directed his attention to the Director for guidance. "You already opened your mouth. You might as well continue."

"Yes, you scare the crap out of me."

"What is your name?" Glogg asked.

"Richard. Richard Comstock. On loan to OEI from SETI."

"SETI is the acronym for the Search for Extraterrestrial Life," Jenny clarified. "It is an organization of scientists searching for life outside of Earth."

"I do not understand," Glogg said. "If you believe other life exists in the universe, why are you afraid of me? Is it because I don't resemble you or because of my size?"

"Believing in something and having ten feet of it stand before your eyes are two different things," Richard said. "And it's not only your stature. You are far superior to us."

"In what way?" Glogg asked.

"In technology," Richard said. "In your knowledge, in your life expectancy."

"Would you feel more at ease if I told you humans are superior to me in some respects?" Glogg asked. "Or my species has flaws like yours?"

"If I knew what those flaws were, I might feel less afraid," Richard said.

"That is not a topic for discussion," Glogg said. "But I will tell you one. I cannot breathe Earth's air. I can never visit your beautiful planet."

"Why?" the Director asked.

"A fact of life," Glogg said. "Thank you, Richard, for your honesty. Your honesty will help me in my talk with humans. Now, I will turn this conversation over to Renn. He will explain to you what will happen. You will receive a feed of the meeting and witness it for yourselves. Until after the meeting, I take my leave." He walked offstage, then stopped. "Richard, I hope you will observe the airing and tell me how I did, if I eased any of your anxieties or not." Then he vanished.

"Renn, the military needs your flight plan so they can allow your approach and landing," Director Santiago said. "We don't want you shot down before you arrive."

"An interesting scenario," Renn half-teased. Beneath his optimism, he knew the President would rather have them blown out of the sky. "We won't be landing in a ship."

"Then how will you attend the meeting?"

"You will have to wait and see." Renn smiled.

THE TALK AT THE UNITED NATIONS

The Assembly Hall at the United Nations was packed. Since there was no press, they opened the Press Room for additional seating. Trusting the message, few brought interpreters, freeing up more seats in the interpreters' room. Even with these additional seats, many stood around the back walls and down the side aisles.

A massive screen draped across the front wall. At precisely twenty-one hundred hours, a small black dot appeared blinking in the middle of the screen. Then a booming voice sounded.

"Please do not be afraid. My name is Renn. I am a human, like you. The only difference between us is I was not born on Earth but on the moon. I will now materialize on the stage. I am no threat to you."

As the various nations kept watch, the air to the left of the speaker's platform vibrated, and a slight hum sounded. A figure took shape. Within fifteen seconds, Renn stood on the stage. Sounds of fear filled the auditorium while their faces showed the terror they experienced.

"We did not feel it was appropriate to show ourselves only on the screen," Renn said. "If you are going to trust us, it is important you see us for who we are."

"You're human like us?" a voice called out.

"Yes."

"You were born on the moon?"

"Yes."

"Were your parents taken?"

"Not taken," Renn said. "Brought to the colony with the choice they could return to Earth if they wanted to."

"An alien captured them?"

"No, two humans brought them to the moon. They recognized my parents as advanced environmental thinkers and realized how much they loved this planet. They thought they would make an excellent addition to their team."

"How many humans are up there?"

"Three thousand, two hundred and one," Renn said. "But two families are expecting births within six months."

"How many aliens?"

"Eight hundred and sixty-four."

"Why were humans taken?"

Renn held up his hands. "I realize you have questions. We will answer them as we tell you about our past, why we are here, and why we have contacted you. To explain this, I have brought with me the leader of our station. His name is Glogg. He is from an ancient alien race we call Caelifera. He appears formidable and frightening, stands ten feet tall. I assure you, he is a gentle giant and means you no harm. Do not fear him. All he asks is for you not to prejudge him and allow him to speak."

Renn waited for a few seconds. "Also, while we come in peace, let me assure you we will tolerate no aggression towards us. At the first sign of hostility, we will end this transmission." The air on the other side of the podium rippled as when Renn appeared. Renn held his breath.

As the image of Glogg materialized, the sounds of fear reverberated throughout the rooms. Those in the first few aisles prepared to run from their seats. Some throughout the audience clasped their hands over their mouths to keep from screaming. Several ran from the auditorium, pushing past the mass of bodies. Others, too afraid to flee, fainted where they sat.

"Thank you for coming," Glogg said as he fully materialized. "As Renn stated, I mean you no harm." He waited until the fright from his appearance settled some. "I come to save your planet. But before I explain, let me tell you about us. My name is Glogg. I am the leader of a colony of humans and five alien species who inhabit your moon."

"Our ancestors arrived in your solar system approximately five thousand years ago," Glogg said. "A race called the Kett had discovered your system. They are a mining race that specialized in destroying planets and solar systems. And they were preparing to harvest your solar system for its wondrous minerals and abundant water supply. To stop their rampage, a group called the Interstellar Space Coalition traveled to your solar system and confronted the Kett. They stopped them, but not before they had obliterated the last two planets. As our ancestors prepared to leave, they discovered the third planet from your sun--a blue planet filled with water, minerals, and a unique assortment of life. They realized why the Kett traveled here, and they would not abandon such a prize. Although you take your planet for granted, Earth is a rare world. Few planets contain the amount of water Earth does. Or the diversity of life. To ensure this rare jewel continued, our ancestors stayed. They built a space station inside your moon. From there, they protected your planet in secret, refraining from interfering with Earth's development."

"Over the past five thousand years, other aliens have come to Earth in exploration. We expelled them and kept you safe."

"Over the millennia, our numbers dwindled. Unwilling to leave your planet unguarded to return to our system to get recruits, we enlisted them from Earth. Please understand, we did not kidnap them nor held them against their will. Anyone wanting to return to Earth could. Those who remained had families. Without human help, we never would have survived."

"So, we have remained hidden from you all this time. Until now. As our ancestor feared, the Kett have returned." The screen behind Renn and Glogg sputtered into life, revealing an armada of spaceships. One could see the vessels were predators, designed for one purpose--destruction. "This is the Kett. Their fleet contains six mining ships, each capable of destroying a sphere the size of your moon in a day. The other nine vessels are cargo ships, giant containers waiting to be filled with the minerals of the planets."

"We have contacted the ISC asking for reinforcements to fight the Kett, but we cannot predict if they will arrive in time. Our fleet comprises a hundred and sixteen ships. If it's enough to stop the Kett, only time will tell. Their weaponry may be far more advanced than our own."

"We have broken our silence because of our fleet," Glogg continued. "We will launch the fleet tomorrow. I tell you of our mission so you will not be frightened. Plus, as sentient beings like ourselves, you deserve to know your future may soon end."

"Are you saying these Kett will destroy Earth?" asked a man in the back.

"The Kett are not people," Glogg said. "They are a violent alien race, like nothing you've ever imagined. Their only want is wealth. We will do all we can to prevent them from destroying this system, but I can make no promises."

"What proof do you have that what you say is the truth?" another man asked.

"None, other than this picture and my word," Glogg said. "But NASA has the Jupiter III satellite heading towards Saturn. We will give them the coordinates to change the satellite's trajectory to take pictures of the ships themselves if they so wish. However, if they do this, the Kett will destroy the satellite the moment they discover it."

"How long before they arrive?"

Glogg eyed Renn. He thought the news might be more palatable coming from him. Why he didn't know.

"Six to seven months," Renn said. "A year at the most. It all depends on if they bypass some moons or other planets. We believe their primary objective is to harvest Earth's water."

"But Earth isn't the only place with water. What about Titan and Europa?"

"They, too, will be processed," Renn said. "But both oceans are buried beneath a mantle of ice. Earth's water is lying there, waiting to be taken. It is more cost-efficient to take what is readily available."

"But don't they realize there is life on this planet? Can't we contact them, reason with them?"

"Kett do not reason," Glogg said. "They have no regard for life, only profit."

"Surely we can negotiate with them."

"Kett do not negotiate."

"So, what are we supposed to do? Simply lie down and die?"

"Our armies have nuclear weapons and missiles," someone said.

"We can shoot them down when they arrive."

Exasperation flashed across Renn's face. "Have you not been listening to what Glogg told you? We might not even be able to stop them with our ships. How do you think your feeble human weapons will cause any harm? The Kett can eradicate you from miles out in space. They can launch their weapons before you can even detect them on your so-called 'advanced' space telescopes."

"Are you saying owe have no hope?" a woman asked.

"There is always hope," Glogg said. "We might get lucky, and the Kett will fill their cargo bays with minerals from the other planets and moons. If so, they will have to return to port and unload their cargoes before striking Earth. Such a delay will give us enough time for our reinforcements to arrive."

"But they'll return?"

"Yes. I would estimate within the next century."

"If I understand you, these other aliens will destroy Earth, and there is nothing we can do about it. Am I correct?"

Glogg surveyed the audience of humans, wondering how he would feel if some stranger came to tell him his life was over. "Remember, there is always hope."

"Is there anything we can do?"

"Prepare for the worst, hope for the best," Glogg said. "If you believe in a higher power, make your amends. Cherish your family and tell them you love them. Put petty disputes aside."

"Wait. You have spaceships," said a male in the back. "You could take a lot of us with you, move us to another planet somewhere."

"I am afraid that is not a possibility," Glogg said.

"Why not?"

"It just isn't. I cannot give you an explanation."

"You state you represent an organization of planets," a woman said. "Couldn't your Coalition speak to these other worlds and get us asylum? Perhaps negotiate for land?"

"Even if they gave us land to live on, we'd be outsiders. I say we opt for somewhere where there is no sentient life."

"If they won't help us, then we'll take what we need," came a voice from the middle of the room. "We deserve a chance to live."

"Taking seems to be the way of the human species," Glogg said. "Take what you want, no matter if it belongs to someone else or not. It is your aggression as a species that almost made us abandon this post several millennia ago. We have not remained here all this time to protect humankind. We protect the flora and fauna of this world." Glogg paused for a moment as he stepped closer to the end of the stage. "Truth is, except for us and a few others in our high command, no one knows or cares that humans even exist. No one will shed tears when your race disappears."

"Are you saying we don't deserve to live?" an angry voice asked.

"No, only that you are not important to others out there."

The sound of angry voices rose as representatives discussed Glogg's words.

"What about your planet?" came a voice above the others. "Why can't we go to your planet? Your world must be close if you came here."

"Although close, you cannot reach our planet in your human lifetime," Glogg said. "Plus, our environment would not support human life."

"Dear Sir, please take some of us with you so our race does not die?" said a soft-spoken woman who walked toward the stage. "At least give us some hope."

"As Renn told you, humans are well-represented on the station. Besides, there are over seven billion humans on this planet. How would we decide who goes and who stays?"

"The leaders of our nations should go," said a gray-haired man with a beard. "They can carry on our laws and way of life."

"The way of the rich, you mean," came another voice.

"What of the ordinary people? Are you saying they should not have a chance too?"

"I don't think they have a lot to offer," said the bearded man.

"Anyone who goes should pay their way."

"The ordinary people made this planet," said another. "The farmers, the ranchers, the metal workers, the coal miners. They have as much right as anyone else for a chance to live. The wealthy should be the last to go."

"Scientists. Our scientists should go."

"But no lawyers." Everyone laughed, breaking the tension.

"Or criminals."

"The children should go," came a suggestion. "They are the hope of Earth. Let them be the hope of humanity in space."

The audience gave more and more suggestions, with occasional arguments interrupting the talk. Unable to take the senseless bickering, Glogg emitted a high piercing sound. When the arguing stopped, he began.

"You must understand we are here only to tell you of what is about to happen. We are not offering you transportation from this world."

"You can't leave us."

"How dare you!"

"You're going to let us all die?"

"That's unthinkable."

Enraged at Glogg's words, a group of humans rushed the stage. When those in front tried to grab Renn and Glogg, their hands went through the air. The alien and human were not real, but holograms projected onto the stage. Both holograms disappeared, leaving those in the room stunned and afraid, with no hope of a future.

———————

As promised, they projected the UN meeting onto the screen in the Command Center. Except for the children, Sally, and two guards, the entire compound attended.

Whispers filled the room. Would they see Glogg as a threat or an ally? Would they listen to what he and Renn said? Or would their fear rule their mind?

The screen switched to a view of those assembled at the UN. There was standing room only. Scanning the faces moving across the screen, they tried to determine the mood. Several minutes later, Renn appeared on the stage. So far, so good. At least the audience seemed to accept the moon-born human. But what about Glogg? They held their breath as Glogg's image materialized. Gasps and sounds of fear sounded throughout the room. Several members fled. Many in the Command Room were surprised at how well the UN attendees accepted the ten feet alien. They believed the meeting would go well. But when the delegates bickered among themselves, their optimism faded. And when the representatives voiced suggestions of who were worthy, they too lost their hope for humanity. The loss deepened when Glogg announced no additional Earth humans would go with them. When the meeting ended, the screen returned to the usual image of the moon. No one spoke a word. The audience sat there, numb, unable to react.

Director Santiago remained silent as she surveyed those under her direction. She saw the helplessness each one felt. She stood with her back to the screen.

"Well, that did not go as we hoped." She tried to give an encouraging smile, but she couldn't. She, too, was devastated by what happened. "Some of you have spouses and children back home. Others may have some business you need or want to finish before the end. Therefore, I am dismissing anyone who wants to leave. I will sign your discharge papers, and you may leave as soon as you'd like."

"Do you have the authority, Director?" Steven asked.

"What are they going to do? Arrest me? I won't even go to trial before the end is here."

"But you can't run this facility by yourself," an officer said.

"Perhaps not," the Director said, this time able to smile. "I am hoping a few of you will stay. But if not, I'll manage."

"You're not leaving?" a civilian asked as she gathered her belongings.

"No, I'm needed here," the Director said. "This facility is the only way to speak with those on the moon. We cannot break the connection. Glogg or Renn will tell us how the battle goes and if Earth has a chance."

"You're right." the female replaced the items on her desk. "Our place is here. Besides, better to be here and aware of what is happening than out there where there is only fear."

"Here, here," rang out the voices of those in the room.

"Surely, some of you want to go?" the Director asked.

"We're staying," Jim said. "Those of us who have families can leave once we know the end is coming."

"Derek, your wife is due next month with your firstborn." Director Santiago addressed the young non-uniformed man sitting a few feet from her. "You need to go home."

"I'm not leaving," Derek said.

"Then I'm firing you," the Director said. "Go home. June, Abdul, Symone, Rashad, you too." The five stated their objections. "I want no discussion on this matter. You are all terminated."

The five individuals stood with heavy hearts, walked over to the Director, hugged her, then left without a word.

"What about you two?" the Director asked Sarina and Steven.

"Our place is here too," Sarina said as Steven put his arm around her shoulder. "Besides, we have nowhere else to go. Here, the children are safe."

"We still have one problem," the Director said. "The President knows the truth of who you are. And I'm afraid of what he might do."

THE STORY OF RENN AND JENNY

As feared, the world's population reacted to the news of the UN meeting with terror, hopelessness, and suspicion. The nations' leaders urged their people not to overreact, to keep hope they would stop the Kett. They stressed the importance of continuing normal activities such as work, school, and family.

It was a time of turmoil and chaos. Adding to the mixture were the scam artists who arose overnight. They lured people into paying hundreds of thousands of dollars for a place in a secured underground bunker where they and their family could survive the Kett attack. Some sold passage to secret government spaceships which did not exist. The most brazen claimed to be friends of the colonists on the moon and could arrange a seat on one of their ships. They charged four million a seat, and they were selling thousands of tickets. But the worst of all were the alchemists who preyed on the poor. For fifty dollars, you could purchase a vial of poison guaranteed to end your life at the moment of your choosing, a swift and painless death. Often the bottle contained water. Or, for the unfortunate, rat poison or a chemical cleaner, giving the recipient an excruciating death. Governments warned people not to buy these vials, advising them most were not what they claimed to be. But people were desperate, afraid of what was to come.

Some realized the moon station was their only chance. They bombarded the moon with radio signals, pleading with anyone to contact them. No answers came.

Russia even began building a space shuttle for launch to the moon. They speculated if they made it to the moon base, Glogg and his people would have to take them under their care.

The world's underground groups went an unconventional route. They believed there were people on Earth who Glogg and/or Renn had contact with, people they might use as ploys to get passage on the spaceship. Since the meeting took place in New York, they calculated the prize they sought hid in the United States, probably under military protection. Millions of dollars exchanged hands as the searchers bribed officials and clerks for information about the aliens, knowledge of communications, or secret operations. In desperation, they searched for someone, anyone with a connection to the aliens. People were taken and tortured for the alien information they did not know of. Mentioned repeatedly throughout the underground was the name of Sarina Spalling. She was their number one priority.

Through this all, the President maintained his silence. He still had a chance to get off the doomed planet if he kept the location of Sarina and her connection to Renn a secret. She was important to the human, a fact he wanted to exploit. His primary concerns were former OEI Deputy Director Samuel MacIntosh and former OEI Director Major General Thomas Hancock. They too knew Sarina's deep connection to the alien base. He would have to silence each of them.

The Director trusted her people with her life. She knew those returning home would keep the secret of what they had seen in the bunker. But as a precaution, she reminded each of their confidentiality oath.

Director Santiago feared for the Spalling family's safety. If anyone in the outside world made a connection between them and Renn, their lives were over. She ordered a complete lockdown the moment the five leaving were outside the bunker. She instructed Chef to harvest everything possible and to destroy his garden. Nothing above ground could testify to what they hid below. Sequestered behind an impenetrable wall, everyone would remain until she figured out what to do, how she could save the Spalling family.

The bunker was the top-ranking security military location in the world. Ten miles below the surface, the bunker sat directly below a volcanic peak named Shiprock on the Navajo Nation Reservation. This peak added another seventeen hundred feet of rock and dirt on top of the bunker. Hidden across the countryside were numerous air shafts, a security measure in case the facility came under assault. No one, not even Director Santiago, knew them all. There was enough food, water, and supplies to sustain a regiment of two hundred people for fifteen years. Because of Washington's budget cuts, they were down to the bare minimum personnel. Subtracting the five people Abigail sent home and adding Sarina's family, the bunker contained eighty-two people. They had more supplies than they could use before the world ended.

The Director debated about severing all communications with the outside world. As she had said, they were their link to Glogg. But if she didn't, would her actions endanger Sarina and her family? After a long debate with herself, she decided outside communication was not a necessity. Glogg would need to broadcast any messages the world required.

———————

"How are you holding up?" Renn asked Sarina that evening when the moon was within range for broadcasting.

"Doing okay," she said. "Director Santiago worries someone might find out about us, so we are on secured lockdown."

Renn diverted his gaze to the Director. "Thank you for protecting my family."

"It's my job," she said. "Besides, she's the only connection we have to you."

"Renn, you're sure there is no way for anyone to trace your signals back to this location?" a worried Steven asked.

"Positive," Renn said. "We've been sending messages all over Earth for centuries with no problems. Not the slightest detection."

"Yes, but no one was searching for them before," Steven said.

"They now know you exist and will be hunting for you. And us."

"This is my fault," Renn said. "We wanted to help the people of Earth, but by doing so, I have put you, my family, in danger. I expected the representatives to react strongly to what we told them, but I did not foresee them reacting the way they did. And I never thought they'd ask us to take a portion of humanity with us."

"You told them their lives would end within the year," an irritated Director said. "What did you expect?"

"I don't know," Renn said. "I've never been around Earth humans much. I guess I didn't realize how they think and act."

"But you spent time with Mom," Sarina said.

"Yes, but only for a few months. And I had little interaction with other people during my time with her. Your mom and I stayed at a quaint little cabin out in the woods, hidden away from the world. The last thing we wanted around was people." He gave his daughter a wink.

Sarina's cheeks blushed slightly at the thought of her mother's romantic involvement with the stranger on the screen. If he was only on earth for sixty-four days, their time together must have been some whirlwind romance.

"You never told us the complete story of how you and Mother met," a curious Sarina said.

Renn slid into deep thought, a smile appearing on his face as he chuckled. His eyes widened and twinkled.

"It was fate," Renn said. "It's the only thing you can call it. We met, fall in love, and had you. I wasn't even supposed to be on Earth. The pilot scheduled for the mission came down with

121

an acute case of poison ivy from an earlier mission. When our commander was on his way to reassign a new pilot, he found me sitting in the garden reading. He figured I needed something to do and told me I was going to Earth to collect some eggs."

"Eggs?"

"We monitor all social media networks. And, as I'm sure you suspect, television and radio transmissions and cell phone calls."

"No military operations?" Director Santiago asked.

"That goes without saying," Renn laughed. "It's our number one listening avenue, filled with doom and gloom." Director Santiago did not laugh. Renn ignored her lack of humor and continued. "One listener picked up a television news segment about birds. The report mentioned the lark sparrow had been declining and was gone from many areas the bird once inhabited. A mating pair was sighted in Monroe County, Michigan, the first since 2015. They sent me to retrieve the eggs and bring them back to our nursery."

"Your nursery?" Steven asked.

"What nursery?" Director Santiago said, now interested in the discussion.

"We are the protectors of your world," Renn said. "With man's determination to eradicate anything alive on the planet, it's a full-time job. Before a species of plant or animal goes extinct, we do our best to capture several and bring them up for safekeeping."

"What's safekeeping?" the Director asked.

"I collected four eggs from their nest. We still preserve them in a state of suspension along with two dozen other eggs found throughout the Midwest of the United States. We hoped humanity would learn to cherish their world one day, and we might return these lost species to the planet. But now, with the Kett coming, it will not happen."

"What will become of them?" Sarina asked.

"The ISC planned to preserve the species, not relocate them. If all life on Earth is destroyed, it will be necessary to locate a suitable planetoid where these creatures and plants can be resettled to multiply and live normal lives," Renn said. "These species must be preserved."

"You told the representatives at the United Nations that there was no habitable planet for light-years, that it would be impossible to reach one," the Director said. "Now you're saying there is a habitable planet?"

"Not exactly. The ISC has been preparing a planet for colonization of the plants and animals we have stored aboard. But it is not meant for humanity to live on it."

"But we could."

"Yes, I suppose if we choose to."

"So, you're just going to let the human species die when you could help?" the Director asked.

"It's not my call," Renn said.

"How many species do you have?" Steven said.

"I don't have the exact number," Renn said, thinking back to what one caretaker had told him. "Let's see. If my memory is correct, the lark sparrow was number five million, seven hundred eighty-three thousand, nine hundred and ninety-eight. We've added many more species in the past thirty-some years since I collected the eggs."

"Your spaceship is that massive?" Director Santiago asked in astonishment. She realized the power the aliens must have and how easily they could have ended Earth any time they wanted to.

"She's a substantial size," Renn said. "But you need to realize we store these plants and animals in their smallest components. We keep plants as seeds, spores, and tubers. We store animals as fertilized eggs, embryos, and polyps. There are also unfertilized eggs and sperm for some species. And some forms of bacteria in Petri dishes."

"Incredible," the Director sighed, taking a nearby seat, contemplating the likely future of life from Earth. Somehow the thought of elephants, flamingos, flowers, and the rest of Earth's life continuing after they destroyed the planet comforted her. But that future did not curb her anger over leaving the world's population to die when something could be done.

"What's the most unusual thing you have?" Steven asked, in a voice almost like a child's. Excitement filled him.

"Hmm, an excellent question," Renn said. "They might not be exotic, but the one I hope to see is the Mammoth. They were almost all gone before the ISC arrived. But about seventeen hundred years ago, we stumbled across a small herd on Wrangel Island off the northern coast of far eastern Siberia. We collected samples before they too went extinct. At thirteen to seventeen feet, they'd be an impressive sight. And their tusks were gigantic. Of course, the dodo bird sounds interesting as well."

"No dinosaurs?" a disappointed Steven asked. Although a Mammoth and dodo sounded fantastic, a dinosaur would have been spectacular.

"The Caelifera arrived almost sixty million years after the dinosaurs disappeared," Renn said. "But we have a few relics." Steven's eyes light up. "There are three plesiosaur embryos the Caelifera discovered right after they arrived. Like the mammoth, a small group survived the extinction inside a small inland sea in the South Pacific. And I believe there is the frozen carcass of a pregnant megalodon we found in Antarctica. It's several millennia old, so it's unlikely the embryos are viable. Or we could clone her." A slightly bored expression appeared on Sarina's face. "But I digress from my original topic of how Sarina came to be."

"Momma lark sparrow hadn't laid her eggs yet when I arrived on Earth," Renn said. "Rather than return to the station, I decided to do a little exploring. I had never been here before and was thrilled to see it firsthand. After securing my ship and setting up a notifier to inform me when momma bird laid her eggs, I walked to the nearest town. I was famished and headed towards the first diner I could find. Well, as you can imagine, I did not know what to order. So, I asked the cute female who came to take my order what she suggested. She was your mother, Sarina."

"I forgot Mom was a waitress in her younger days," Sarina said.

"She suggested black coffee, a cheeseburger, and fries," Renn said, laughing as he remembered his reaction to the food.

"The coffee tasted like something out of the bathroom. And I spit the cheeseburger out immediately. I almost became violently ill. We do not eat animal flesh at the station -- only synthetic foods and vegetation. I did like the fries. Still, have a hunger for them occasionally."

"Mother told me you didn't like meat," Sarina remembered. "She said you were some advanced vegan hippie."

"She couldn't tell you the truth, could she?" Renn said. "Once Jenny realized I had an aversion to the meat or any of its byproducts, she finally brought me something I could eat--a huge garden salad. After I had finished, she brought me the most delicious thing I had ever tasted--a hot fudge sundae."

"But we make ice cream from milk, which comes from a cow," the Director said.

"So, I found out later," Renn said. "But that night, in my ignorance, I chowed down. I ate one form of ice cream each night I was on Earth. I justified my consumption by thinking it was a natural product of a LIVING cow, not a dead one. And I wasn't hurting the cow. Glogg put me straight when I returned to the station, explaining how dairy cows produce milk and their mistreatment."

"The diner was slow the night we met, so Jenny and I talked a lot. I asked her where to find a place to stay for a few days. She told me the closest motel was about fifteen miles away, too far to walk. She invited me to stay in the loft of her barn. I did not understand what a loft or a barn was, but I accepted."

"It got a little cold during the night, so Jenny invited me to come into the house and sleep on the couch. Neither of us got any sleep." Sarina's cheeks flush again. "And it's not what you think. We stayed up all night talking. She was so fascinating to listen to. I could have spent the rest of my life listening to her. The next morning, she called into work sick, and we spent the entire day together walking through the countryside. It was so beautiful. For the first time, I utterly understood why the Ancestors chose to protect Earth. That night we slept in the same bed, and I told her the truth of who I was."

"She wasn't scared?" Sarina asked.

"Not in the least." Renn glanced lovingly at the android off-screen who held her memories. "We fell in love that night, a deep, fulfilling love. The next morning, we packed up her car and drove up north to her grandfather's cabin in the woods."

"What about the sparrow eggs?" Abigail asked.

"The lark sparrow had laid her eggs, so I hurried back and retrieved them. I placed them in a freeze-unit to keep them safe. Got hell from Glogg when I got back with them almost two months later. Thankfully, they were okay. Two weeks after we met, I married Jenny. And the rest, you know. I returned to the moon and could never find her again."

"How did you get back to the moon?" Sarina asked.

"Fearing someone would discover my craft, Jenny insisted I bring my ship close to the cabin, which I did. Good thing I did, too, because I would never have made my way back to where it was. I stayed on Earth too long. My body rebelled to the air and soil pollutants your bodies are accustomed to. The constant exposure to them made me deathly ill. And to make matters worse, I was too ill to fly home. Jenny helped me get a message to the station, and Xavier came and brought me back. You haven't met Xavier. You need to. He's something unique. But a bit more intimidating than Glogg."

"Is he an alien?" Sarina asked.

Renn laughed. "Not exactly. But he is an alien design." He had opened a can of worms by mentioning Xavier. Now he had to finish the explanation. "Xavier is a shiny, nine-foot police robot. Timmy would love him. I haven't brought him out for anyone to see because I was afraid of the reaction. Having a race of aliens on the moon is one thing. Having a race of aliens with an army of military robots is something totally different."

"Wise call," Steven whispered. He wondered how the Director was taking this new piece of news.

"If you did not know where Mom was, how did you learn of her death and me?"

"I monitored the area around where we had met for any news of Jenny," Renn said. "It was time-consuming listening to radio reports, listening to town gossip on telephones. When the Internet came to be, my job became a little easier. Then one day, I found a notice on the Internet stating my Jenny had passed. The announcement gave the location of where her body would be, and the times people could visit. I got permission from Glogg to return to Earth and see her one last time. That was when I learned I had a daughter--you, Sarina."

"You were the stranger who cried at her casket," Sarina said. "No one knew who you were. I remember you hugged me so tenderly, so lovingly. You disappeared before I could talk to you."

"I was so emotional. I feared I would blow my cover, so I left immediately after hugging you," Renn said. "Plus, I was already having trouble breathing Earth's polluted air. I waited until they put my Jenny into the ground. Then I retrieved her body from the grave and brought her here to have her memories stored inside the android. I couldn't be with her while she was alive, but I could have a piece of her when she was dead. I don't expect you to understand."

"No, I do," Sarina said. "If Steven were to die today, I couldn't go on. I'd give anything to have his memories stored in a unit like her. A piece of him is better than nothing at all."

THE FLEET LAUNCHES

"The bunker is sealed tight," Rear Admiral Paine announced as he walked into the Oval Office. "No communications are coming out. No way to comprehend if they are receiving our communiques or if they're ignoring them."

"Christ, Mack, you're the one in charge of the damn operation," the President said. "You must have a way inside."

"Not when they're on lockdown," the Rear Admiral said.

"Then we'll break the door down," the President said.

"It, too, is secured," the Rear Admiral answered. "You can't break it open with a nuclear warhead. Besides, the bunker is on Navajo land. We have no authority for such a strike."

"What are you talking about," the President bellowed. "I'm the damn President."

"Sorry, Sir," Major General Hancock stated. "Only the Tribal Council has jurisdiction over those lands. And since they resent the current administration for allowing drilling beside their lands, I don't think they'd be too accommodating."

"Hell, this is ridiculous," the President roared. "I'm expected to sit here in the dark while that woman talks with those aliens? Have we heard anything more from them?"

"We received a message an hour ago. It stated the alien fleet would emerge tonight at twenty-two hundred hours," the Rear Admiral stated.

"The bunker is sealed tight," Rear Admiral Paine said as he walked into the Oval Office. "No communications are coming out. No way to comprehend if they are receiving our communiques or if they're ignoring them."

"Christ, Mack, you're the one in charge of the damn operation," the President said. "You must have a way inside."

"Not when they're on lockdown," the Rear Admiral said.

"Then we'll break the door down," the President said.

"The door, too, is secured," the Rear Admiral said. "You can't break it open with a nuclear warhead. Besides, the bunker is on Navajo land. We have no authority for such a strike."

"What are you talking about," the President bellowed. "I'm the damn President."

"Sorry, Sir," Major General Hancock said. "Only the Tribal Council has jurisdiction over those lands. And since they resent the current administration for allowing drilling beside their lands, I don't think they'd be too accommodating."

"Hell, this is ridiculous," the President roared. "I'm expected to sit here in the dark while that woman talks with those aliens? Have we received any new communications from them?"

"We received a message an hour ago. The moon's statement said the alien fleet would emerge tonight at twenty-two hundred hours," the Rear Admiral said.

"So, we will see it from the United States?" the President asked.

"Yes, as long as the skies remain clear."

"How many vessels are to be launched?"

"The beings who referred to themselves as Renn and Glogg never specified a number," Major General Hancock answered. "They only reported their fleet would emerge."

"And you're positive there is no way to use those hidden nuclear missiles to blast their operations to hell while they're gone?" the President asked.

"No, Sir," Rear Admiral Paine said. "We designed the rockets to strike Earth, not the moon. The rockets are short-range and can't reach such a distance. Besides, you don't want to blast apart the moon."

"Why not?" the President asked. "Afraid someone will find out what we have up there? Since chances are Earth will end soon, I don't think it matters if the whole frigging world knows."

"Destroying or even damaging the moon would have tragic consequences on Earth," Major General Hancock said.

"It will be darker at night," the President said. "Dogs won't have anything to howl at. What's the difference?"

"What's the difference?" a horrified Major General asked. Did this president know nothing about science? "The moon controls our tides, Mr. President. Its gravity affects countless things on Earth. The moon keeps the Earth's spin stable on its axis. Without her stability, the Earth's tilt would change, causing dramatic climate change, huge tidal bulges, and coastal destruction. The animals and plants who depend on the lunar cycles for their livelihood would perish. Plus, the probability is high that huge chunks of the moon would crash into Earth, destroying our planet before the Kett even got here. Trust me, Mr. President, we need the moon to survive."

"A lot of scientific mumbo-jumbo," the President grumbled. "The next thing you will tell me is the moon's responsible for life on Earth."

"Actually, Sir, it is a theory," Major General Hancock said.

The President stared at him, pursing his tiny lips together. "I don't care how you do it, but I want inside that damn bunker."

"Might I ask why it is so important for you to gain access to the bunker?" Rear Admiral Paine asked.

The President saw the confusion on the Rear Admiral's face. "Damn, Mack, don't act like you don't know."

"Know what, Sir?"

"That woman."

"You mean Director Santiago?"

"No, the other one. I don't remember her name. The one whose father is one of the moon people." The President's face tightened. Did he have to explain everything? Was no one in his cabinet competent?

"Her name is Sarina Spalling," the Rear Admiral said. "But we have no confirmation she is his daughter."

"He thinks she is, and that's all that matters," the President said. "And if she's his daughter, those kids of hers are his grandkids. He'll never leave her or them behind if this planet is going to be destroyed. I guarantee you he will come for her. And when he does, we will be waiting."

"To do what?"

"Negotiate for a seat on their spaceship."

"I don't believe either Renn or Glogg negotiate," Rear Admiral Paine said.

"Oh, they'll negotiate," the Present said, a smile of determination on his face. "With the Spalling family as our bargaining chip, we can get anything we want. Find me a way inside, and I promise there will be room for you and your families too."

"What about the Vice President and the cabinet members?"

"Let them find their own ride."

As the launch time came closer, the degree of excitement, curiosity, and fear intensified worldwide. In the Eastern Hemisphere, daylight prevented direct viewing. People in Tokyo, Hong Kong, London, and other significant cities gathered by the thousands around the giant advertising screens. In the Western hemisphere, where it was night, people filled the streets and their yards, many with telescopes, eager to glimpse the alien fleet emerging from the lunar globe above. People filled Times Square, the Las Vegas Strip, Toronto, and Rio de Janeiro hoping to see the event on their gigantic screens.

The International Space Station would broadcast the fleet's emergence to the billions of humans on Earth glued to their televisions and tablets. Because of the extraordinary occurrence, even those incarcerated watched the event.

The Hubble, Spitzer, and the other telescopes around the world were reset to monitor the moon. All except the Kepler Space Telescope. Because of its capacity to discover planets, the Kepler Telescope searched space to find confirmation of the Kett fleet and verify Glogg's claims.

Ten minutes before the launch, a hush spread across the globe. Even the crickets and other night animals remained silent, waiting for the impossible to happen.

Back at the White House, the President waited also, but for a different reason. He wanted proof Glogg told the truth about the Kett and the ISC fleet. If the ISC fleet was real, so was the space station. And, if it too was authentic, then he had a way off the doomed planet. The President was positive he could manipulate Glogg into granting him a seat. Part of him hoped nothing would happen, and the Kett was all a hoax. Then, perhaps, life could return to normal. He could engage his followers on Twitter again and remind them how marvelous of a President he was.

At exactly twenty-two hundred hours, an enormous section of the moon appeared to open. It seemed as if someone had sliced into the top area of a block of cheese and peeled it back. Those on Earth could not tell how extensive the opening was, but the watching telescopes measured a space thirty miles across. Earth held her breath, waiting for the first ship to emerge.

After what seemed like an eternity, the nose of the first ship emerged. As it advanced, the ship increased in size and substance. Shaped like a naval destroyer, but twice the size, the craft contained a pointed bow behind which three rows of artillery guns were mounted. Behind the guns rose a square bridge made of glass. Attached to its sides were numerous fighters, bracing to launch when needed. A faint red glow emanated from the end, heat from the massive engine vents which powered the spacecraft.

Next emerged forty smaller vessels, the real fighters and defenders of Earth. They would defend the larger ships. Each was swift and sleek, able to get in and attack before being fired on. Although similar in design, several distinct differences were noted among the smaller fliers. The variances represented the distinctive configurations of alien nations or casts.

Following the fliers were five bright red ships with an insectile design. They were more extensive than the first destroyer which had emerged. Its top bowed forward and down, reminding one of the alien from the *Alien* franchise movies. A substantial circular cockpit bulged out the front as if it was the head of the beast. Emerging from behind the cockpit were mechanical arms with claws capable of grasping and ripping an enemy to pieces. Two sets of wing-like appendages extended out from the sides a third of the way back from the front. The vessel's bodies ended in a short tail straight across. Many wondered in what world one would need such a machine to defend its occupants.

After a swarm of thirty more fighters, vessels of another design emerged. They appeared to be two ships in one, about double the size of a fighter. The bulk of the vessel consisted of two long cannons. A dorsal wing with alien writing protruded from the back of each. Cables connected the cannons to the heart of the ship, a separate flier. Artillery guns covered its back and front. The airman sat high above the cannons so the pilot could see over them. The ship appeared capable of going up and down as needed and possibly detaching. Although formidable attackers, it was apparent they did not have the smaller fighters' speed and agility.

For the next forty-five minutes, more ships emerged, a combination of the styles already seen. When the last ship appeared, people gasped in awe. Even those on Earth witnessed how enormous the flagship was without the aid of a telescope. Four times as powerful as the destroyers, it was long and cylindrical with two vast round sections orbiting the middle's cylinder. The front of the barrel was cone-shaped with a flat front. Its body contained no wings or fins. Ten enormous engines lined up in two rows of five in the back, driving the ship forward. On its side were the flags of many alien nations, signaling the Interstellar Space Coalition command ship. If the mother ship was that immense, how enormous was the space station which housed it?

The ships spread out and took their place in front of the command ship. The formation moved forward and prepared for flight. In the blink of an eye, one by one, the space vessels disappeared as they folded space en route to engage the Kett. The hangar door closed, making the moon whole again. As had been the norm for thousands of years, nothing gave testimony to the fact aliens lived inside the glowing circle of light.

The people on Earth who believed in a higher power prayed the fleet would be victorious. Those who didn't believe hoped for the same outcome. The future of Earth was in the hands of the alien fleet who had emerged.

––––––––––––

For four long days, the citizens of Earth waited for any news about the alien fleet. People kept their eyes on the skies at night, hoping to see something of the fleet, praying they didn't see the Kett. NASA took Glogg's proposal and rerouted Jupiter III to fly by the Kett fleet.

It was a time of reflection, a time for making amends and forgiving old wounds. For the first time, there was peace where war had raged for decades. People put hatreds aside. Opposing sides made and kept peace treaties. Except for the swindlers and those trying to make a fast buck, humanity lived as it was meant to. Neighbors helped neighbors. Those who had lots gave to those who had nothing. Some even opened their homes to the poor and homeless. Humankind prepared for his judgment day.

On the fourth day, Glogg sent a worldwide transmission. He gave an update on the fleet's position and a countdown until they would engage the Kett. He could also relay one piece of welcomed news: two of the Kett cargo ships and several fighters had left, presumably returning to port with full bellies of the resources they had stripped from Uranus and Neptune. Now, only twelve of the planet-killers needed destroying. But, even if the fleet could destroy all twelve, Earth's days were numbered. The Kett now knew firsthand of this solar system's riches, and they would not abandon such a rich haul. Earth's waters alone were worth the fuel it would take to bring another fleet. Glogg thought how ironic it was--for centuries, humans took whatever they wanted, having no heed if the land belonged to someone else or if it was detrimental to the ecosystems, plants, and animals. Now their planet faced destruction, their lives ending. At last, humanity understood the ramifications and errors of their actions.

Renn talked with his daughter and family each evening when the moon was in the range of the United States. He started each session with the latest news. The remainder of the time was spent talking with the grandchildren and answering their questions. They wanted information about the colony, what beings lived there, and what it was like to live in space. To help answer the questions about aliens, Renn brought several of the alien children to the sessions. The alien younglings were as curious and excited to meet real Earth humans as were Jeremy, Timmy, and Mary were to meet them. Somehow, they seemed different from the moon humans. Timmy was especially thrilled to meet an alien his age who had green scaly skin and six eyes. As the adults listened to the children's conversations, they realized they all possessed the same qualities of empathy, acceptance, understanding, and childhood curiosity. Although different species, they were all children whose primary purpose in life was to have fun. It made no difference if one was green, and one was white or how many arms or eyes they had. It was a humbling experience.

After the last transmission on the night before the fleet would meet the Kett, Director Santiago asked Renn and Glogg to remain for a moment. She wanted to speak privately with them. Not even Steven or Sarina could stay. Once the Command Center was empty, Director Santiago locked the entrance door and turned off all recording equipment. Her actions did not go unnoticed by Renn or Glogg.

"I fear you have something dreadful to tell us," Renn said.

"Not dreadful, but important." The Director stood before the two towering figures on the screen. "And time is of the essence, both now and later. What I am about to tell you must remain with us three."

"We're listening," Glogg said.

"It is about the Spalling family," Director Santiago said. "You must come and get them."

"I don't understand." Renn took a step closer to the screen.

"I'm afraid your announcement brought attention to Sarina and her family," the Director said. "People are now searching for them."

"People? What people?" Renn asked.

"For what purpose?" Glogg inquired.

"People in power," Abigail answered. "Leaders of underworld occults, people of significant financial means, you name it. They want off this planet. And they believe she and her family are their ticket to do so. It won't take them long to figure out where they are."

"What can we do?" a terrified Renn asked, understanding the danger.

"I put the base on lockdown. Nothing comes in; nothing goes out. This includes communications."

"We are aware of that," Glogg said.

"What you are not aware of is the fact one of these people in power is already here," the Director said. "The President has repeatedly ordered me to open the bunker and has an army outside trying to find a way in. He is determined to go with you and will use Renn's family as a bargaining chip to secure himself and his family a place on your station. Nothing will stop him from getting to them. Your family is no longer safe."

"I have been working on a plan," Renn said.

"No, you don't understand," the Director shouted, pacing before the screen. "They're out there. I can't keep them out much longer. I estimate they will find a way inside within thirty-six hours." She stopped and stared at the human and alien on the screen. "You must get them by twenty-four hundred tomorrow."

"But how?" Renn asked. "I have been working for a week trying to calculate the exact method to get inside your bunker. It takes precise calculations. If we're off by so much as a microbe, we're dead."

"There's a secret tunnel," the Director blurted out. "One no one is aware of."

"A secret tunnel?" Renn asked.

"I only discovered its existence yesterday," the Director said. "I was going through some old Directors' files hoping to find something to help keep the military out, and I came across it. The tunnel opens about five miles from here, on the north side of the installation. It's flat land. If you can bring your fliers in undetected, you can get your family and leave before the military realizes you're here."

"Avoiding detection is no problem," Glogg said. "The way we travel guarantees your radar will not pick us up."

Director Santiago smiled slightly. "Perhaps one day you will explain your mode of travel to me."

"Why are you doing this?" Renn asked. "Putting your career and life in jeopardy for a family you just met?"

"Being forced to accept your own upcoming death puts things in perspective," Director Santiago said. "I never had children of my own, but I have nieces and nephews whom I love dearly. Jeremy, Mary, and Timmy remind me of them. I can't save my own, but I can save yours. Someone who was born and raised on Earth should survive this tragedy to tell future human generations what their home planet was like."

"I cannot thank you enough," Renn said.

"Getting your family safely to the moon is all the thanks I need. So, we agree?"

"Yes. We will be at the coordinates tomorrow at twenty-three hundred."

"These are the coordinates." she held up a piece of paper with the Earth coordinates written on them. "I don't want to say the coordinates out loud or send them electronically. Someone may be listening. Can you understand what I wrote?"

"Yes." Renn jotted down the longitude and latitude.

"The emergence point is far enough away from the mountain so the President's men will not notice your ships," Director Santiago said, tearing the paper into small pieces. "I will create a diversion by pretending to open up the front security doors. That should keep the army focused on the bunker and not the surrounding terrain."

"We'll be ready for them," Renn said.

"We had best end this conversation before my staff becomes suspicious," Director Santiago said.

"Before you go, Director," Renn quickly said. "If the President discovers a way into the bunker before your designated time, I will need to retrieve my family early. If that happens, have Sarina squeeze the stone around her neck. I will come immediately."

"What if she can't emit the signal?"

"A possibility," Glogg said. "We need a backup plan."

All three thought, desperately trying to figure out a signal which would be undetected by others.

"The phone line!" Director Santiago said. Renn and Glogg stared at her inquisitively, not understanding what she was talking about. "The phone number Sarina called the first time to reach you. We'll call home if we are in trouble."

"Call home it is."

The screen went dark. An eerie silence filled the room with no one inside. Even the computers and recording system were silent. The Director walked over and reactivated the security equipment. As she turned to open the door and allow the staff back inside, a shape in the back corner moved. The silhouette advanced out of the blackness, yet still silent. Abigail held her breath, fearing who had witnessed her conversation with Renn and Glogg. Was the Spalling family now in danger? Had she failed?

"So, you plan on releasing the Spalling family?" Sally asked, stepping into the light. "I don't believe the President will be pleased to learn of your decision."

DAY FIVE

Day five: The day which would determine all their futures. At thirteen hundred hours, they received a message from the Command Ship. It contained only two words--KETT CONTACTED.

Sarina rechecked her watch. Fourteen hundred. She was sitting with the family in the dining hall, trying to eat lunch. She, like most, was too nervous and preoccupied with the thoughts provoked by the message Glogg had sent. Even probably hopeless, the ISC fleet would try to talk with the Kett and inform them this was a protected area, and mining was forbidden. Would the Kett listen and withdraw? Or would they fight? And if so, who would win?

She surveyed the almost deserted mess hall. Both Director Santiago and Sally were missing, which Sarina thought curious. On such an important day, she thought they'd be with the family. But then, why should they? They were probably in the Command Center waiting for some news. Both had more important things to do than to babysit them.

"Not hungry?" Stephen asked, noting his wife barely touched the delicious catfish Chef had made for them.

Sarina smiled at her spouse. "Guess I'm too nervous to eat."

"I know what you mean," Steven said, pushing away his lunch.

A massive "boom" filled the room, and everything shook. Sand and fine pieces of rock rained from the ceiling, falling onto their plates of food. Bottles fell off the tables. The lights overhead flickered and swung as if pushed by invisible children. Mary screamed and dove into her father's protective arms.

"Awesome." Timmy smiled. "I've never been in an earthquake."

Sarina focused on Steven, doing her best to hide the panic she felt inside. Both parents realized this was no earthquake, but the army outside trying to blast their way in to seize them.

"Now you have something to tell your friends about." Steven tried to lighten the situation. He witnessed Sally and Fred enter the dining hall. "Here comes Sally. She's probably got information about the earthquake."

"You guys okay?" Sally asked as she drew nearer.

"It's our first earthquake to experience," Sarina said, hoping to stop Sally before she said it was a bomb. "Mary's a little unnerved, but Timmy's enjoying the experience."

"Will we get more?" a delighted Timmy asked.

"Possibly," Sally said. "Sometimes, there are some aftershocks after the initial earthquake. Some feel as strong as the first one." Another boom rattled the room. "See, that was another one."

"Make them stop, Daddy," Mary cried.

"We're safe down here, Pumpkin," Steven said.

"That should be the last one for a while," Sally said. "Stephen and Sarina, Director Santiago would like to see you right away in her office. Sargent Hawkspoon will escort you. I'll see to the children's safety and take them to a secure place."

"Don't leave me, Daddy," Mary said.

Sally knelt beside Mary. "I promise, Mary, you will be safe. The room I'm taking you to is the most protected area in the compound. Nothing will happen to you or your family. I promise."

"Cross your heart and hope to die?" Mary asked.

Sally crossed her heart with her fingers. "Cross my heart and hope to die." She held out her hand to the frightened child. "Let's go so your Mom and Dad can meet with Director Santiago."

Sarina studied Sally's face, trying to detect any deception. She trusted Sally with the children, but once more, doubts made her question her decision. Whose side was Sally on? The President's or theirs? Was she trying to separate the children to get them to the President?

"Perhaps I can stay with the children, and Jeremy can go with Steven," Sarina said.

"No, she needs you both," Sally said.

Steven realized something was amiss. Circumstances necessitated the children be separated from them for the moment. Before Sarina objected, he stepped forward. "You kids go with Sally. Your mom and I will be along shortly. Kiss your mom."

Sarina returned each kiss, fighting the horrible impulse to grab her children and refuse to let Sally take them. For a second, she thought a voice spoke inside her head. "It's okay. They must go with Sally to be safe." Then the voice disappeared. Had she imagined the words? Or had her dad gotten through to her again? But the voice didn't sound like her dad's. Terrified, she fought against the urge to grab her children as they walked out of the dining hall.

"If you would follow me, please," the Sargent said. Steven and Sarina fell in behind the soldier. Sarina wanted to voice her objections to her husband, but Fred was too close to talk freely. She hoped Steven was correct.

Fred led them down several hallways they had never traveled before. Weren't they going to the Command Center? Finally, he stopped before a metal door with a nameplate reading "DIRECTOR". He knocked once and entered.

"Steven and Sarina, please sit down," Director Santiago said, gesturing towards two chairs. "Thank you, Sargent Hawkspoon. Dismissed."

The soldier saluted the Director, then closed the door behind him. "Have there been some fresh developments?" Sarina asked.

"No news yet on how the battle is going," the Director said. She stepped out from behind her desk and walked towards the couple, holding her fingers up to her mouth. "Ears may be listening," she whispered.

Both Steven and Sarina thought it odd the Director would be afraid to speak in her own office. Was this entire place bugged?

"The President asked me to speak with you. He was hoping you would talk to Glogg about him and his family going to the moon," the Director said. "The President realizes you three didn't get off to an agreeable start before and apologizes. He hopes you will understand, as parents, how worried he is about his own family."

"I suppose," Sarina said, not sure what was happening.

"He's on a secured line down the hallway in a separate Communications Room," the Director said. "If you would follow me, I'll take you there."

Once more, Sarina was going to object. Then the voice returned. "Go with her."

Sarina noted from Steven's expression he was not aware of the voice. Only she did. They needed to trust the voice. She took his hand and squeezed it. "I don't think it would hurt to listen to what he has to say."

"OK," Steven said.

The last thing Director Santiago did before leaving her office was pick up the phone. She dialed the number Sarina had called the first day. Setting the receiver on the desk, she and the Spallings walked out into the hallway. No one remained behind to discover if anyone answered the call.

For thirty minutes, the three children followed Sally down various winding dark rock corridors, climbing up several stairways made of granite. The air was stale, and the lighting inadequate. "How much further is this place?" Jeremy asked. He was getting nervous, wondering where Sally was taking them.

"My feet hurt," Mary whimpered.

"I promise kids, it's only about ten more minutes," Sally said.

"That's what you said last time," Timmy grumbled. "I'm tired. Let's go back."

"No, we can't," Sally said. "Tell you what. If we're not at the place in, oh, let's say fifteen minutes, we'll turn around and go back."

"I thought you said ten," Jeremy said. As the oldest brother, he had to keep his siblings safe.

"I thought best to give myself an extra five minutes in case I was in error." Sally turned her flashlight so the children could see her face. "I understand you three are tired. I'm exhausted too. But we're almost there." The ground shook as another explosion sounded in the distance. Mary screamed, grabbing onto Jeremy's leg. This time, even Timmy was afraid as sand rained down from the ceiling. The tunnel they were in was cramped. If the rock above them gave way, they'd all perish.

"That was no earthquake," Jeremy said with defiance in his voice. "What is going on, Sally? We're not going another foot unless you tell us the truth."

"I don't have time for this," Sally said. "We have to hurry. Time is getting short."

"No, Sally," Jeremy said. "Not another step until you tell what is going on."

Sally didn't have time to explain what was happening or what was about to happen. She, too, feared the President's bombing would bring down the mountain upon them. But she realized the children would go no further without some explanation.

"Alright," Sally said. "The truth. You are in danger. Those weren't earthquakes but bomb blasts. The military is outside trying to get in to capture you and your parents. I'm taking you out a secret way to meet your grandfather. He's taking you to the moon, where you'll be safe. Now, hurry, we have to go."

"What about our parents?" Timmy asked.

"They will meet us up ahead," Sally said. "Director Santiago is bringing them." The children still didn't move. "Jeremy, I'm telling you the truth. Believe me."

"Why should I trust you?" Jeremy asked.

"I don't have an answer for you," Sally said. "But if we stay in this tunnel, we are all going to die. Is that what you want? Your sister and brother buried beneath a mountain of rock? Now, let's go before it's too late."

Jeremy wasn't sure what to do. He wanted to believe Sally but was afraid to. She was part of the operations team that had initially brought them there. She was the Director's secretary. But he didn't want himself or his siblings to die inside the tunnel either. "Come on, Mary, it's not much further."

"I can't go any further," Mary said.

"Me either," Timmy said, sitting down on the bare floor.

Jeremy sighed, an inkling of helplessness flowing over him. "You can do it, Tim. I can't carry you and Mary both. Get up."

"Five more minutes," Timmy said.

More sand fell from the ceiling as another blast shook the ground. Behind the children, two rocks the size of Jeremy's fist fell from the ceiling.

"Jeremy, help Mary on my back," Sally said. "I'm shorter than you are and can get Mary through the tunnel without her hitting her head. You help Timmy."

Jeremy helped Mary climb onto Sally's back. He took off his sweatshirt and placed the shirt below her butt, creating a seat, tying the arms around Sally's front. Secured in place, Sally headed down the tunnel.

"Get up, Tim," Jeremy said.

"Okay," Tim eyed the two fallen rocks behind them. Fearing more rocks might come down, he pressed on, running to keep up with Mary and Sally.

In thirteen minutes, the four travelers arrived at a steel door ornately decorated. Sally untied the sweatshirt and lowered Mary to the floor. Reaching inside her shirt, she removed a small, wrapped towel. Unwrapping the cloth, she revealed a metal key.

Running her hand across the door, she searched for the hidden keyhole. It only took seconds to discover the opening. Holding her finger over the hole, she inserted the key with her other hand and turned the lock. Upon hearing the lock click, she grabbed the handle and pulled the door open. It creaked loudly, the hinges protesting its opening for the first time since installed. She slipped her fingers inside the space, grabbed the door, and tried to pull the unwilling door open. It barely budged. Jeremy and Timmy rushed forward and grabbed the handle. Together, they tugged on the door, and it slowly opened. Once the opening was extensive enough, Sally braced her back against the door to hold it and told the children to go through. Sally slipped in next, allowing the door to swing back shut. She re-locked the door.

"What about my parents?" Jeremy asked.

"They will have a key." Sally walked over and turned on the lights. "We don't want anyone bad having access to this room."

The children inspected the room. It was ample but cold in appearance. The walls and floor consisted of cement blocks and painted a dull gray color. The ceiling appeared to be one colossal piece of steel. In the right corner were six cots, each with a sheet, blanket, and pillow sitting on top. The children were astounded to see their backpacks sitting on the beds. Did Sally pack and bring the bags without their knowledge? Fearing things were worse instead of better, Jeremy turned to Sally.

"When will our parents be here?" Jeremy asked.

"As soon as they can," Sally said.

"Mr. President, I have Major General Hancock on the line for you." The aide handed the President a phone.

"I hope you have agreeable news, Tom," the President said.

"Yes, Sir," the Major General said. "I received word from Director Santiago stating she is opening the front door. She reports an electrical malfunction in the security system put the entire bunker on secured lockdown. It's taken this long to get control back and reopen the bunker. We should have the Spalling family within the hour."

"Excellent," the President said. "Air Force One should arrive at your location in approximately forty-five minutes."

"Arriving?" the Major General asked, slightly confused. "I thought you were waiting in Washington for my call."

"I brought the family down early in case your men succeeded."

"Your wife? Do you have your family with you? I thought you planned to leave tomorrow. I have not advised my wife to bring herself and the children down to this location."

"Plenty of time to notify her," the President said. "I'm sure once we negotiate our departure, they will bring several planes down to pick up the families. I'll see you shortly."

"Mr. President? Mr. President?" The line was dead. Anger boiled inside the Major General. The President, Rear Admiral Paine and he had all agreed on a plan of action: get control of the bunker, use the Spalling family to negotiate transportation to the moon for their families, and arrest Director Santiago. There had been no talk of the President and his family coming first. Surely, the President wasn't trying to back-stab them, was he? The idea of a double-cross now in his mind, the Major General ordered the Lieutenant to call Rear Admiral Paine at the Pentagon. He wondered if the Rear Admiral was in on the deception.

"Rear Admiral Paine's office," came the voice over the phone.

"Major General Hancock. Is the Rear Admiral in?"

"Yes. One moment and I'll connect you." The phone went silent as the clerk put him on hold. A few moments later, the clerk returned on the line. "I'm sorry, Major General, but I believe the Rear Admiral has stepped out for the moment. Would you like me to have him call you upon his return?"

"Where is he?" More suspicions grew in his mind.

"His itinerary says he's in the office this afternoon," the clerk said. "The President called him early today. Perhaps the Rear Admiral went to meet him."

"Something came up, my ass," the Major General muttered. "Have him call me as soon as he returns. Tell him it's vital."

"Yes, Sir, I will."

Fearing the worst, the Major General asked the Lieutenant to get him Rear Admiral Paine's home phone number. While he waited, he dialed his wife. "Margaret, I'm sending a chopper to pick you and the kids up. Be ready in thirty minutes." (Pause.) "I don't care if he's got a game tonight or not. I want all of you on the chopper." (Pause.) "Tell them we're going on a brief vacation. Pack for a four-day trip." (Pause.) "Never mind where. Be ready to leave in thirty minutes." He disconnected the line, then dialed another number. "Commander Hollingsworth, Major General Hancock. I need my family picked up at home and flown out to the bunker in Shiprock, New Mexico." (Pause.) "No, I don't have clearance. Do as ordered." He hung up the phone, wishing it were the old-fashioned kind so he might slam down, taking out some of his frustration.

"Sir, I called Rear Admiral Paine's home," the Lieutenant said upon his return. "I spoke with his maid. She reported the family left early this morning. They took suitcases and would be gone for several days. She was not told their destination."

"Damn him," the Major General grumbled. More and more, he believed he had been double-crossed by both the President and Rear Admiral Paine. Well, he'd show them.

"Lieutenant, advise Director Santiago I am coming in," the Major General said. Two can play the President's game. He'd go in, take control of the Command Center, and negotiate his own deal with Glogg before the President even arrived.

"Sir, with the blasting they did, I'm not sure the tunnel is safe," the Lieutenant said. Upon seeing the anger on the Major General's face, he stopped. "Yes, Sir. I'll notify her right away."

The Major General waited in the nearby air-conditioned tent for the Lieutenant's return. After twenty minutes, the soldier nervously returned. "I couldn't advise Director Santiago of your arrival, Sir. She wasn't available, so I spoke with a Sargent Hensley. He stated they cannot locate Director Santiago."

"What do you mean they can't locate her?"

"That's what the Sargent said. No one has seen her for several hours."

"And the Spalling family?"

"Gone as well."

"Get me the Sargent on the line. And get me a jeep to take me inside that damn bunker."

"Mary, why don't you sit over here on the couch," Sally said, patting the couch. "I brought your *Mary Poppins* DVD. You can watch it while we wait for your parents."

"No, thank you." Mary clung to Jeremy's leg, frightened to be in the secured room.

"How much longer do we have to wait?" Jeremy asked. "Timmy and Mary need something to eat."

"You will find some food in your backpacks. As for how long we need to remain, we'll leave the moment your parents arrive."

"When is that?"

"I can't say for sure," Sally said. There was no reason to lie to the children. She did not know how long it would take Director Santiago to bring Steven and Sarina through the passage if she could get them through at all. The blasting might have caused some of the corridor to collapse, preventing them from reaching the room. Or worse yet, captured or killed. If they weren't there in the next twenty minutes, she'd have to take the children out herself. Their grandfather would be waiting, and he couldn't remain in plain sight for long. She'd have Renn take them while she would sneak back inside and locate the parents. The plan wasn't the best, but at least it was something.

As if reading Sally's mind, Jeremy said, "We're not going without our parents."

"You may not have a choice," Sally said. "Once your grandfather arrives, we will only have minutes to get you aboard. If your parents aren't here when it's time, take Mary and Timmy to him. You need to protect them. It's what your parents would want you to do, wouldn't they?"

"Yes." Jeremy knew that was what his parents would want and expect him to do.

"I'm not going without Mommy and Daddy," Mary said.

"Hush, Mary," Jeremy said in a loving voice. "You'll do as I say."

"You can't tell me what to do," Timmy declared.

"Yes, I can. I'm in charge when Mom and Dad are gone. So, all three of us will leave when Sally tells us to."

"We'll leave in eighteen minutes, with or without your parents. Last stop for the bathroom."

THE RESCUE

"Why don't you and the kids wait inside the pavilion, Mrs. Smithridge," the Lieutenant said as the President and his family stepped off the helicopter. Air Force One was too wide to land on the short runway at Shiprock. Plus, the elders refused to give the President permission to land on the Navajo Reservation. The President needed to land at the nearest Air Force base, then board a helicopter for the rest of the trip. "It's much cooler than out in the sun. I'll have someone carry your bags inside. This way, please."

"Henry, what are we doing in this awful place?" Mrs. Smithridge asked her husband. "It's hot and dusty. You can't expect us to stay out here."

"Don't worry, Kate, you'll be somewhere cooler soon." The President scanned the area for the Major General, but he was nowhere to be seen. "Lieutenant, where is Major General Hancock?"

"He entered the bunker thirty minutes ago," the Lieutenant said. "The moment I told him Director Santiago and the Spalling family were missing, he rushed inside."

"What do you mean missing?" screamed the President.

"It's all I know, Sir," the Lieutenant said.

"Are communications with the bunker re-established?" the President asked.

"Yes, Sir."

"Then get the Major General on the phone, NOW."

Without delay, the young Lieutenant put a call into the Command Center under the mountain. Within seconds he had the Major General on the line. He held the phone out to the President. "Here you are, Sir, Major General Hancock."

"What in the hell is going on, Tom?" the President screamed.

"You tell me," the Major General yelled back. He didn't care if he was talking to the President or not. He was mad at being double-crossed.

"I understand the Director and the Spalling family are gone?" the President asked.

"Are Rear Admiral Paine and his family with you?" the Major General asked, ignoring the President's question.

"What? What are you talking about?" the President asked. "No. Why would they be with me?"

"I tried calling him when I learned you were coming with your family. He wasn't at work, and his family wasn't at home. Their maid reports they left for a vacation. I figured they were coming with you."

"Is that what has you all uptight?" the President asked. "You think I brought his family and left yours behind? John, you know me better than that."

"That's the problem. I know you too well," the Major General said.

"We can argue this point when we're safe on the ship," the President said, trying to regain control of the situation. "Right now, none of us are going anywhere if we can't find his damn family. Doesn't anyone have information about where they went?"

"No, Sir," the Major General said. "This is a gigantic place, with lots of dark places to hide. They could be anywhere."

"No, not anywhere." The President thought for a moment. "Everyone is concentrating on the fleet preparing to engage the Kett today. It's the perfect time to slip in and try to retrieve them. They're outside someplace." He scoured the surrounding area, hoping to catch a glimpse of the missing family or a spaceship. "Cleaver lady. The Director opened the front gate to keep us preoccupied. Tom, find out if there was a malfunction."

The Major General left then returned several minutes later. "Those inside report they don't know if there was a malfunction or not,"

"The hell they don't," the President said, running the scenarios in his head. "The bunker has another way out. A secret passage somewhere, a passage only Director Santiago knew. Hell, she's probably one of them and planned the escape all along."

"So how do we find them?"

"I don't have the faintest clue, but we'd better find them soon," the President said.

The temperature around Shiprock was stifling hot. The sky was a robin-egg blue with no clouds in sight. One could see across the plains in all directions for miles. From nowhere, three spacecraft appeared, hovering twenty-five feet from the ground. Without a sound, each drifted downwards and landed in formation on the dry New Mexico soil. The only testimony to their arrival was a tiny cloud of dust rising two inches from the ground. Their appearance did not even disturb two nearby squabbling horned lizards.

For sixty-eight seconds, the ships sat there, motionless, their occupants safe inside. Then, in unison, the three side hatches opened without a sound. From each vessel stepped out a single being. A covering of alien metal encased each pilot from head to toe. The end two were loftier in stature by three feet. Their shoulders were broader, their chests more muscular, and their waists smaller. Like their arms, their thighs bulged with chiseled muscles. The middle pilot stood six feet tall and had an exquisite physique, but one could see he was not the operation's brawn. Each pilot wore a face mask of the same metal as the suits. A one-inch band cut across the front of the helmet, behind which a red light glowed. No eyes were visible to offer a clue what type of creature occupied the suits. The two heftier aliens each carried a formidable weapon of an advanced design, ready to use at a moment's notice. For protection, they kept the smaller one between them. He, too, carried a weapon, only smaller.

As they advanced toward the specified coordinates, their spacecraft seemed to disappear. The ships refracted the rays of the sun to render their vehicles invisible.

Renn scoured the landscape for any sign of the President or his military. He checked his readout and detected no human life forms. He nodded to his two companions to continue.

"I'm picking up movement." Xavier held out his arm to stop Renn's advancement. "There." Xavier pointed to the south. A half-mile ahead was an isolated mound of rock, dirt, and scrub brush, thirty feet tall, designed to resemble an ordinary bank. The aliens' visors detected movement amongst the ruble as a door slide open. His heart racing, Renn strained his eyes to see who was emerging. Was it his family? Or the President, or worse?

The door ground opened loudly with metal grinding on metal, complaining at being moved after so many years of being silent. A single man appeared, holding his arm up to shield his eyes from the brightness of the sun. He inspected the terrain, then turned and motioned with his hand. Three children and three human females followed: Sarina and her family. Renn waved at them, then took off running towards them. They waved back.

Renn had barely gone half the distance when, from behind the mound, several soldiers sprang forward. They grabbed the children first, putting each in a neck hold. Steven's military training took control. He grabbed two of the soldiers, disarming them and dropping them to the ground, unconscious. He aimed his confiscated assault rifle at the soldiers holding his daughter hostage.

"Let her go."

"Watch out," Director Santiago yelled, but she was too late. Another soldier had snuck behind Steven and hit him with the butt of his rifle, knocking him out cold. Steven collapsed to the ground.

The sound of clapping filled the air as the President stepped out from behind the mound. "Heroic attempt, I must admit. But, as you can see, you did not outsmart me. I expected you'd attempt a rescue, Renn." The advancing human slow his approach to a brisk walk.

"What do you want, Mr. President?" Renn asked, reaching up and removing the helmet covering his face. The President paused for a moment. He didn't see a human, but a determined father, a soldier ready to do anything necessary to obtain his goal to get his family. Renn kept his attention on the President's eyes while keeping tabs on the two soldiers at his side.

"You guys grow them big up on the moon."

"We didn't grow these two; we made them," Renn said. "They are police androids to retrieve my family."

"Another little secret you kept from us." The President's face flushed red. Once more, Renn had anticipated his moves and surprised him. "Is this how you will take over our world? Bring down an army of space robots to slaughter us?"

"I have no time for your nonsense," Renn said. "I'll ask you again, what do you want in exchange for my family?"

"The same as you," the President said, waving his wife and four children to come forward. "To save my family."

"Your family?" Major General Hancock shouted. "What about my family? They are on their way as we speak."

"I'm sure Renn will be accommodating enough to return for your family once we're secured on the moon base," the President said.

"Why should your family go and not mine?" the Major General asked, anger swelling inside him. The President WAS trying to double-cross them. He had been using him and the Rear Admiral as pawns in his plan to escape Earth's destruction. "Renn can come back for YOUR family!"

"I'm sorry, Tom, but the fact is, I'm the President, which means my family and I are a bit more important than yours. Besides, as you said, your family hasn't arrived yet. These alien planes can't wait forever. They will detect them, and then none of us will get off this doomed planet."

The Major General's frustration rose. Sweat was forming on the President's forehead and dripping down his face. His hands trembled, even though he tried to hide them behind his back.

"Mr. President, aren't you needed in Washington to run the country?"

"Vice President Hollingsworth can do it," the President said. "At least until the Kett come and rip this country apart."

The Major General stared at the President in disbelief. "You're leaving the Vice President behind?" The President smiled. "I thought you were kidding the other day when you stated he could find his own ride. What about Rear Admiral Paine? Have you forgotten your promise to take him and his family? You are such a sleaze-ball. I'm ashamed to call you President."

"Oh, shut up, Tom," the President yelled. "You were all too willing to go with him a few moments ago. Renn, if you want your family saved, you must take mine with you."

"I don't have the authority to take you to the base," Renn said, his demeanor relaxed. He still had the upper hand.

"Exceptions can be made when needed," the President said. "I can break the rules for the right price."

"And what price is that?" Renn asked.

The President moved with lightning speed. He grabbed Mary and pulled her into his arm, holding a knife at her throat. "The life of your only granddaughter."

"Don't hurt her," Sarina said as she rushed forward.

A soldier raised his rifle to protect the President. The Director reached out and grabbed his arm, pushing the gun skyward. The bullet whizzed by Sarina, grazing her arm as it passed. Sarina dropped to her knees, realizing how close she had come to death. Several soldiers rushed the Director, forcing her on her knees as well. They held their guns to the two women's heads, cocked and ready to fire if either tried something again.

"Enough," Renn forcefully screamed.

"I agree," the Major General said. "This is getting out of hand. Henry, no one needs to get hurt, especially the children."

"Let me take my family to safety." Renn controlled his speech, talking loudly but calmly. He realized how unstable this President was, how fearful of dying. "As soon as I drop them off at the station, I will return for you and your family with two more planes."

"You must think I'm a fool," the President said. Why wasn't this alien doing as told? "The moment you take off, I'll never see you again."

"I give you my word," Renn said.

"Words are nothing but dead air," the President said.

"Keep me." Sarina placed her hand over the bullet graze on her arm. Bright red blood oozed out between her fingers, sliding down her arm. "Father, you can take the kids and Steven, then return for the President's family and me." She looked at the President. "Don't worry. He won't leave me behind."

The President didn't even consider the offer. "I'll make this simple: Either you take me with you, or the kid dies, and you die." He pushed the tip of the knife blade into Mary's throat, causing a tiny droplet of red blood to trickle down the edge. Mary let out a little whimper of pain.

"I can only take three." Renn's heart raced as a new drop of Mary's blood slid down the blade. He had to keep control of the situation if his plan was going to work. "Only three can fit inside an airship, including the pilot. And before you even suggest it, I won't leave any of my family behind. If they don't go, I don't move my plane."

"I could shoot you and take the plane myself," the President said.

"Good luck trying to fly one of our ships." Renn laughed. "Or even reaching one. When one of your soldiers fires a weapon, Xavier and Juaquin will shoot each of you in the head, starting with you, Mr. President. And, in case you were wondering, the metal they're wearing is completely bulletproof. Not even a shot from a bazooka can penetrate their shielding."

"Alright," the President said, hastily thinking of a solution to his problem. Sweat flowed down the side of his face. An irritating ringing filled his ears. "Your family, you and the two pilots make eight. I'll be the ninth person."

"Henry, you'd leave us behind?" a shocked Mrs. Smithridge asked.

"Only for a little while."

"If he's willing to leave his own family behind, do you believe he cares about yours?" A voice sounded inside the Major General's mind. He shook his head, trying to dispel the words. "He's already betrayed the Vice President and Rear Admiral Paine."

"Shut up," the Major General said silently to himself.

"Stop him before it's too late. Stop him before he hurts the little girl."

The President pushed the blade a little deeper into Mary's neck. She cried out loud in pain as more blood dripped out onto the blade.

"Xavier, if the President pushes the blade any further into Mary's neck, shoot him between the eyes," Renn said.

"Yes, Sir." Xavier raised his assault weapon. A small red bead of light appeared in the middle of the President's forehead.

"Stop," Sarina said. "He's won. Take him with us."

The President lifted the blade point back out of Mary's skin but kept the knife at her throat. "Everyone has a price." The President smiled.

"He will leave you and your family to die," said the voice inside the Major General's mind.

"I said shut up," the Major General said, this time in a whisper. Who was in his head?

"Let my granddaughter go, and we'll board the aircraft," Renn said.

He laughed. "I don't think so. As soon as I release your grandchild, you'll order your killer robot to assassinate me. I keep the child with me. And we go first."

Renn realized he had no choice. "Tell your soldiers to put their weapons on the ground."

"No," the President said.

"Then we have no deal." Renn stepped up to the President and stared into his eyes.

"You're bluffing," the President said.

"Xavier, the operation is a no-go. Send the ships home."

Positive he had the upper hand, the President gazed in disbelief as the three ships lifted off the ground with no pilots inside. "Once they reach twenty feet, they will return to the base. Then none of us will have a way home."

Was Renn bluffing? "Stop," the President screamed when the airships reached fifteen feet. "Men, put your weapons on the ground."

"But, Sir," the Major said.

"Do as I say," the President yelled.

One by one, the soldiers dropped their rifles to the ground.

"Their sidearms too," Renn said. He pointed to two soldiers. "You two, the one with the red hair and the guy to his left. Gather all the weapons and pile them fifty yards to the east."

"Do as he says," the President said.

The two soldiers walked among their comrades, gathering the assault rifles and handguns without saying a word. Once their arms were full, they walked fifty yards away and laid them on the ground.

"Pile sand on top of them," Renn said.

The soldiers nodded in agreement. Taking handfuls of coarse, fine sand, they buried the weapons. Upon completion, they returned to where they had been standing.

"I did as you asked," the President said. "Now, return the planes."

Renn touched his comm-link again. "Xavier, you transport the two boys. Juaquin, you get Sarina and Steven. I'll take the President and Mary. *Roerewuu @,$#ilifi* IOeoriu jouotu**#eu(e fr weorui*#% hyyyt.*"

"What did you say?" the President asked, not understanding the alien words.

"I had to give him the code word stating I was not being coerced," Renn lied. "He won't land the ships without the correct code."

The President kept his eyes on the airships as they landed without a sound on the ground. "I don't care what kind of signal he needs; you speak only in English."

In the distance, the sound of approaching helicopters filled the sky. "I believe your reinforcements will soon be here," the Major General said. Hopefully, his own family was on one of those choppers.

"We have to leave before they get here."

"Agreed." Renn held up his hand to signal for Xavier and Juaquin to get their charges.

"You are not going anywhere." An angry Major General walked over and stood before the President, determined to keep him from leaving the planet.

Seeing his chance, Renn reacted. He and the two androids moved so fast no one had time to respond. As if in a dream, the President saw Renn grab onto the arm holding the knife to Mary's throat and yank it away. The scenery turned into a swirling sea of misshaped objects, blurred lines, and flashing colors. His skin tingled, and his stomach became violently upset. A few seconds later, he was throwing up beside an alien aircraft. Renn was beside him, helping Mary into the spaceship.

Xavier grabbed the boys and brought them to his plane. Juaquin did the same with the parents. Before folding space, he winked at Sally. "Ready?"

"Definitely," Sally said. "Hold on, Director Santiago. You're about to go for a ride." The ground disappeared beneath the Director's feet as Sally whisked her away.

Not sure what to do, the soldiers watched as Renn grabbed the President and child and vanished. Thirty seconds later, Renn appeared back where he had been with a vomiting President. Then Renn disappeared a second time. Timmy, Jeremy, Steven, and Sarina also vanished in a blink of an eye. Sally waved and then disappeared with the Director.

"What happened?" the President tried to stand up straight but was still fiercely ill. He waited as the three spacecraft sat on the ground, not moving. Then, from behind the image, the actual ships rose and vanished. After thirty seconds, the holograms of the three vessels dissolved into the hot desert air.

"I'd say you were outsmarted." Major General Hancock laughed. "By a better man than both of us." He helped the President stand up straight. Then, reaching his arm behind his back, he brought his fist forward and punched the President in the face, knocking him out cold. "You're impeached, Mr. President." He walked over the unconscious body of the man to Mrs. Smithridge. "As soon as the helicopters arrive, I'll have one take you and the children home."

Mrs. Smithridge listened to the quietness of the air. "I don't hear the helicopters anymore."

"Huh, neither do I." The Major General scoured the blue sky for the aircraft. "Must have been one of those freaky things which happens out in the desert." But the phenomena did not fool him. Renn had fabricated the sound of approaching helicopters to make the President react. And his trick had worked. "So, back to Washington?"

"I think the children and I would be much happier at my parents' home in Texas," Mrs. Smithridge said. She turned and walked away without even glancing at her disgraced husband.

"Major General, what about the President?" a Lieutenant asked.

"There should be something inside the bunker you can use as a brig," the Major General said. "Haul him in there. And don't let him out until I tell you to."

"But he's the President," the soldier said.

"Not anymore." The Major General held up a recorder. "Not after Congress and the people of the United States listen to this."

"What's he guilty of," the soldier asked as the Major General walked away.

"Treason and failure to fulfill his duties as President of this United States."

ARRIVAL ON THE MOON

"How are you two feeling?" Xavier asked the boys. He didn't remember ever seeing humans that shade of gray before.

"Not too good," Jeremy said.

"I think I'm going to throw up," Timmy said.

"Don't mess up my ship." Placing the airship on autopilot, Xavier walked back to the boys with a syringe. "This will help with your nausea." Within seconds, the effects of their ordeal disappeared.

Jeremy peered out the window and saw they were only a few miles from the moon. He checked his watch. "It can't be. We only left Earth ten minutes ago. There is no way we can travel to the moon in such a short time."

"We didn't," Xavier said. "At least not in the way you are familiar with. Our alien associates discovered eons ago we can travel faster and easier between two points by folding the space between the two."

"I've seen space folding," Timmy said. "It's how they traveled in the movie *Dune*. But I never dreamed folding was real. This is so cool."

"Perhaps the author had contact with our colony," Xavier said. "But if you are familiar with folding space, why have you Earthlings not used such technology to travel?"

"*Dune* isn't real," Jeremy chuckled. "It's make-believe, a work of fiction."

"I do not understand," Xavier said.

Holding on to the seats, Timmy walked to the front where the robot was. "It's a story someone fabricated."

"But folding space is real."

"We didn't know it was," Timmy said. "Are you a real robot?"

"I am an RZ-47G," Xavier said. "I am an advanced artificial life form designed to keep you from harm."

"Awesome. Do you have a name?"

"I'm called Xavier."

"Grandpa's Xavier?" Jeremy asked.

"Since I am the only RZ-47G of that designation, I must be. But he does not own me. We are friends."

"Do you have to do what I tell you to do?" Timmy mischievously asked.

"No. I am not programmed to take orders, especially from children."

"Shucks. Can I touch your suit?"

"I see nothing objectionable about your request." Timmy ran his hand across the muscles in Xavier's arms. He thought the metal would feel cold and slippery, but the covering was warm and smooth, not much different from his skin.

"Are you the same model as Jenny?" Jeremy asked.

"No, Jenny is a deluxe 34F model created specifically for Renn," Xavier said. "I have no memories of a human's life. But we have similarities."

"Like what?" Jeremy asked, sitting in the copilot's seat.

"I can make my own decisions," Xavier said. "I can weigh the pros and cons of a situation and make a logical decision. My body does not need food. My sleep requirement is only ten hours a week."

"Are you sentient?"

"Your word has no meaning to me," Xavier said.

"Are you self-aware? Do you know you exist and who you are?"

"Yes."

"Is Jenny?" Timmy asked.

"Of course."

A monolithic blue arch appeared as they descended. The interior of the arch vibrated, then became translucent.

Sally injected Director Santiago and herself with medication to stop their stomachs from churning and to help clear their heads. She walked over to Mary, who was asleep in the back. Sally cleaned Mary's neck wound and placed a bandage over the cut. Sally then gave her the same shot she had taken along with one of antibiotics.

"Still have trouble with your stomach when you fold?" Renn asked.

"Hey, give me a break," Sally belched. "I've been on Earth for the past four years. My body is no longer accustomed to jumping around the universe."

"I don't understand," Director Santiago said. "How did we get away? The President had the upper hand. And how are we at the moon already?"

"We needed him to think he was in control," Renn said. "Otherwise, we couldn't have gotten any of you out. We used the same method to get in and rescued you and the others and to reach the moon in minutes. We folded space."

"You what?" a skeptical Director asked.

"We folded space," Renn repeated.

"Ok, let's say for a moment folding space is possible. How would Sally know about folding?"

"Because I'm not from Earth."

"You're an alien?" an astonished Director asked.

"No, I'm human, like you." She giggled at the expression on the female's face. "I was born on Earth ninety-six years ago. But I've been living on the moon for sixty-eight of those years. It's amazing what good space life will do for you. Your aging process will slow down, too. Might even reverse itself some."

"Not me," Director Santiago said. "I have no intention of staying here."

"You can't go back," Sally said. "They'd arrest you the moment you stepped foot on Earth for treason, disobeying a direct order from the President, abandoning your post, helping and abetting fugitives, and who knows what else."

"I forgot about the possible criminal charges," the Earth human said.

"Do you have a family who you left behind?" Renn asked.

"My parents are deceased. I never married and never had children. I have a brother somewhere. My sister and I haven't spoken in several years. I always land the 'sensitive' jobs where communications were a no, no. It's hard to be close to family when you can only see and talk with them every five or six years."

"Then you have nothing to go back to," Renn said. "Stay with us for a while. If you don't like living here, I'll take you back to Earth and place you somewhere where you can begin a new life. At least until the Kett arrive."

"I don't understand one thing," the Director said. "Why was Sally assigned as my secretary?"

"It's a long and complicated story, too detailed to go into now," Renn said. "For now, the simple version is I inspired Sarina to write her novel. We arranged circumstances so your agency would realize she was divulging top secrets and bring her here for questioning. I planted Sally to make sure my family was safe and to get them out when the time came."

"How long have you known the Kett was coming?"

"Three years," Renn said.

"So, I guess the OEI wasn't as intelligent as I thought we were," the Director said.

"If it's any consolation, we couldn't have rescued my family without your support."

Renn pushed a button on his console. "X-148 returning. One female human child in need of undetermined medical attention. Stretcher needed. Saill-Nee Luna is accompanying us."

"Noted, X-148. Glogg asked me to congratulate you on a job well done. I'll tell Master Kim his wife has returned. Welcome home."

"How's Steven?" Sarina asked as Juaquin injected both with medication for their stomachs.

"He's still out," Juaquin said, "The soldier hit him pretty hard."

He tore Sarina's shirt sleeve open and inspected her wound. "Appears to be a flesh wound. I'll apply antiseptic and bandage your wound. You will be okay until I get you some medical attention."

Juaquin opened a jar of green goop and spread some over the wound. The ointment stung, but Sarina didn't complain. She was thankful her family was safe and alive. The android placed a bandage over the cut, then returned to the pilot's seat.

"Thank you for saving us." Sarina reached down and took Steven's hand in hers.

"All in a day's job, Ma'am," Juaquin gave her a warm smile. "Besides, you are Renn's family. We couldn't leave without you."

"Do you understand the concept of family?" she asked, surprised a synthetic lifeform comprehended the idea.

"I have a mate and child of my own," Juaquin said as if such a thing was the most normal thing in the world.

"I have much to learn," Sarina said. She caught sight of the blue arch rising from the moon. The formation was identical to the description in her book. She also recognized it as the arch Director Santiago had shown her when she first arrived at the bunker. She smiled when the interior of the arch shimmered, then disappeared. Yep, exactly like her book.

"Fighter X-47 returning from Earth mission," Juaquin said into his mike. "Medical assistance and stretcher needed for an unconscious male. Also, a female adult has a superficial injury and is ambulatory."

"Noted, X-47," came a voice. "Medical assistance standing by. Welcome home."

Sarina slid into the copilot's seat and watched as they disappeared into the bunker opening. The illumination of a well-lit hangar replaced the darkness of space as they descended. Upon reaching the hanger floor, she spotted several aliens awaiting their arrival. Among them was Glogg.

"Welcome to your new home, Mrs. Spalling."

The spacecrafts slid through the arch and landed on the hangar floor. Once they docked the ships, the doors opened. Two medical personnel waited outside Renn's ship for permission to enter. One resembled Glogg, only taller, and the other mimicked an extended version of a human, but with teal skin.

"She's in the back," Sally said. "She has a small puncture wound in the neck under the chin. Not deep. I gave her a sedative, so she cannot walk."

The teal-skinned alien walked to the back and lifted the sleeping Mary in his long arms. He carefully carried her out the side door and laid her on a stretcher. The Caelifera entered data into the bed's side control panel. Checking on the child one last time, the medical technician pushed the gurney forward.

"After you, Ladies," Renn waved his hand towards the door.

Upon exiting their ship, the Director, Renn, and Sally saw Steven being carried out on a stretcher. Sarina and the two boys were following at his side.

Renn ran over and took his daughter into his arms. "Thank goodness you are alright." He stepped back and did a visual inspection of Sarina to ensure the flesh wound was her only injury.

"I assure you, Renn, I am fine." She watched the medical personnel pushing her unconscious husband down the hall.

"What were you thinking?" an angry Renn asked. "Your little stunt almost got you killed."

"I couldn't stand there and let him kill my daughter," Sarina shouted back.

"Xavier would have shot him dead before he pushed the knife in any further," Renn said.

"But I didn't know." Sarina's anger subsided as she realized that was precisely what would have happened. She should have trusted him. "I'm sorry."

"No, I am." Renn hugged each boy. "I should have explained to you what I was doing. I forget you aren't familiar with our ways."

Glogg walked up to the small group. "Welcome to the moon. It is so wonderful to meet you in person. I am glad you have arrived and are out of danger." He held out his two-fingered hand.

The alien towered above them. He appeared even taller in actual life. Without hesitation, she took his hand. "Thank you for rescuing my family."

"I merely agreed to the operation," Glogg said. "Renn and Xavier planned all the details. Although I see from the injuries, everything did not go according to plan."

"It never does," Renn laughed.

Glogg walked over to Director Santiago. Even though she stood over six feet, she too was dwarfed by the insect-like alien.

"A special thanks to you, Director Santiago. I fear without your help, this happy meeting would not be taking place."

"It was the right thing to do." The Director's face briefly flushed with embarrassment.

"True, but many still would not have endangered themselves to protect innocents," Glogg said. "Your sacrifice is the reason I offer you a place amongst us."

"She hasn't decided if she wants to stay or not," Renn said.

"Why?" Glogg couldn't imagine anyone not wanting to stay.

"Renn assured me I can return to Earth if I don't like living here," the Director said. She feared she would never go home, even if that home meant prison and certain death.

"He spoke the truth," Glogg said. "We keep no one against his, her, or its will."

"This place will take getting used to," the Director said.

"Any news regarding the battle?" Sarina asked.

"So far, we are holding our own," Glogg said.

Glogg walked over to Sally, putting his long leathery arms around her. "Saill-Nee Luna, what a joy to see you again. Master Kim has greatly missed you. Your return will delight him. Thank you for bringing Director Santiago to us and helping Renn secure his family."

Sally hugged the insect-like creature back. "It's wonderful to be back." She took a deep breath. "I forgot how wonderful healthy air smells. It's so much better than the polluted air on Earth."

"If I may impose upon you, would you show the Director to her room before joining your mate?" Glogg asked. "Be sure she gets a bite to eat. Suite 1473B. We'll get together later and talk." The two women were almost out of the hangar when Glogg shouted, "Saill-Nee, I need Master Kim to help with the calculations for the station's launch. Don't wear him out completely."

"No promises," Sally said as she skipped down the hallway.

"Now, let's get you reunited with your husband and daughter," Glogg said to Sarina. "And get your arm attended to. Renn will take you to the medical unit. Perhaps if Steven and Mary are up to it, your family will join me for dinner."

Sarina walked over and, standing on her tippy toes, reached up with her arms and brought Glogg's face down to her level. She kissed him on what she presumed was his cheek. "I can never repay you for what you've done for us. Thank you again."

Glogg smiled as Renn and his family walked away. He reached up and caressed the spot where Sarina had kissed him.

"Are you okay, Glogg?" the purple, six-eyed alien beside him asked.

"She is the first female to kiss my cheek since my Azillee died those many years ago."

Jeremy and Timmy were disappointed there were no aliens to see on the way to the medical unit. Both boys had been anticipating with excitement at seeing what the aliens looked like. They didn't get a good view of the two who had taken Mary. And two humans retrieved their dad, which was a major disappointment. They had counted on the walk to the medical wing to show them the station's aliens.

Sarina, too, wondered why the halls were so deserted. Were the hallways always this quiet, or had most gone to fight the Kett? Would there be an abundance of injured aliens? If they blow apart your spaceship in space, is there a way to get back to a ship?

Renn made small talk as they walked down various corridors and took a lift to a lower floor. When the elevator stopped, a creature with a long nose, at least they thought it was his nose, and blue skin, stood outside the door waiting to get on the elevator. Timmy's eyes widened in amazement, holding in his laughter. The creature grunted, to which Renn grunted back. As soon as the door closed, both Jeremy and Timmy burst into laughter.

"Did you see his nose?" Timmy asked.

"What was the gunk oozing from it?" Jeremy asked.

"Caladrine from the Orion System," Renn said before anyone asked. "Excellent farmers. Unfortunately, they're allergic to many Earth plants, so they're always in the medical wing for treatment. Two more corridors to the right, and we're there."

"Boys, you cannot react that way to the beings who live here," Sarina scolded as she picked up her pace. "If he had seen you, I'm sure he would have been insulted."

"But he looked so funny, Mom," Timmy said in his defense.

"Even if true, you need to hide your reactions."

Finally, the small group arrived at a set of double doors bearing a sign written in various languages. The last words were English. The sign read "Medical Unit." Sarina pushed through and walked over to the desk. When the nurse turned around, Sarina came face-to-face with an alien with four eyes. He had purple skin and a flattened, broad yellow nose that covered over half of the face. The lips were also yellow. Its head was smooth; not a strand of hair was visible. Momentarily startled by the alien, she let out a scant scream.

"May I help you?" the alien asked.

"Way to go, Mom, on hiding your reaction."

"We're here regarding the two humans brought in," Renn said.

"They are down corridor 2F, room 16 The desk alien motioned to the right. "Dr. Robinson is expecting her."

"Thank you." Renn ushered his small group down the hall.

"Who's that?" Timmy asked upon seeing a female waving.

"That's My Jenny," Renn waved back. "I asked her to stay with Steven and Mary until we arrived. You boys stay with her while I take your mom back to see your father and sister and get her arm medically tended to."

"Do we have to?" Timmy whined.

Renn scanned the nearly empty waiting room. There wasn't much to keep the boys occupied. He thought for a moment, then came up with a brilliant idea to keep the boys entertained. "I bet you two are hungry. How about I have Jenny take you to the medical cafeteria for something to eat? On the way, you can pass the maternity ward and visit the new babies."

"Why would we want to see babies?" Timmy thought seeing newborns was a stupid thing to do.

Renn leaned closer and whispered, "Because most of them aren't human."

"Let's go," Timmy ran over to Jenny and took her hand, pulling her towards the hall. "I've got to see this."

"Jenny, I'll bring the others to the cafeteria as soon as I have Sarina's arm looked at," Renn told Jenny. "This was the boys' first experience with folded space, so their stomachs might be sensitive. Don't let them eat anything too heavy or spicy."

When the boys left with Jenny, Renn walked Sarina back to Mary and Stephen. Mary was sitting on the edge of her bed with her feet dangling over, eating a large container of what appeared to be ice cream. A broad bandage encircled her throat. Steven was in the bed beside her, awake but still lying down. A crown of bandages covered his head, his reward for fighting the soldiers.

"Are you two okay?" Sarina asked, sitting beside Mary.

"Mary's not allowed to talk," Steven said. "The doctor said the knife didn't penetrate past the outer skin, but he wants her to rest her vocal cords until tomorrow. He ordered her to eat lots of ice cream to keep them from swelling."

"They have ice cream up here?" Sarina asked. She peered into the container Mary held and was surprised it contained ice cream.

"Shocked the hell out of me," Steven said.

"And what about you?" Sarina asked.

Steven raised his hand and rubbed his head. "Head hurts some. And my vision's off. But I'm not sure if it's from the whack on the head or the drugs the doctor gave me. What about you?"

"Only the bullet graze on the arm," Sarina said.

"We have another doctor in the room, I see," laughed a blond-haired, clean-cut human male as he walked into the room. He was wearing white pants, a white lab coat, and white shoes. An unfamiliar instrument hung from around his neck. "I went through this routine with your husband a few minutes ago. And I will tell you what I told him--I am the doctor, and you're the patient. So, if you would hold still while I unwrap your injury, I will see if you have 'only a bullet graze'."

"Sarina, meet Dr. Robinson," Renn said. "He is one of two human doctors who we have here at the station. And don't let his youthful appearance fool you. He's easily three times your age."

"So, you better do what I say," Dr. Robinson teased.

The doctor pulled out an arm extension from above the bed and laid Sarina's injured arm on it. He then brought down a viewing tablet. A beam emanated from the device, scanning the arm. Soon an interior view of the limb appeared on the screen.

"Whoever did your field dressing did an outstanding job," Dr. Robinson said. "I doubt you'll even have a scar left to give testimony to your ordeal." He turned off the screen. "As you diagnosed, Mrs. Spalling, only a flesh wound. The nurse will re-bandage it, then you and your family can leave." He turned to Renn. "I recommend rest for the remainder of the day and plenty of fluids. As Mr. Spalling reported, Mary should eat lots of ice cream and keep a cold pack on her neck. I don't expect any swelling, but better to be safe. Mr. Spalling suffered no permanent damage, but he should be careful for the next twelve hours. The drugs I gave him will make his judgment a bit off. Nothing strenuous or too exciting for the lot. I'll swing by when my shift's over at twenty-eight hundred and check on them." He

174

turned to the newly arrived humans. "And in case you were wondering, you heard correctly - twenty-eight hundred. We run on a thirty-hour day."

"Thanks, Doc." Renn reached out and shook the human's hand.

"Yes, thank you," Steven said.

"That's what I'm here for," the doctor said. "Make sure you get some rest."

"They will." Renn helped Sarina off the bed. He then helped Steven, who was still wobbly on his feet. The medication the doctor gave him was more potent than Steven realized. "Gliisteel, I believe our new human might need a transporter until the medicine wears off."

"I can walk," Steven said as a green-skinned alien left. Nurse Gliisteel returned with the transporter several moments later. The moment Steven saw the cart, he changed his mind. A carrier was precisely what he needed. It was like a mini spaceship - round with a seat in the middle. There were controls in the front, and the damn thing floated on air. If this was what the sick got to move around in, he might think about getting sick more often.

Steven felt a tug on his sleeve and looked down. Mary pointed to the hovercraft.

"There should be room inside for both of you," Nurse Gliisteel said. Mary smiled.

After a few quick lessons, Steven managed to steer the craft down the hallways without bumping into the side walls--or his family. With Steven and Mary in the front (in case his driving got terrible again), Renn led the small group to the cafeteria. After joining Jenny and the two boys, they had a light meal before retiring to their rooms for some much-needed rest.

FIZZLEWIGGS AND GILLYHOPPERS

"Have the Kett responded to any of our hails?" Commander Oglich asked.

"No, Commander. They continue to go unanswered."

"Are we sure they are receiving our signals?" Vice-Commander O'Neil inquired.

"To our knowledge, yes," the Corpsman said. "The newest diagnosis states our communication equipment is operating correctly. Our ships are having no trouble receiving our communications."

"Which means they're too arrogant to reply. Waddo, bring up a picture of the Kett fleet," Commander Oglich said.

"Aye, Commander." Within seconds, a picture of the advancing alien ships appeared on the screen.

"Our initial assessment of their ships was correct," Vice Commander O'Neil stated. "They've got some pretty big guns on those cargo ships."

"They've used the time since our last confrontation to upgrade their weaponry. It's top-notch," Commander Oglich stared at the enormous ships. "I was afraid of this. They expected us to be here, still ready to defend this system."

Vice-Commander O'Neil squinted his eyes as he walked closer to the screen. "Something's odd. The configuration of the mining ships doesn't appear right. Waddo, zoom on the forward ship. Section 34-18." Immediately, the screen narrowed in on the specific location and zoomed in.

"Is that what I think it is?" Commander Oglich rose slightly up in his seat for a better view.

"Fighters."

"Zoom out and pan to the left."

The screen operator slowly zoomed out, revealing numerous small craft alongside the side of the mining ship. "There has to be twenty-five to thirty-five fighters along her side."

"You can bet they have the same number of ships on the port side."

"That means fifty to seventy fighters per mining ship, times four ships. I believe we've got at least two hundred and fifty fighters we did not expect," the Commander said. "Our odds of stopping the Kett have taken a major reduction."

"Your orders?" Vice-Commander O'Neil asked.

"Prepare the fighters for launch," Commander Oglich said. "Inform the squadron leaders we will meet in my briefing room in one hour to discuss an alternative plan of battle." He turned to the Communications Officer. "Advise Glogg of our findings."

"Stare straight ahead at the wall," Dr. Robinson checked the reflex in Steven's eyes with a small flashlight. "Slept okay last night?"

"Are you kidding?" Steven asked. "I didn't wake until 0-eight thirty this morning. I may sleep here forever."

"I think that's the plan, Dad," Jeremy grumbled.

Steven ignored his son's comment. "This morning was so peaceful, although I did miss earing the birds singing."

Dr. Robinson put his flashlight back into his pocket. "You can program your room to wake you each morning with whatever sound you'd like. It appears there are no side effects from yesterday's skirmish. You're free to resume normal activities."

The doctor stepped over to Sarina. He removed the bandage on her arm and inspected the injury. "Healing nicely. No infection." He placed a new wrap over the wound. "Let's give it one more day before we discard the bandage."

Lastly, Dr. Robinson walked over to Mary. He carefully removed the bandage under her neck. "Looks good." He ran an electric medical instrument over her throat and down her neck. "No swelling. Can you say something, Sweetie?"

"Something." Mary smiled. Everyone laughed except the doctor and Renn. Both appeared confused.

"You told her to say 'something', so she did," Steven said.

"And that's funny?" Dr. Robinson asked

"On Earth it is."

Dr. Robinson turned his attention back to his patient. "Mary, say '*Fizzlewigs* do as *fizzlewigs* want, while *gillyhoppers* ooze mountains of snot'."

Trying not to laugh, Mary repeated the words. But when she got to the last word, she burst into laughter. She couldn't say "snot" with a straight face.

"What are *fizzlewigs* and *gillyhoppers*?" Sarina laughed.

"Pesky little nuisances which, hopefully, you'll never meet," Dr. Robinson said, listening to Mary's heart. "Mary, you can resume normal activities like your father."

"No more ice cream?" The thought of not eating mountains of ice cream was unbearable to the ten-year-old.

"Most certainly. Even if you repeat my *fizzlewig* phrase, I recommend another two days with as much ice cream as you want."

"Hurray," Mary said.

"I recommend you all have a light breakfast," the doctor said. "Your bodies are still trying to cope with the effects of space and ridding your bodies of yesterday's medications. I recommend a bowl of cooked barley, oats, or *knipper* would be beneficial."

"No eggs and bacon?" Jeremy asked.

Now Renn and the doctor laughed. "You'll find no meat for consumption on the station," Renn said. "And eggs are a product of reproduction, not a food source. We make our food from plant material."

"You mean you guys are vegans?" Timmy asked. "No more hamburgers or tacos?"

"Our chefs can make you hamburgers and whatever tacos are." Dr. Robinson picked up his medical instruments to leave. "You can make some delicious eats from vegetables and fruits." He chuckled at their surprised faces. "It was wonderful meeting you, but hopefully, it will be under social circumstances the next time we meet. Good day."

"Thanks again, Doc," Renn said as the doctor left. "Now, let's get you five some breakfast."

"Whoopee," Timmy said. "Can I have ice cream like Mary?"

Jeremy leaned in towards his brother as they walked into the hallway. "You'll be surprised to know Tim, the ice cream Mary's been eating is made from plants too."

"Is it really?" Timmy asked.

"As I said, we have no animals to harvest for food," Renn said. "So, no dairy products either. With no way to receive supply ships, we must produce all our food. Occasionally, someone brings up something tasty from Earth. Besides, can you imagine what this place would smell like if we had hundreds of chickens, cows, and pigs?"

"I never thought of that," Timmy said.

"Couldn't you get supplies from Earth?" Sarina asked.

"Possibly, but we would risk being detected," Renn said. "Most of the station's inhabitants are plant eaters by nature, so we decided the inhabitants would be vegetarian. But trust me, you will be surprised at how scrumptious some plants taste, plants from other worlds."

"Not one being eats meat up here?" Steven asked, already craving a huge, juicy grilled steak.

"There is a small group of high-backed riders," Renn said. "I understand they weren't part of the original inhabitants of the station but arrived back in the 1700s. Their systems can't tolerate plants. Luckily, they brought a small amount of their food with them. Our caretakers discovered a way to reproduce their nutrition. But I don't think their food sources would interest any of you."

"Why? What do they eat?"

"Sillian tube worms, giant Aries beetles, golden slugs, and other such creatures." The thought of a bowl of cooked oats sounded terrific.

On the way to the dining area, Renn explained how to follow the directions inscribed on the floor to get where they wanted to go. He also showed them how to access a wall map showing which airlifts and rolling walkways to use. It was a twenty-minute walk to the area of the station where the main eatery was.

As the doors to the last airlift opened, a sight was revealed that was so magnificent it brought tears to the Spalling family's eyes. There, in all its magnificence, was planet Earth. The western section of the United States was slipping into night. The Pacific Ocean was a vivid, almost indescribable blue. A variety of land colors, ranging from forest green mountains to green grass plains to tan deserts filled the screen. As one looked east and the light of day diminished, the landscape progressed from a murky gray to a deep black. Spattered across the blackness were thousands of lights, the illuminations from the homes and streetlights of cities and neighborhoods. The entire planet floated amongst a background of millions of stars twinkling in a sea of black.

Renn smiled as the family stopped. Each gasped at seeing their home planet from space. "One of the first things the original builders of the station did was construct this wall so they may see our beautiful planet. She's something to see, isn't she?"

"She sure is," Sarina said.

"Is that Earth?" Mary asked.

"Yes, Mary, that is Earth," Renn said.

"From here, you'd never think strife, hatred, and destruction existed down there." Steven took two steps forward, trying to soak in the magnificence of his planet.

"No, you wouldn't," Renn replied. "The Blue Planet appears to be the most wonderful place in the galaxy to live. And, in some respects, she is. Come. Let's get something to eat."

As suggested, the family had bowls of cooked oatmeal. Sarina and Steven drank something passing for coffee, but it left a foul after taste in their mouths. Steven decided he needed to spare the crew and themselves the torture of consuming such liquid. He planned on explaining to the kitchen workers how to brew a "good" cup of coffee. Hopefully, somewhere amongst the vegetation growing in the station's belly were some coffee plants.

After breakfast, Renn took the family and Director Santiago on a tour of the station. The first stop was the massive airship hangar where the fleet was typically housed. The sounds of their boots echoing across the vast expanse made a lonely, haunting sound, reminding them why the fleet wasn't there. They encountered more of the long-nosed creatures at the farming unit. This time, Timmy controlled his laughter. Somehow, among the diversity of plants, the long-nosed aliens didn't seem out of place. Stephen asked the Farming Supervisor about the coffee plants. He was ecstatic to hear there were several bags of coffee beans stored in the back shed. The Supervisor promised to bring some out and start them growing but reminded Stephen they would take two to four years before they could be harvested.

"Don't worry, Stephen. " Renn chuckled at seeing Stephen's sad face. "We just received a rather large shipment of coffee beans from Earth. You'll be able to drink your coffee each morning until the new plants are ready. "

"I thought you didn't get supplies from Earth? " Sarina asked.

"We usually don't. There are only a few items we don't produce ourselves, one of which is coffee beans. Most Earthlings and some aliens up here couldn't live without their daily jolt of coffee. I believe Glogg would have a mutiny on his hands if the brown liquid stopped flowing. "

After the farm, Renn showed them the library, which interested Steven. Its shelves contained literature and knowledge dating back eons from across the galaxies. Renn told the family he would get them a reader that would translate any book of their choosing into English. Next, they visited the recreation area. The room contained various exercise equipment, games, and holographic images one could mold into any shape. They were several other stations whose purpose was unknown. Next was the education area.

"Jeremy, Timmy, and Mary will need to be tested to see where they fit in our school program," Renn said.

"You mean we have to go to school?" Timmy asked.

"Of course," Renn said. "Did you think your school days were over? Here, some students study for thirty to forty years."

"Thirty to forty years?" Timmy was in shock. "Why would anyone want to go to school that long?"

"For many reasons," Renn said. "Living in space triples, sometimes quadruples, your life expectancy, so you have the time to learn all you ever wanted to know. Plus, we have science from hundreds of alien civilizations which contain things you can't even imagine. But most of all, you will tell us about Earth. If she's destroyed, you will be teachers, the historians of our past, the last humans amongst us to be born on Earth. Others will rely on you to learn what life on Earth was like, how they did things, and so forth. You will also learn about other worlds and civilizations if you want to live amongst them one day. You can't decide where you want to go if you don't know what's out there waiting for you."

"I can leave and explore the galaxy?" Jeremy asked.

"When you get of age, if you choose," Renn replied. "Remember, we hold no one against their will. There are some worlds out there who love sports as much as you do. They would be thrilled to have you come and teach them the games of basketball and football. Or you might join an intergalactic team."

Jeremy's thoughts drifted away to what it would be like to be on a real live intergalactic sports team. He had been moping for days about missing his game on Friday night. The missed game seemed trivial when contemplating future possibilities. He could introduce the entire galaxy to Earth's sports.

"Can I learn to fly a ship as you do?" an excited Timmy asked.

"If you want to," Renn already imagined his grandson following in his pilot steps. "But not only fly them. You can learn how to design them, how to build them. Our fleet has thirteen different models of airships. But there are thousands of types out in the universe. And thousands waiting to be designed."

"Thousands," Timmy echoed, trying to wrap his mind around what he could design.

"What about me?" Mary asked. "What can I learn?"

"What do you like?"

"I like animals."

"We don't have a lot of those here, but you can still learn to become a veterinarian. When the day comes to release the animals we have in hibernation on a new world, they will need someone to take care of them, someone who understands them."

"I'd like that."

"One more stop," Renn said. "I saved the best for last. Our crown-jewel." Renn led the group down several floors. This time when the lift doors opened, they peered through an enormous pane of glass at a massive room, several miles across. "Our pride and joy. This room is where we house the specimens we've collected these past five thousand years. And the lark sparrow eggs I brought back."

"It's breathtaking," Sarina's eyes roamed across the scene before her. To the right were countless rows of shelves extending from the floor to the ceiling. Each shelf contained hundreds of sealed jars. The frames extended back further than she could see. To the left were gigantic white units with a single door. They appeared to be freezers. Down the middle of the room were massive tanks of water. The water inside was almost frozen solid. Amongst the various divisions were beings in white suits floating amongst the units, checking the instruments that controlled the stored life forms and making sure everything was in order.

Renn smiled at his family's reaction. He was proud of this room. "To the right, we house all the seeds. Behind them are the tubulars and spores. In the back, where it's dark, we keep the fungi and bacteria. To the left are the freezers housing our animal collection in suspended animation. There are eggs, embryos, sperm, zygotes, and more. We even have a few full-grown animals suspended. The middle contains both fresh and salt-water life. We keep the water at freezing to ensure the fry, larva, jellyfish polyps, zooplankton, and phytoplankton survive. Like with the animals, there are some larger animals in the back."

"Very, very impressive," Stephen said.

When a beeping sounded, Renn reached into his pocket and removed his communicator. "Glogg wants us in the Control Room. He may have some news from the fleet." He sent a message of his own. "Jenny will meet us on the way and take the children. She can take them to the recreational area where children their age meet and mingle, if they like. There they can meet other humans and some alien children."

Renn had been around Glogg long enough to notice the subtle difference in his face when he was upset.

"I wish I had better news," Glogg said as the four stepped onto the bridge. "Commander Oglich reports their hails have gone unanswered. This is as expected. As I told the humans in New York, Kett do not negotiate. What is unexpected and troubling are Commander Oglich's findings. The Kett ships are more sophisticated than when our ancestors fought and defeated them. Besides the upgraded weapons, they have a new series of small fighter planes. Oglich estimates about two hundred and fifty of them."

"Two hundred and fifty?" Renn repeated. "Our surveillance estimated somewhere between twelve and twenty. Are you now saying there are two hundred and fifty? How were we so wrong?"

"They have learned to hide the bulk of their fighters along the sides of their larger ships."

"How many fighters do we have in our fleet?" Sarina asked, unable to remember.

"We have a hundred and ten fighters," Glogg said. "Eight destroyers, five Caelifera, ten double cannons, and the ISC command ship. Roughly two Kett ships to our one."

"Can our fleet defeat them?" Steven asked.

"Doubtful," Glogg said. "All we can hope for is they can cause enough damage to make them retreat."

No one asked what the alternative was because they knew; it would be the destruction of the solar system, including Earth.

"Any word from our reinforcements?" Renn asked.

"Nothing good." Glogg walked up to a map of the galaxy on one of the giant screens. Using his long leathery finger, he indicated an area. "An ion storm is raging through the *Tantibam* area. They estimate it will last another four to six weeks. They are trying to cross, but the going is slow."

"Can't they go around?"

"Impossible," Glogg said. He motioned his hand over to the right. "This section is where the Kett live. They would never give us safe passage. And this area," he motioned to the left, "is uncharted territory. We don't know what's out there and if it's passable. As for going up or under, the storm is too massive and would take longer than to go across."

"They can't fold space as Renn did on Earth?" Sarina asked.

"That was the plan," Glogg said. "Unfortunately, the ion storm makes folding space impossible. The ions make the calculations unpredictable. The fleet could find themselves four galaxies away when they emerged, making it unlikely they'd ever return home. While folding space is a wonderful way of transportation, it has limitations."

"What happens if the reinforcements don't arrive in time?" Sarina asked.

Glogg said nothing. Sarina thought a tear had formed in his dark eyes. "I think you know the answer."

"Earth will die," she whispered. "And your fleet."

"Yes," Glogg said. "Our citizens will die, the Kett will arrive, and Earth will be destroyed. I've already given the orders to formulate the calculations for departure."

"Departure?" Director Santiago asked.

"This station is not at operational military unit," Glogg said. "It may have been once, but no longer; too many millennia of peace and complacency. We have weapons, but they are no longer sophisticated enough to defend ourselves against the Kett. If our fleet cannot stop them, we will be forced to take the station out of this solar system." He turned to address the Director specifically. "If you're still thinking about returning to Earth, you must make your decision within the next twenty-four hours. After that, I cannot return you."

"You can move the entire moon?" Steven asked.

"No, such a feat is impossible even for us," Glogg said. "The station is exactly that - a space station inside a lunar body. To leave, we must break apart the outer rock walls surrounding us. Once we are no longer confined, we will lift the station out of the moon, then set sail for another destination."

"Are you saying you will blow the moon up?" a horrified Steven asked.

"Not all of it, but about a third of its mass," Glogg said.

"You can't tear away the moon," Director Santiago said. "All hell will break loose down there. Earth will die."

"If it becomes necessary for us to break free, she will already be on her deathbed. The cargo we have inside the station is too important to allow it to be destroyed.

THE BATTLE

In the openness of space, there is nothing to hide behind to mask your approach. Your enemy is aware you're coming hours, even days before you arrive. The only advantage the ISC fleet had was their ability to fold space, giving them a small surprise element. Commander Oglich and his leaders developed a battle plan that allowed the fleet to appear and attack from different directions to expand on the slight advantage. This maneuver will be something the Kett would not expect.

"We have no chance against so many fighters," Commander Oglich said as he addressed the leaders of the various squadrons. "So, if we can't defeat the Kett, we'll slow them down. We must inflict as much damage on their ships as possible, forcing them to make repairs before proceeding to Earth. It will also give our reinforcements a few extra weeks to get here."

"The cargo ships are our primary targets. Captain Onk, I want you to fold to area 2B." He pointed to the specified area on the map. "As soon as you emerge from your space fold, concentrate all your firepower on this cargo ship." The Commander moved his finger to an empty circle. "You'll only have about five minutes before the Kett realize you're there and send their fighters. From our analysis, the cargo ships are weakest in two areas. The first is the belly where the cargo doors open. Although the doors are made of two-inch *niirillythium*,

188

there appears to be a flaw in the brackets holding the doors closed. Blast the brackets, and the weight of the doors will pull them off." Punching in several commands, he brought up a picture of the cargo ship, zooming in on the aft section. "To carry more cargo, the Kett designers sacrificed shielding for profits. The area in front of the engines contains the ship's air vents. That section is extremely light and vulnerable. If you can get your torpedoes past the engines, a direct hit there will do immense damage."

"My team can do it," Captain Onk said.

"Captain Ehrotuh, you do the same with the cargo ship here," Again, he pointed to a large empty circle. "Emerge from section 4B."

"Aye, Sir."

"Captains Jay and Blint, emerge from section 1C. I want both of your squadrons to concentrate on this big cargo ship here. She appears to be of a newer construction and made of a lighter metal alloy. She does not have the weaknesses of the other ships and is more heavily guarded. Our analysis shows her only weakness is the bridge behind the heavy artillery gun. With luck, your double-cannon ships should open the ship in that location. Once opened, our fighters can drop their bombs inside to do sufficient damage."

"We can't disable her any other way?" Commander Jay asked. "We can open her up with no problem but getting fighters in close enough to drop bombs will be almost impossible."

"I understand, but we can discover no other tactic to disable her." Commander Oglich punched in a code, bringing up a picture of four mining ships. "Now, for the real troublemakers. Of the six mining ships, these four marked with a yellow 'X' seem to be older models, like the cargo ships Captains Onk and Ehrotuh will be attacking. The extensive mining machinery covering the vessels makes them basically impenetrable."

"Commander, we will inflict more damage if we attack from behind and target those engine ventilation shafts," Colonel Quet said. "Their ships appear to be like the ones the Rockbins used to manufacture. They had a major flaw in their construction - the engines overheat easily. If we can cut off the air supply to the engines, we might blow the vessel to smithereens."

"Agreed. Your group, along with Captain Ziiger, will emerge in the rear, section 3H. See what damage you can do. Now for the commanders of the destroyers and Caelifera ships. Since you have the strongest weapons, I'd like you to target the newer mining and cargo vessels. If anyone can damage them, your ships can. The rest of the fighters will defend the Command Ship, Caelifera, and the destroyers. Try to keep those small Kett ships from causing too much damage to us."

"Commander, our fliers can defend us against those Kett fighters," Captain Ligg said. "Have the remaining fighters concentrate on the Command Ship and the destroyers."

"As you wish." Commander Oglich paused for a moment. "This is the last time many of us will see each other. Chances are, more than half of our fleet will meet their maker today defending this system. But it is and has been our mission for five thousand years. We protect the Blue Planet and the other worlds of this system. We will not tolerate another race destroying planets for their own profit."

"Here, here," rang a cry.

"I want to thank each one of you for your dedication and say it has been my pleasure to lead you on this assignment. May your god of choice be with you. Forever freedom."

"Forever freedom," yelled those in the room.

––––––––––––

"You don't understand." Jeremy quivered, his face flushed. "I have to return to Earth. I can't leave Rachel behind to die."

"Jeremy, we can't return to Earth." Steven once more tried to explain to his son. "We have no way to return."

"Renn can take me," Jeremy said. "Or Xavier. They snuck in under the radar and saved us. Why can't they do the same for Rachel?"

"What about her family?" Steven asked. "Would she leave them behind?"

"Probably not. I don't see why Rachel's mom and brother can't come too," Jeremy said. "What difference would three people make on this vast station?"

"It's too dangerous," Sarina said. "Those on Earth will be waiting for a ship and attack it."

"Your mother's right," Renn said. "It's a death sentence to return to Earth."

"Just because you left Grandmother behind to die doesn't mean I'm willing to do the same thing to Rachel," Jeremy screamed, too desperate to choose his words wisely.

"Jeremy, enough," Steven said. "You will not treat Renn with such disrespect, not after all he's done for us."

"He's done nothing for me but ruin my life." Jeremy stormed out of the apartment, slamming the door hard behind him.

"I'd better go after him." Steven followed his son.

"I'm so sorry," Sarina said. "He doesn't realize the danger involved."

"No, he's right. I deserted the woman I loved, and I've regretted the decision every day since the day I left Earth. Now, I'm sentencing my oldest grandson to the same future."

"He's young," Sarina said. "He'll understand one day."

"Did you?" Renn asked. "Even though you thought I was dead, did your resentment against me lessen as you grew older?" Sarina didn't answer. She couldn't because she had carried ill feelings toward her father until after she met him. Time did not always take the pain away.

"Preparations for the launch have already begun," Renn said. "Everyone on Earth has returned to the station already. I don't have anyone I can contact and ask to bring Rachel and her family up. No one can go back down."

"People from the moon visit Earth?" Sarina asked. "Why?"

"For many reasons. Some gather specimens for our collection. Others further their Earth education to teach future generations. Others, believe it or not, are simply on vacation. At any given time, there are somewhere around a hundred moon humans on Earth. Even a few aliens, although they are hidden well."

"I never realized that." A seriousness covered Sarina's face. "Will it be necessary to launch and leave Earth behind?"

"Unknown. But we must be ready to leave the moment we receive word that Commander Oglich and his fleet have failed to stop the Kett. If you would excuse me, I told Glogg I would cover his shift so he can attend his daughter's birthday party this afternoon."

"I must admit I was surprised to learn Glogg was a father," Sarina blushed. "Or aliens celebrate birthdays."

"Glogg has four children," Renn said. "His daughter is the youngest. She was a surprise. His mate died several years after her birth because of complications from an earthly virus."

"Are the other three on the station?"

"Not anymore. Glogg's three sons are each commanding a Caelifera ship fighting the Kett."

"But most of the fleet will die," Sarina said.

"Yes."

"Why would all three sons go?" Sarina couldn't imagine all three of her children going off to fight for a planet that wasn't their own. "Shouldn't at least one have stayed behind?"

"Perhaps. But Caelifera are bound by duty and responsibility. Glogg's race vowed to protect this system. The vow extended from his great-grandparents to him, to his children, and their children. Had Una been old enough, she, too, would be in the fight."

"Poor Glogg."

"Never say those words to him," Renn said. "His children's dedication to duty is a great source of pride to him. Don't get me wrong. He loves his children as much, if not more, than humans love theirs. His sense of obligation and purpose is a lot stronger than ours. As for the birthday celebration, that is something the alien races learned from the humans. Most never celebrated the day their offspring was born. The idea caught on, and many now celebrate their children's yearly birth date. However, once they reach their teen years, most of the aliens discontinue the celebration. Now, I must go, or Glogg will be late for the party."

Six minutes after Renn left, Steven returned alone. "I can't find Jeremy anywhere. These dang kids know their way around this part of the station like it's their home backyard."

"I'm sure he's sulking somewhere," Sarina said. "He can't go anywhere."

"True, but he's upset enough to try," Steven said. "I don't mean he'd try to fly a ship himself, but he might try to talk someone into returning him to Earth."

"Do you think anyone would take him?"

"No. Glogg has given the order stating no one may return to Earth. I am sure a flier would not go without Glogg's permission."

"Should we ask security to find him?"

"Not yet. Let's give our son time to cool off. I'm sure he'll return when he gets hungry. If he's not back by bedtime, I'll have security find him."

―――――――――――

Jeremy returned an hour later, but not alone. Two police androids escorted him home. They found him trying to start a small flier in the hangar. Thankfully, his feeble attempts to start the engines set off the alarms, and the androids apprehended him before he did any damage. Without saying a word to his parents or the officers, Jeremy walked into his bedroom and locked the door. Steven thanked the androids for their help.

"Crazy kid." Frustrated, Steven plopped on the couch beside his wife. "I can't believe he thought he could fly one of those things."

"The officer said he tried to get someone to take him down," Sarina said in defense of her son. "I guess he figured if no one would take him, he'd take himself."

"And probably kill him and do considerable damage to the station before he even got out the hangar door."

Steven stood to go speak with his son. Sarina grabbed his hand and stopped him. "Wait. Give him time to think about what he did. Rachel must mean a lot more to him than we thought. Besides, we yanked him out of his life with no say-so on his part. We destroyed his planned future."

"We didn't," Steven quickly said. "It's those damn Kett."

"It's not the way Jeremy sees it."

"Are you saying we should let him go back?"

"No. I'm suggesting we try to understand his point of view. He's devoted his entire life to earning an athletic scholarship to college. That future was yanked out from under him. The place he calls home is about to be obliterated. And with her dies the current love of his life." She saw Steven was still angry. "What would you have done if it was me down there and you up here?"

Steven squeezed her hand. "Probably got myself killed trying to steal a flier."

When it was time to go to Una's birthday party, Sarina knocked on Jeremy's door, announcing they were leaving and wondering if he wanted to go. When there was no response, she told her son there was food in the kitchen if he got hungry. They'd be back in several hours. Even though Jeremy was too old for a babysitter, Jenny was asked to stay in the apartment in case Jeremy needed something. And to ensure he attempted nothing crazy again.

As the lift doors opened, the sound of children laughing filled the room. Inside, thirty youngsters representing all six races clustered around a table. Seated in the middle of the group was a smaller version of Glogg.

"Thank you for coming," Glogg said as he walked over to the Spalling family and extended his hands to the parents. "Timmy and Mary, go join the children at the table. They are playing a Game of 'Nonsense'."

"Oh, I love Nonsense." Timmy hurried to join the game.

"You do?" Sarina asked. "When did you learn to play the game?"

"When Jenny took us to the recreation area the other day when you met with Glogg." Mary ran after her brother.

"Any word on how the battle's going?" Steven quietly asked, not sure if it was appropriate to bring the subject up at the party.

"Not yet," Glogg said. "I'm not sure if it's a good thing or not."

———————

As feared, the fleet's surprise attacks only fooled the Kett for a few minutes. Somehow, they soon anticipated from where the ships would emerge to counterattack. But they did enough destruction in the first two assaults to destroy two cargo ships and heavily damage two more.

When the squadrons emerged again from folding space, the Kett released a hoard of two hundred and thirty-six small enemy fighters. Although not as fast as feared, they were outmaneuvering the ISC fliers and causing a heavy toll.

The planned attack on the mining ships did not go as planned. The ISC had miscalculated the immense amount of mining machinery covering the vessels and its ability to make the spaceships too thick to penetrate. Wave after wave of torpedoes were fired into the massive vessels destroying much of the digging and hauling equipment, but the vessels' skin remained intact. The melted metal added to the spaceships' armor. Even the attack on the engine's air vents caused minor damage. They blew the outer sheathing away, but the engines themselves were recessed too far inside the crafts to be reached. The fliers bombarded the air shaft vents with explosives, but they did not produce the damage hoped for. Evidentially, the Kett fixed the air shaft flaw.

The indestructible mining ships concentrated their cannons on the destroyers. Their weapons' range was greater than the ISC's, hitting their target without being hit themselves. Within fifteen minutes, they obliterated two of the destroyers, the crew floating dead amongst the debris.

The cargo ships determined the fate of the double-cannon ships. Although they possessed limited gun power, their marksmen were accurate. They soon discovered a flaw in the double-cannon construction - eliminate the cable holding the ship to the cannons, and they would fall away, leaving a flier with little firepower. One by one, the double-cannon ships were targeted and destroyed.

"Do you want the fliers to fall back and protect the destroyers and Command Ship?" Vice-Commander O'Neil asked, seeing the damage being caused. He realized they only had minutes until all their fliers were destroyed.

"Have the remaining fliers concentrate on the remaining five cargo ships," Commander Oglich said. "They can find some cover around the enemy vessels. The smaller fighters won't fire on them if they're near a cargo ship. They won't risk hitting their own. This is the only chance we will get, so we need to inflict as much damage as possible. We need to buy enough time for the other fleet to arrive."

As the fliers moved from protecting the larger ships to attacking the cargo vessels, the enemy fighters attacked like hungry wolves. The Kett hammered the Caelifera ships as if they had a personal vendetta against the race. They didn't stop until they destroyed two and badly crippled the other three, then turned their attention to the Command Ship.

"Lieutenant, send an urgent communique to Glogg," Commander Oglich said. "Tell him we have failed. We could not defeat the Kett and suffered heavy losses. Chances are none will survive."

"Aye, Sir."

"Vice-Commander, let's make our death count for something," the Commander said. "Let's take out at least one of those mining ships. Push the throttle forward, and let's ram this vessel down that mining ship's throat."

"Yes, Sir." As Vice-Commander O'Neil prepared to ram the closest ship, the small fighters attacking them exploded.

"Sorry we're late," came an unfamiliar voice over the intercom as forty ISC ships emerged from folded space.

"Delay the order," Commander Oglich shouted upon seeing the new arrivals. Although not a massive army, their presence was enough to turn the battle to the ISC's side. Realizing they lost, the Kett retreated.

"They're leaving," said the Vice-Commander.

"Commander Oglich, we're picking up a reading. The innermost cargo vessel is almost full of *pinrite*," Captain Hun from the main Caelifera ship said as his image appeared on the display screen. His skin was burned and torn. Black blood flowed from an enormous gaping hole in his chest. Flames were everywhere. Fragments of the ship and Caelifera bodies covered the floor. "If we hit her hard, the explosion will cause extensive damage to those mining ships. It will take them months to make repairs."

"We don't have enough power left to cause that kind of damage," Commander Oglich said.

"Most of my crew is dead," Captain Hun said. "Our remaining three ships are compromised and are being held together with spit and luck. Captain Org, Lieutenant Vill, and I will follow your plan. We will ram our ships into the ship."

"Captain, no," Commander Oglich said. "Don't all three of you sacrifice yourselves like this."

"Commander, it's the only thing to do," Lieutenant Vill said. "We're beyond the point of being saved. We want our crews' and our deaths to count for something."

"I can give you five minutes," Captain Hun said. "You need to be a hundred miles from here by then. Tell our father we said Forever Freedom."

"Forever Freedom," Commander Oglich said. "Vice Commander O'Neil, give the order to retreat to section 23c/45a. Space fold to commence in three minutes."

While the fleet prepared to withdraw, Commander Oglich observed the three brothers power their ships. In high throttle, they zoomed forward, plowing through the few enemy fighters who remained. Pieces of spacecraft flew into space as they started to disintegrate from the power of accelerating. The remaining ISC fleet reached safety as the three ships hit the volatile cargo vessel. Upon impact, the *pinrite* ignited, creating an enormous fireball. The mining vessels' equipment turned red hot, then white as the metal melted into lumps. Vast chunks of the Caelifera vessels flew into space as they exploded, tearing into the mining ships' sides. Although they destroyed only one ship, they caused enough damage to halt their advancement for a while. Hopefully, the entire ISC annihilation fleet would arrive before they rebuild.

DEVASTATING NEWS

"Vice-Commander O'Neil, what's our assessment?" Commander Oglich asked when they arrived at section 23c/45a.

"We lost all the double-cannons and the Caelifera ships," the Vice Commander said. "Four destroyers survived, but two are too heavily damaged to make it much farther. A fifth destroyer's hull integrity was too compromised and exploded. The Hellens have two ships working. The Goots have three, one of which probably isn't salvageable. We have thirty-one fliers operable."

"No others?" the Commander asked, the magnitude of their loss weighing heavily upon his heart.

"No, Sir," Vice-Commander O'Neil sadly said. "We wouldn't even have this many ships remaining if Captain Quid hadn't shown up with his small relief fleet."

"What damage has the Command Ship sustained?"

"The last attack of fighters shot her up pretty bad. We lost decks twenty-two B through twenty-five D. We also have a breach outside of Engineering. Repair crews are reinforcing the areas as we speak. We need to take it easy until we make some repairs."

"Can she survive another fold through space?"

"Not now, Commander. I can't explain how she survived the one here. The two destroyers won't take another journey either."

"Understood." The trip back to the space station would be long and slow. "Get me Captain Quid on the screen."

Several moments later, an alien of unknown origins appeared on the screen. His skin was a mossy green with turquoise stripes, reminding the Commander of the pictures he had seen of Earth's zebras. He was tall, easily ten feet, with a long neck rising from his bony shoulders. The neck curved forward and ended at a large breathing hole set in the front of what appeared to be the creature's face. His face was a pinkish color. Two pairs of small eyes, devoid of eyelids, sat on each nasal cavity side. The eye closest to the opening looked forward while the other gazed to the side. From its mouth hung six-round tentacles stretching halfway down its neck. He appeared to have no lips or teeth.

"Captain Quid, I presume," the Commander said.

"Guilty as charged," the alien said, his tentacles moving as he talked. "I assume you are the Commander in charge of this fleet?"

"Yes, I am Commander Oglich from the Moo-in delegation. I thank you for your assistance. Without it, we surely would have perished. How were you able to get through the ion storm?"

"We didn't. My race lives on this side of the expanse. We only joined the Interstellar Space Coalition five hundred years ago, so you probably don't recognize my species."

"You are a stranger to me."

"We received ISC's call to defend this system from the Kett destroyers. When we learned of their inability to arrive in time because of the ion storm, we came on our own. We may be few, but our ships can give a good punch."

"Yes, they did."

"I offer any help you may need: supplies, repairs, whatever. I can spare only three craft to help escort you back to your station.

The rest will need to remain with me to keep track of the Kett and be ready to join the primary fleet upon their arrival. It will take all of us to destroy those mining ships."

"Thank you, Captain," Commander Oglich said. "We will get back to you within the hour on what help we need. Command Ship out." When the screen went blank, the Commander ordered an updated message be sent to the space station to advise them of their situation and losses. He made sure their communique contained the news about Glogg's three sons and their heroes' death. He wished he could be there in person to tell Glogg of their bravery and how they sacrificed their lives to protect the blue planet.

A group inside the dining area gathered around Una and sang "Happy Birthday", another Earth custom adopted by the aliens on the space station.

After the traditional song, Glogg and a small group of Caelifera sang a melody in their native tongues. A mixture of chirps and clicks, Sarina thought the song was beautiful.

When the singing finished, a Caelifera female cut the cake into pieces. They passed out the cake with another female's help, giving Una and Glogg the first pieces.

Sarina pressed her fork into the piece of cake, cutting off a small portion. She placed the morsel in her mouth, cautiously chewing, not sure what she expected a vegan cake to taste like. To her surprise, it was delicious. She quickly finished her piece and went back for seconds. While she finished her dessert, she noted how the children interacted together, having fun. She scanned the mess hall. Intermingled together were the five different alien races and the humans brought to the station throughout the years. All lived together without prejudice, strife, or hostility. Sarina wondered if these beings, who were so different from each other, could live in harmony, then why couldn't humanity?

Gifts were not a part of the birthday celebration on the station, but Glogg had two gifts for his last born. The first was a bright red stone on a golden chain, a gemstone from their homeworld Glogg had given to her mother when they became pledged mates. He slipped the necklace over the young Caelifera's head. Even from where Sarina and Steven stood, they witnessed the brilliance of the stone. The inside glowed as if a small flame burned inside, sending rays of soft umber across Una's clothing. The second gift was a painted representation of their home planet, an image of a field of exotic flowers stretching across the plain. The flowers appeared so real one could almost smell their fragrance. The field ended at an enormous mountain of greens with a golden waterfall flowing over its top. Behind the mountain was a sky with a mixture of reds, oranges, and yellows, reminding Sarina of a sunset she had seen several years earlier while vacationing in Hawaii. The one significant difference was the three moons visible in the heavens.

"Glogg, what a gorgeous painting," Sarina said.

"It's of my homeworld. Or, at least, I believe it is. I have never been there, but I hoped one day, Una, her brothers, and I would have time to return."

"Did you paint it?" Steven asked.

"Painting is something I like to do in my spare time." Both humans wondered when he ever had any free time. He was always on the bridge. And when he wasn't, he was with them or his family.

"How did you know what to paint?" Steven asked.

"My grandparents, from many generations back, were on one of the original Caelifera ships that fought the Kett," Glogg said. "They remained to protect your planet. Before they left our homeworld, they realized they might never return home, and future generations of our family would be born who would never have the joy of seeing our beautiful planet for themselves. He brought a book of pictures with him showing the wonders of home. We have passed the book down to each generation of our family. I will pass the book on to my oldest son, Quid, who will pass it on to his oldest, and so forth. Since Una will not have the photos, I wanted her to have something of her world. I plan on..." Glogg stopped when his communicator sounded. "Renn reports we have received a message from Commander Oglich and the fleet." He walked over and kissed his daughter, telling her he had to leave.

"If you'd like, I can see the children get back to your apartment if you'd like to go with Glogg," said the female who had helped pass out the pieces of cake. "My son has become fond of your two youngest, and I would hate to break up their fun."

"Are you sure?" Sarina asked, not sure if she should leave her children under the care of this alien. She looked at Steven for guidance.

"We only live three apartments down from you," the alien said. "It is no problem."

"Thank you. We appreciate your help." The children would be safe with the neighbor. After all, where could they go? They were on a sealed space station.

Both Steven and Sarina had to run to catch up to Glogg, who developed a brisk walk with his long, thin legs. The airlift door was closing when the couple reached it. Glogg held out his hand, stopping the doors from shutting.

The three rode in silence to the Control Room floor. As soon as they entered, Glogg felt the silence in the room. Too nervous to sit in his command seat, he nodded to the communications clerk to play the message.

A picture of a battle-scarred Commander Oglich appeared on the screen. A bandage covered his left eye. His clothes were torn and dirty. The bridge was in shambles, and the screens were dark. Consoles were smoking as if they had been on fire. Wiring hung from the ceiling. The floor was littered with debris.

"Commander Oglich here. Hopefully, you will receive this message. Our power supply is low, so I'll be brief. Once we complete repairs and restore power, I will send a more detailed account."

"As you may have surmised by the condition of the bridge, our confrontation with the Kett did not go well. Their weaponry was far superior to anything we imagined. They cut us down with no mercy. We would have lost the entire fleet if it had not been for the surprise arrival of a small ISC squadron."

"Our casualties are high. Only thirty-one fliers remain intact; six are damaged. Four destroyers survived. Two are not salvageable, and we will destroy them once we reassign their crews to other ships. The Hellens lost all but two vessels, and the Goots have two left. I am sorry to report, Glogg, we lost all the Caelifera ships." Glogg stepped backward, collapsing into his chair at the Commander's words. "Your sons gave their lives to destroy one of the mining ships and severely damaged several others. Without their sacrifice, we never would have escaped. They asked me to give you a message." Glogg looked into the commander's eyes. "Freedom forever."

"Freedom forever," Glogg repeated. He remembered the day he had taught each of them the Caelifera saying.

"They and the rest of your people were all heroes. Their attack has slowed the Kett's advancement enough to allow the ISC fleet to arrive. The Command Ship has suffered severe damage. Our hull integrity is compromised, and we can no longer enter folded space. We're making repairs, but she can't make the journey back to the station. We'll need to meet you on an intercept course as you leave this system."

"Commander Oglich signing off for now."

No one uttered a word as the screen went blank, then returned to an image of the Earth. Silence filled the room as those on the bridge digested what they had just witnessed; the reality of losing their friends and family entered their consciousness. Each waited for their distraught leader to speak. After several minutes, Glogg stood and spoke briefly.

"Captain Henry, advise the inhabitants the station will leave the moon in eight hours," Glogg said, his voice broken and sorrowful.

"Sir, we're ready now," Captain Henry said. "We can depart within the hour."

"Eight hours, Captain." Glogg kept his vision transfixed on the floor. Renn noted the slight tremors flowing through his body, his limbs weakening, his eyes filling with liquid. He feared his friend would collapse there on the bridge, but his friend was too proud to accept assistance to leave the Command Center. When he left, he had to do so under his own power. Renn stood there and waited, ready to rush in if needed. "Not a minute before. Renn, you're in command." Somehow Glogg found the strength to turn to leave. When he reached Renn, he paused momentarily, his eyes still looking downward. "Have it done." Without another word, Glogg walked off the bridge.

"You heard the orders," Renn bellowed as soon as the door closed. "Send out the message and get everything locked down. Notify anyone who hasn't returned from Earth as ordered that they have four, after which I will lock the station tight, and they will have to fly home on their own."

"Does this mean you're giving up?" a tearful Sarina asked.

"No, it means they beat us. We gave it our best shot, lost a hell of a lot of good beings, and now we must save those who remain. And the special cargo of plants and animals in storage. They are our number one priority now."

"What will happen to Earth?" Steven asked, looking up at his home planet on the screen.

"Hopefully, Glogg's sons' sacrifice caused enough damage to keep the Kett in repairs for months," Renn said. "With luck, they may even have to return to port for new ships. By then, the ion storm will pass, and the rescue fleet will arrive in time to save Earth."

"And if not?"

"Then she, like many other places, will be no more."

"Can we do nothing?" Sarina asked. "We can't abandon her."

"We only have one thing that can be done," Renn sadly said. "Inform the people of Earth we failed."

Sarina and Steven wandered the hallways, not sure where to go, not wanting to return home. They passed by the mess hall to check on the party, but everyone was already gone. The sight of the blue planet shining brightly through the glass wall only made them more depressed. They went to the nursery and watched the newborn aliens and humans. The new lives gave them some comfort to know life was renewing itself even in this disaster. Unable to think of anything else to do, they returned home.

"Jeremy came out of his room and ate dinner," Jenny said.

"Mrs. Gonk brought Timmy and Mary home after the party. They've been asleep for about an hour. It appeared they had a fun time. I wish I could say the same for their parents." Jenny gave them a warm smile.

"I'll go check on the kids," Steven said. "Why don't you sit down and relax."

"I thought you might like some tea upon your return from the Command Center." Jenny rose from the sofa. "It's on the stove. If you have no further need of me, I'll return home."

"You don't have to go, Jenny," Sarina said in a soft voice.

"My presence upsets you," Jenny said.

"Are my mother's memories really inside of you?" Sarina finally asked.

"Yes. Would you like me to tell you some of my memories?"

"Yes, I would like to hear them."

"Come, lay beside me with your head on my lap like you used to do as a child," Jenny said. Without hesitation, Sarina complied. She was an adult, and it was silly for her to do this, but tonight she felt like a lost child afraid of the dark.

"What do you remember?" Sarina asked.

"Everything. I remember the day Renn walked into the diner. He was so confused over the menu and didn't know an egg from a pork chop. I remember the taste of his lips when he kissed me, the tangy smell of his skin when we made love. The hours we spent talking about everything and anything. The plans we made for our future. My surprise when he told me the truth of who he was."

"Weren't you afraid?"

"No, I could never be afraid of him." Jenny reached down with her hand and stroked Sarina's hair. "I remember the moment the doctor told me I was pregnant. I was so happy. The best memory was the day you were born. I was only in labor for a little over an hour. You were in such a hurry to come out and meet the world. You looked so much like your father. Even had a head full of strawberry-blond hair. It brought me joy knowing a part of him lived on through you. I can remember the sensation of you nursing at my breasts, the times you snuggled up to me in my bed when you became scared. Every Halloween costume you wore, every birthday party you had, every Christmas present you opened is stored in my circuits. Do you remember when you were six and found an injured bunny in the Spring? You swore he was the Easter Bunny in disguise."

"Mr. Whiskers," Sarina said, recalling the memory. "I forgot all about him."

"I remember all your pets. Mr. Whiskers, Patches, Lillybean, Scout, and Cat."

"Do you remember Billy Greene?"

"How could I not? He was your first crush. You cried for a week when he took Kathy McMasters to the school dance instead of you."

"I was so devastated," Sarina laughed. "He attended your funeral. He was bald and fat. His wife had finally had enough of his running around and drinking and divorced him. I was so lucky he took Kathy to the dance instead of me."

"Yes, you were. And years later, you found a wonderful man to marry, Steven. I died before you married him."

"You remember dying?"

"Yes. I remember you laid beside me and held me in your arms as I drifted off. It was, and still is, one of my fondest memories."

"Are you able to love, Mom?"

"No, not in the true sense of love. I remember the fuzziness of love, the warmth inside me when you hugged me as a child, the racing of my heart when I was with your father, the ache inside my body when I didn't see you for a while. I can remember the experience and feelings of love, joy, fear, anger, and all the other emotions, but I cannot feel them for myself."

Sarina snuggled up closer to Jenny, stifling a yawn. Upon seeing her actions, the android sang the lullaby Sarina's mother had sung to her when Sarina was a child. The song always calmed her, made her feel loved and safe.

Steven returned from the children's bedrooms to find Sarina asleep on the couch, her head on Jenny's lap. Jenny held her finger to her mouth to instruct Steven to be quiet, never skipping a note of the lullaby. Steven reached over, removed a blanket from the back of a nearby chair, and laid it over his sleeping mate.

"Wake me if she needs anything," he whispered.

Jenny nodded, continuing to sing her song softly.

"Steven, I need for you to wake up," Jenny said as she tapped the human's shoulders.

"Hm? What? Is Sarina okay?"

"Yes, she's on the couch trying to come around," Jenny said. "Renn needs you, Sarina, and the kids to meet him right away."

"What time is it? Have we left the moon yet?"

"It's 0-three hundred. You've been asleep for just under five hours. Departure is in three hours. You need to wake up."

"I'm awake. I'm awake." Steven sat up in bed, trying to open his eyes. "What could Renn want at this late hour?"

"He didn't say. He only said to bring your family to section 14F."

The children grumbled at being woken at such an early hour. Jeremy particularly was not pleased and had no intention of meeting Renn. Jenny informed him she would physically carry him if he did not go willingly. She reminded him she was an android of unbelievable strength and determination. Under protest, Jeremy joined the group.

The family followed Jenny down several corridors and into an airlift. When the doors opened, they walked down another two hallways to where Renn was standing.

"I realize it's early, and you're tired, but I wanted to give you some happy news after what's happened," Renn said.

"You couldn't tell us the news in our apartment?" an angry Jeremy asked.

"I don't think it would have the same effect." Renn smiled. "If you would follow me."

"We have to go further?" Jeremy groaned.

Ignoring the sulking teenager, Renn led them through a doorway into a room with a glass wall. Below was the hangar. Replacing the spacecraft were hundreds of people of different ethnicities, colors, shapes, and ages.

"Who are all those people?" Timmy asked, pressing his face against the glass.

"Representatives of our race," Renn said. "I thought Jeremy would be interested in the three beneath the third blue light." He pointed to the small group.

Jeremy moved his gaze to where Renn gestured. He saw Jenny walk up to three humans and speak to them. The android pointed to the room behind the glass. Then Jeremy's heart almost stopped beating when the one female raised her hand and waved at him.

"It's Rachel," Jeremy screamed. "With her mom and brother. How?"

"You were right about me leaving My Jenny," Renn said. "I couldn't condemn you to the same life of regret I lived. When I told Glogg I had to rescue Rachel and her family, Glogg realized there might be others worthy of rescue. He sent out a message asking if there were people who should be saved. If so, he gave permission to bring them to the ship."

"Thank you." Jeremy threw his arms around Renn and hugged him.

"If you go through the door there, you can take the lift down to the hangar," Renn said, pointed towards a side door. "Don't break your neck getting down to her."

Before he said another word, Jeremy left. Moments later, he emerged on the floor below, running into Rachel's arms.

"That was a wonderful thing you and Glogg did." Steven saw his son kiss his girlfriend.

"She may or may not be his one genuine love," Renn said, watching the pair. "They will have time to discover if they are, and if not, go their separate ways. It is better than never knowing. As for the other people, Glogg felt it was the right thing to do. If he couldn't save the entire planet, he could at least save some of them."

"How's he doing?" Sarina asked.

"Not well, I would imagine. As soon as I leave, I'm stopping by to check on Glogg. Those three boys were his life. I can't imagine what it must be like to lose all three at once."

"Lost trying to save a world where most of the sentient beings care nothing about their sacrificed lives," Steven said.

"I don't believe that's true," Renn said. "There are many wonderful humans on Earth. Director Santiago showed me. Plus, Earth is the only home they ever knew. Although most never set foot on her, they loved her all the same. They gladly gave their lives hoping to prevent her destruction."

"Hey, look," Timmy pointed to a woman in red. "There's Director Santiago."

The Director walked across the floor to a familiar-looking male. It was Fred from the bunker.

"Fred?"

"Yes. Fred, like Sally, was a plant to protect you," Renn said. "I couldn't find any of the Director's family in the short time I had, but I found something she loves very much, something she regretted leaving behind."

Fred lifted several furry objects out from beneath his jacket. The first one was black and white, and the next was blond. Dogs. Lastly, he raised a small kitten. Fred had retrieved the Director's beloved pets. "Meet Hambone and Sheila. I don't remember the kitten's name. I know we don't allow live animals on the station, but I thought they might make an exception this time."

"I don't think two small dogs and a kitten will create much of a problem," Stephen said.

"I wouldn't say that," Renn chuckled. "From what I was told, Hambone and Sheila are about to become parents."

"Hurray, puppies," Mary said. "Can I have one?"

"That will be up to Director Santiago," Sarina said. But she, too, relished the thought of puppies on the station.

"Unfortunately, I have the hunch many beings are going to want a puppy," Renn said.

A FINAL MESSAGE TO EARTH

Renn exited the airlift and strolled down the corridor. Stopping at the fourth apartment door, he reached out to push the doorbell. His hand trembled. He withdrew it and took a deep, cleansing breath, hoping to calm himself. Glogg mustn't see him this way. He was a captain, there to inform his commander of the space station's departure status. But more importantly, he was a comrade there to comfort his best friend, to give him whatever support he needed to cope with the loss of his only three sons. Renn wished he could allow Glogg to grieve longer, but, as the station commander, protocol mandated the alien be on the bridge.

His insides calmed once more, Renn pushed the button. He waited for sixty seconds, then pushed the button again. The door opened. Before him stood Tiinew, Glogg's sister.

"How's he doing?" Renn asked as he entered the apartment. Because of their enormous eyes, Caelifera usually kept their apartment lights dim, but this was beyond that. The room was almost pitch black.

"As our leader and a Caelifera bred into our philosophy of service, he is unbroken," Tiinew said, using a cloth to wipe tears from her eyes. "As a father whose sons gave their lives for the welfare of all, heartbroken. I don't know how he's holding it together. He's in the study."

Renn knew the Commander's apartment's layout like his own, so the lack of light did not impede his walk to the study. As he entered, he distinguished his friend sitting in a chair with his back to him, the illumination of a small lamp beside him casting ghostly shadows around the room. Glogg appeared to be staring into nothing but the blackness surrounding him. Knowing there were no words to express his immense sorrow for his friend's loss, Renn walked over and placed his hand on Glogg's shoulder.

"I've been sitting here for hours trying to figure out what to say in the message to Earth," Glogg softly said. "How do I tell over seven billion humans I failed, and they have less than a year to live?"

"By not telling them you failed," Renn said as he walked around the chair and took a seat on the nearby couch, facing Glogg. "No one did, most certainly not you."

"It was my command."

"Doesn't count. It was a joint effort."

Glogg lifted his head. His eyes did not shine as they always did. They were dull and cold looking, the color of death itself. "How can you say we didn't fail?"

"The mission was to slow down the Kett. We accomplished that. From the latest report we received from Commander Oglich, Quid, Org, and Vill did enough damage to the mining ships to keep them in repairs for at least ten months. Possibly longer. Hell, there's even the possibility the Kett may have to scrap the entire mission and bring back different ships. We destroyed the cargo the haulers carried, making this a costly operation for the Kett. Our fleet and your sons bought us the time needed for the ISC to arrive."

"At what cost, Renn?" a sorrowful Glogg asked. "So many are not returning to their families, to their friends."

"But some are. We must find joy in this small piece of successful news." Renn paused for a moment before asking, "Have you told Una?"

"No, I didn't want to wake her. I will tell her when she awakens."

"And Dii?"

"I delivered the news myself. Dii had the right to hear of his death from me, his commander and father. As a true Caelifera, she thanked me and said Quid and his two brothers would live through Una and the twins Dii is carrying."

"Your species never stops amazing me," Renn said. "Even with such a devastating loss, she beheld the good. How do you do it?"

"It is our way. We are bred for duty and its consequences. What is the status of our departure?"

"All inhabitants have reported in," Renn said. "All the fliers sit in the hangar and are tied down. The bulkheads are locked, all outside shield coverings are in place. I have advised personnel to secure themselves and their belongings. The primary thrusters are warming up and should be ready to take us out of here in two hours. Explosives will ignite thirty minutes before takeoff."

"Have we taken precautions to ensure no large debris plummets to Earth?"

"Yes. Ming and his engineers have manufactured an explosive that will vaporize most of the rock. The laser cannons will pulverize any huge pieces breaking away. The most Earth should get is a spectacular meteor shower."

"And a massive chunk of their moon missing," Glogg added.

"Something we cannot avoid."

"And what of our new passengers?"

"We brought aboard two hundred and forty-eight new humans, along with Jeremy's girlfriend, Rachel, and her mother and brother. Jeremy and his parents asked me to convey their deep gratitude."

"As you told me, it was the right thing to do." Glogg stood and laid the pen and paper he held on the nearby table. He seemed shorter in status, perhaps weighed down by the loss of so many. "I need to get to the bridge. Perhaps, if you don't mind, you could write the message for Earth and have it sent."

"I have it right here," Renn said, handing his commander the brief message he had written as he also stood. "I thought it might be easier for a human to tell humanity it's about to end. Make any changes."

Glogg glanced at the communique, barely comprehending what it said. He handed the message back to Renn. "You've sort of exaggerated the time of their repairs."

"Had to give them some hope."

"Broadcast the message immediately."

"If you'd like, Glogg, I can handle the departure. No one would think less of you if you remained here to be with Una."

"I would think less of me," Glogg said. Then, for a moment, the slightest hint of a smile crossed his face. "Are you bucking for my job again?"

"You have to retire sometime?" Renn laughed, glad to see a little of his friend returning. "Besides, I'm determined to be the first human commander of this space station."

"Not going to happen."

A worldwide communication went out to the people of Earth.

The engagement with the Kett fleet has ended. Their ships took heavy damaged and will need substantial repairs. We estimate it will take a year before they can get underway again. This delay will allow our reserve ISC fleet time to arrive and stop the Kett advancement for good.

This is not a triumph, nor a defeat. We lost Seven hundred and eighty-two brave soldiers and over half of our ships. We pray they did not sacrifice their lives in vain.

We are leaving this system. We can no longer defend it or your planet. The Interstellar Space Coalition will decide if they will assign another station to this quadrant. Currently, the actions of humans do not warrant such a move.

If you want your planet protected from future attacks by the Kett and other marauding species, you must show the ISC you are capable of change. The petty fighting amongst your cultures, countries, and governments must cease immediately. Empathy, caring, and coexistence must replace violence, hatred, and greed. The use of all fossil fuels must end, and global warming halted. Deforestation must stop and destroyed forests replanted. Humans must learn to live as one with nature, not against her. I know this is a massive request, but if you don't heed our words and change, your planet is doomed. Already your world is dying. Your oceans are faltering because of your aggressive overfishing, the toxic wastes you continue to dump in them, and the rising water temperatures caused by global warming. You teeter on the precipice where, if you do nothing, the entire food chain will collapse. Once you go over this edge, nothing, not even our advanced technology, can save your world.

Without the ISC's protection, this system will be consumed in the near future for water and mineral resources. You cannot defend yourself alone against those who are coming. Show us you can be the creatures you were meant to be. If you do, we will help you return your planet to the Garden of Eden it once was. We will return with a new station that we won't have to hide. It will circle the Earth as a warning to others.

At 0-four hundred Greenwich Mean Time, we will depart your world. It will be necessary to remove a portion of the moon's top and side section facing the Earth for our vessel to emerge. We will minimize any danger to Earth.

We wish you well and hope you will change. The future is in your hands.

Farewell,

Command Glogg, leader of the ISC Earth guard space station.

Around the globe, people with heavy hearts gathered to monitor the space station's emergence. Those experiencing night gathered outside to see the spectacle firsthand. Those in daylight waited inside, their vision fixed to their television, computer, tablet, or phone. Anxiety ran high as people discussed the upcoming event.

Those who believed the aliens were benevolent assured those who worried. Others were not so sure. Skeptical, they argued there was no proof of anything the aliens had said was accurate. What evidence was there of the conflict or the Kett themselves existed? They predicted it was a ploy to deceive Earth's citizens, and the moon would be destroyed. Still, others went about their daily business, stating what would be would be. So why do anything?

Amongst the speculations and questions rose another louder discussion, a dialog of the ordinary citizens' desire to change as Renn's words had suggested. For days, Earth was a planet of peace as its inhabitants awaited to learn their future. Why couldn't peace continue? Why couldn't they put differences aside and end century-old confrontations? For the first time, they had proof of what existed in space, and they were doomed without the ISC's protection. Change was the only thing that would give them a future.

At precisely 0-four hundred GMT, a bright light emerged from the upper part of the moon. It started small, then enlarged like ripples on a pond. As the illumination spread, its intensity grew, then quickly weakened, disappearing entirely after five minutes. The scene was a little clearer for those watching the International Space Station and the Hubble Telescope feed. The side of the moon seemed to be pushed outward when the light appeared. Huge chunks of rock let go of their holdings, drifting out into space for several seconds before being engulfed and consumed by the intense light. When the brilliance ended, a prominent dark crater was visible in the moon.

Another fifteen minutes passed before the first glimpse of the ISC space station became visible. The station rose from the newly formed crater inch by inch as its long-dormant engines woke from their long sleep. Even with only the tip showing, it was clear the space station was enormous. The structure continued to rise for another thirty minutes before its body cleared its once rocky home.

All doubts of their existence now put aside, the alien vessel's size and shape captivated the people of Earth. Fears turned to excitement as they witnessed once more the confirmation of other intelligent life existing in the universe, life capable of intergalactic flight.

The ship hung in space a little way above the torn moon. It was elliptical, not round as speculated. Scientists estimated its diameter to be from ten to twenty miles across and at least five miles high. Exhaust vents protruded from the middle-bottom, encircled in several protective rings, two of which displayed a circle of either white or blue lights. Rectangular protrusions stacked in sets of two covered the sides: the inhabitants' living quarters and various offices. A small domed section sat on the top of the vessel containing the bridge. It, and the rooms along the side, were covered with protective sheathing, thus blocking any insight into what was inside. The entire vessel glowed with a luminous blue haze from the many lights attached around the ship. The station was a vision worth beholding. The sight of such a spacecraft gave many watching the hope for a better future and the possibility of building Earth's station one day. Its existence renewed their resolve to change so the Interstellar Space Coalition would return and continue to protect their blue planet and launch them into a new future.

The space station blinked off and on three times, signaling their goodbye to the inhabitants of Earth. They moved away from the moon, heading to a new destination somewhere in the vastness of space. Many spectators wished them a successful voyage and a swift return. Those who viewed them as a threat to Earth and their way of life were glad to see the vermin leave.

When the all-clear was given, most of the ship's humans rushed into the dining area. Both moon and earth-born came to say their final goodbyes to the Earth, along with a few aliens. They anxiously waited for the shield doors to reopen and cried when they did, revealing the beautiful blue planet. As they moved away towards their new home, the planet grew smaller and smaller.

"Do you think she'll survive?" Sarina asked.

"She will for a while," Renn said. "If her people change, the ISC will send another space station to protect her. And, now that humans have proof aliens exist, they won't have to hide as we did. Perhaps they can work together and build her a wonderful future filled with space exploration and new knowledge."

"And if they can't?" Jeremy asked, holding Rachel in his arms.

"Then we are the last people who will see this magnificent sight," Renn said. "One day, the Kett or another race will come and harvest her wealth of water and minerals. Only a small barren rock will remain. All life will end."

"Where are we going?" Rachel's mother asked.

"To a new planet not too far away," Renn said. "It's in the Proxima Centauri system. It's called XR15. She's larger than Earth and has the same chemical nature and atmosphere."

"What about the life living there now?" Sarina asked. "Won't we be altering their lifestyle?"

"Not at all," Renn laughed. "The planet contains no indigenous life. The plants and animals which live there have come from Earth." He laughed again upon seeing the confused expressions. "I had the same reaction. Long ago, the ISC realized if the day ever came where we needed to move Earth's life forms to another living world, it would disrupt that world's life cycle. So, to prevent this, they took a barren rock planet devoid of life, like Mars, and terraformed the sphere into a breathing, livable planet. Once the principal components of the planet were in place, our scientists shaped the world. Some plants stored in our incubation facility were taken there twelve hundred years ago, along with some insects for pollination, fish for populating the seas, and a few animals to colonize the land. "

"About five hundred years ago, they were ready for part two of the project. A small shipment of larger animals was sent - beavers to create marshlands, predators to keep down the vegetarians who were thriving, scavengers to keep the system in check. Today the planet is a positive representation of Earth with oceans, mountains, valleys, and flatlands. It even snows in the mountains and has two polar caps. But the one thing it doesn't have is humans - and that is where all of us come into play. We are assigned the task of caring for this world, introducing the rest of Earth's life into the ecosystems, and making it into the Eden Earth was always meant to be.

"How long will it take to arrive at this new Earth?" Steven asked.

"The one drawback to the project," Renn said. "Since Earth is so far out in the galaxy, any place is far away. We estimate the journey will take about six point seven years to reach New Earth."

"Isn't this station able to go through folded space?" Stephen asked.

"Thankfully, yes, or the journey end with our grandchildren's grandchildren's grandchildren arriving." Renn chuckled. "Even though folding space is a technical wonder, the distance still limits us on how far we can fold. Right now, we can go no further than a million miles, after which we must wait two or three days before attempting a new fold. One must give space a chance to resettle before going forward. And since the journey is trillions of miles, it will take us some time to get there. The trip will give us time to mourn our many losses, to rebuild lives, and meet the new Earth arrivals and them to know us."

"When will we slip through our first space folding?" an excited Timmy asked. He had all kinds of ideas of what the experience would feel like.

"Not for a few days," Renn said. "The space station hasn't been outside of its imprisonment for thousands of years. She's like an old car; still fit and operable but has a few kinks in her from sitting so long. A slower course will allow us to find her kinks and repair them before they cause any problems. Plus, we need to rendezvous with Commander Oglich and the others. Their ships are too severely damaged to space jump and are proceeding along an interception course to meet us. Once we have them aboard, I imagine Glogg will give the okay to fold space."

"Is he doing better?" Sarina asked.

"His heart is broken, but he will never let you see it. He will devote his life to his daughter and soon-to-be-born twin grandchildren. And, as always, to the inhabitants of this station."

As Earth's image grew smaller until it was nothing but another twinkling star in the darkness of space, the human gathering dispersed. Each wondered what it would be like to sit in the mess hall eating their meals without the beautiful blue planet below. For many, Earth had been their meal companion for many centuries.

As the Spalling family left, they wished their world the best. Each hoped humans would somehow change, would find the strength to put aside their petty differences, live together as one, and survive.

Sarina turned to take one last glimpse at the tiny dot of light which was Earth. In her mind, she doubted humans could abandon their need for wealth, power, and fame. But in her heart, she hoped the best of humanity would win out. She wondered what Earth's future would be - and her own.

Guardians of Earth II: The Watcher

Arriving December 3, 2021.

Order your advance copy today

ABOUT THE AUTHOR

P.R. Garcia is the author of the Europa Saga, a compelling, six-part sci-fi series of intrigue, suspense, and mystery. It is a retelling of who the Atlanteans were, how they arrived on Earth, and what happened to them. Told through the eyes of a twenty-year-old human female named Europa, she learns upon her mother's assassination that she was never meant to be human. She was to be the next leader of the Oonock race of aquatic beings from Jupiter's ice moon, Europa. With the help of ancient Orbs, she is transformed into the Oonock she was destined to be, ends a six-thousand-year-old battle, and unites her people into a magnificent nation once more.

Global warming, deforestation, pollution of our air and water, species loss, and Earth itself are all subjects dear to Ms. Garcia's heart. The three-book subseries in the Europa Saga about Europa's son, Prince E.J., deals with corporate corruption and their destruction of our planet. Her book *Extinction 2038* also deals with these subjects, except this time, global warming has caused the re-release of the original strain of the Ebola virus. It is destroying animal life across the planet.

If you'd like information on ways, you can help global warming and the other topics, sign up for her newsletter HERE:

https://prgarcia1.ck.page/8712f666de

Ms. Garcia also writes children's books. *A Cat for William* is about a stray cat who helps a man cope with a disabling disease. Coming Christmas, 2022, two more children's books will be released: *The Story of Sudan: The Last Northern White Male Rhino* and *The Christmas Crayons*, a story about a homeless boy who finds happiness in a box of crayons. For more information, go to her web page http://www.prgarcia1.com.

THE EUROPA SAGA

She was never meant to be human.

When a young woman regains consciousness, she is told her mother has been assassinated, and she is the next target.

The Europa Saga is a fresh telling of the myth of Atlantis, who its people were, and why they sank the city. Told through the eyes of a twenty-year-old human female named Europa, the saga covers four generations and spans over two thousand years.

As Europa tries to come to grips with her mother's death, she discovers the truth - her entire life has been a fabrication, an intricate weave of lies and omissions. Her parents are thousands of years old and have been on Earth, along with her caregivers, for over two thousand years. They are not human but the royal leaders of an aquatic race of aliens from Jupiter's ice moon, Europa. Forced to flee their homeworld due to civil war, they remain hidden in the Pacific Ocean's depths in the technically advanced City of Atlantis. But their numbers are dwindling. Because of a chemical attack by their mortal enemy who tracks them to Earth, no Atlantean child has survived past the age of five. When Queen Medaron miraculously becomes pregnant, the child's only hope is to be born as a human.

Europa must discover who and what she is and learn the authentic story of her people. As the new queen, she protects them from the enemy that still hunts them and the world of humans. But to do that, she must become an Atlantean herself and lose her humanity. If she fails, she will die, and the Atlanteans will be no more.

For more information and a free eBook copy of the first book, go to http://www.prgarcia1.com.

OTHER BOOKS

Extinction 2038: Much of the ice in Antarctica has melted, revealing the corpse of a dinosaur. A group of paleontologist stumbles across it, believing they have found the find of the century. But inside the corpse is the original strain of Ebola. As the disease spreads across the globe, killing most animals and man, society breaks down. Three scientists with a possible cure are stranded in Antarctica with no one alive to rescue them and no internet to call for help. This book is available to be read for free on Kindle Unlimited: https://www.amazon.com/Extinction-2038-P-R-Garcia/dp/1948060019

The Bounty Hunter: On Proxima Prime, the Bounty Hunter, BiiJun, lies dying in a pool of blood. While pursuing a bounty, he made a fatal mistake and is paying the price with his life. For twenty years, the Huntsman's armor has been part of him, protecting him, giving him an advantage over his quarries. This time, however, his armor cannot save him. Only a stranger can.

Thrown together by fate, BiiJun and the stranger fight side-by-side in an attempt to stay alive. For the first time, the Hunter glimpses a different life, one without his armor. If they survive, which life will he choose.

This book is available to be read for free on Kindle Unlimited: https://www.amazon.com/dp/B08C8YXCPN

Video: https://www.youtube.com/watch?v=F-IVYkQtIl4

BONUS MATERIAL

Wondering what decision the ISC made on if they would send another space station to guard Earth? Was humanity able to change their ways to warrant the station? To find out, subscribe to my newsletter.

https://prgarcia1.ck.page/36dfd1e874

Honest reviews help others find my books.

If you enjoyed this book, I would be very grateful if you could spend five minutes to leave a review. (It can be as short as you like.) Just one or both click the links below:

https://www.amazon.com/Guardians-Earth-P-R-Garcia-ebook/dp/B08XQVKCG2

https://www.goodreads.com/book/show/57462217-guardians-of-earth

www.ingramcontent.com/pod-product-compliance
Lightning Source LLC
Chambersburg PA
CBHW051458170626
46811CB00002B/536